Stay With Me

Getting her back will be the toughest deal they've ever negotiated.

On the night of her fifth anniversary, Catherine Cullen-Wellesley intends to break the news to the two men in her life. She's pregnant with their child. It'll be the perfect preamble to the vacation they've promised her: Two weeks on a Jamaican beach. No cell phones, no emails, no business.

But when Logan and Rhys blow off the trip for yet another "business emergency", Catherine faces some difficult truths. She hasn't come first in her busy husbands' lives in a long time. Defiantly, she packs her bags for her long-awaited vacation—alone. It'll give her a chance to figure out what the hell she's going to do with the rest of her life.

When Logan and Rhys come home to an empty house, they realize two things: One, it was a mistake to take Catherine for granted. Two, they're not willing to just let her walk out of their lives.

Winning her back will be the most difficult battle of their lives—more important than any business deal they've ever negotiated.

Warning: This title contains explicit sex, ménage a trois, a polyamorous relationship, graphic language, and sex near a beach (and in the shower).

Songbird

The voice of an angel, a husband who loved her—she had it all...until a tragedy took it away.

They called her their Songbird, but she was never theirs. Not in the way she wanted.

The Donovan brothers meant everything to Emily, but rejected by Greer and Taggert, she turned to Sean, the youngest. He married her for love, and she loved him, but she also loved his older brothers.

Her singing launched her to stardom. She had it all. The voice of an angel, a husband who loved her, and the adoration of millions. Until a tragedy took it all away.

Taggert and Greer grieve for their younger brother, but they're also grieving the loss of Emmy, their songbird. They take her back to Montana, determined to help her heal and show her once and for all they want her. They're also on a mission to help her find her voice again. Under the protective shield of their love, she begins to blossom... until an old threat resurfaces.

Now the Donovans face a fight for what they once threw away. Only by winning it—and her love—will their songbird fly again.

Warning: Explicit sex, ménage a trois, multiple partners, a committed polyamorous relationship, adult language, and sweet loving.

Look for these titles by
Maya Banks

Linger

Maya Banks

A Samhain Publishing, Ltd. publication.

Samhain Publishing, Ltd.
577 Mulberry Street, Suite 1520
Macon, GA 31201
www.samhainpublishing.com

Linger
Print ISBN: 978-1-60504-549-8
Stay With Me Copyright © 2010 by Maya Banks
Songbird Copyright © 2010 by Maya Banks

Editing by Jennifer Miller
Cover by Natalie Winters

Stay With Me, ISBN 978-1-59998-934-1
First Samhain Publishing, Ltd. electronic publication: May 2008
Songbird, ISBN 978-1-60504-661-7
First Samhain Publishing, Ltd. electronic publication: September 2009
First Samhain Publishing, Ltd. print publication: May 2010

Contents

Stay With Me

Dedication

To Jennifer who is every bit as nitpicky as I am, a fact I am extremely grateful for. This wouldn't have a chance of being near as good without you.

Chapter One

They weren't coming.

Catherine Cullen-Wellesley dropped her gaze to the rumpled table napkin in her hand and swallowed against the lump in her throat. Tears burned her lids, and she blinked rapidly to dispel the liquid threat.

Beside her, the waiter hovered, asking for the fourth time in the last hour if he could get her anything. No, not unless he could hand-deliver her husbands.

She waved the young man away and brushed defiantly at the corner of her eye. Her trembling lips betrayed her, though.

How could they have forgotten their anniversary? Again.

She checked her watch and winced as she realized they were an hour and a half late for their reservation. No, not late. Absent. Just like they'd been absent from every other date she'd arranged in the past several months.

Each time they promised to be there, swore they'd make it up to her, and each time she was left to wallow in her misery.

But tonight...tonight was special. Her palm smoothed over her still-flat abdomen, and a sad smile curved her lips. She was going to tell them on the night of their fifth wedding anniversary that she was pregnant.

Only now she was stuck alone with no one to share the news with.

Alone. It amazed her that even though she was in a relationship with two men, she'd never felt more alone in her life. At a time when she wanted to feel so much joy, her heart ached with sadness. How could she rejoice in her pregnancy, at impending parenthood, when she couldn't even be sure that her baby would have a father to rely on?

Desolation clogged her throat and tightened her airway. She couldn't breathe around the growing knot. When had she lost hope? Looking back, she couldn't remember the last time she'd felt any.

Placing her palms down on the table, she bolted upward. She motioned impatiently for the waiter to bring her the check. When he presented it to her, the sole item on the receipt a glass of wine she hadn't drunk because of her pregnancy, she fumbled in her purse for a few bills and dropped them on the table.

She hurried for the door where the maitre d' snapped to attention.

"Shall I summon a cab for you, Mrs. Wellesley?" the older man asked.

She smiled wanly. "Yes, please."

Compassion shone in his eyes before he turned away. She hated that look. Hated the way it made her feel. Forgotten. Negligible.

A moment later, the doorman escorted her into a waiting taxi and shut the door behind her. She supplied the address to the driver in a shaky voice then sank back against the seat.

"This is a goddamn mess," Logan Wellesley said as he threw his cell phone across his office. After hours of playing phone tag and one botched conference call, nothing had been solved.

Rhys Cullen made a grim sound of agreement from the doorway. "The question is, what are we going to do about it?"

Logan eyed his partner and shoved his hands deep into his slacks pockets. He turned to stare over the glittering Manhattan skyline, anger and frustration pounding his temples.

He turned back to Rhys. "I'll tell you what we're going to do. We're going to get on a goddamn plane and fix it."

Rhys nodded. "You taking Kingston or Montford?"

Logan sighed. Catherine wasn't going to like it. Hell, *he* didn't like it. But she'd understand. She always did.

"I'll take San Francisco. You fly to Atlanta and pin down Montford. You shove those plans in his face. Once he sees them, there's no way he can turn down our proposal. I'll do the same with Kingston. I'm not going to let a year's worth of planning go down the toilet. We've got too much time and money riding on this."

Rhys stepped further into Logan's office as Logan punched the call button for his personal assistant. In a few moments, Paige Stanton made a punctual appearance. He was really going to have to increase her salary. Having to work well into the night was becoming increasingly habitual for her.

"Yes, sir?" she said primly.

"Call our pilot and have him ready to depart within the hour. I'll be traveling to San Francisco. Then I need you to book the first available flight to Atlanta for Rhys."

She blinked in surprise. "But sir, have you forgotten?"

"Forgotten what?" he barked. He didn't have time to play guessing games. Not when his company was on the brink of the ultimate success. Or failure.

Her lips drew together in a disapproving line. "You and Mr. Cullen are supposed to be flying to Jamaica tomorrow. With Mrs. Wellesley."

"That's Mrs. Cullen-Wellesley," Rhys said mildly.

Logan's chest tightened, and a dread he couldn't quite dispel settled over him. He exchanged glances with Rhys but couldn't read into Rhys' expression.

"The trip will have to be postponed. Something has come up."

"Doesn't it always," Paige murmured.

Logan stared, sure he hadn't heard her correctly. Maybe he'd rethink that pay raise. He decided to ignore whatever it was his assistant had muttered under her breath.

"Get the flight arrangements made. Now. Report back as soon as you have."

Paige turned and walked briskly from the office.

"Cat's going to be disappointed," Rhys said softly.

Logan closed his eyes. "I know. It can't be helped, though. We can't turn our backs on this. We can reschedule. We'll take her wherever she wants to go just as soon as we get the lockdown on this new hotel."

"I'll call her," Rhys said, reaching for the phone.

"I'll call her from the car," Logan said. They didn't have time to spare, and if he was honest, he knew he didn't want to face Catherine right now, even over the phone. If he allowed himself to think too long about her, he'd say to hell with the hotel and get on the plane with her to Jamaica.

"Call our driver instead. Tell him to be out front in ten minutes. We can ride together to the airport."

As Rhys picked up the phone, Logan looked up to see Paige return.

"Your pilot is filing flight plans as we speak and will have the jet fueled and ready when you arrive at LaGuardia. I booked Mr. Cullen on a ten-thirty flight. You'll need to get moving if you're going to make it on time."

Logan nodded approvingly. Paige turned to go, but he called her back.

"You need something else, sir?"

He swallowed. "I'd like for you to call Catherine tomorrow. See if there's anything she needs."

Annoyance flashed in Paige's eyes. "Of course, sir."

Catherine let herself into the apartment and kicked off her shoes before trailing across the living room toward the balcony. She was already packed for their trip, so she had nothing else to do with her evening except wait for them to come home.

She consoled herself with the idea that they'd probably gotten caught up with last-minute details. It had seemed a miracle when they'd agreed to the two-week trip to Jamaica. No phones, no email, no business, just the three of them on a tropical beach.

God, she missed them. Missed touching them, talking with them, snuggling into their arms after lovemaking. She touched her stomach again. She was three months pregnant. Three months ago had been the last time either man had made love to her. Before that? She couldn't even remember.

She'd hoped that tonight, and their impending vacation, would go a long way in recapturing what was lost in their relationship. Somewhere along the way to making their business a success, Logan and Rhys had sacrificed themselves—and her—in the process. She knew it, had known that things could only be allowed to go so far, but now that she was pregnant, it seemed the most important thing in the world to gain that reassurance that she still came first with them, that their child would come first.

She was about to open the sliding glass door when the flashing red beacon on the answering machine caught her attention.

Her heart sped up, and she cursed the fact that she was so willing to forget and forgive at the mere idea Logan or Rhys had called to leave a message. They had her cell phone number, damn it, and if they'd left a message here, it just showed them for the cowards they were.

She blinked in surprise when the phone rang. She stood, staring at it, refusing to cross the room to answer. After four rings, the answering machine picked up, and her own voice filtered across the room.

She held her breath as Logan's voice sounded.

"Catherine? Baby, pick up the phone. You must have let your cell phone go down again. I've been trying to call you."

She vaulted for the phone, simultaneously reaching into her purse for her cell. As she yanked up the receiver, she fumbled with the cell, turning it over in her hand to see that it was, indeed, dead.

"Logan?" she said as she punched the on button.

"Catherine. Finally."

"Logan, where are you?" she asked.

"I'm in the car. Something came up." A long silence descended over the line, and she heard him suck in his breath. "About the trip, Catherine..."

Oh no. No, no, no. He wouldn't.

"I'm afraid we're going to have to postpone it. Rhys and I have to fly out. Why don't you see if you can reschedule it. We'll go wherever you like as soon as we get back."

Numb to her toes, she stood, hand gripped tight around the phone. She began to shake, and she gulped back the sob in her throat.

"Catherine, are you there?"

"Y-yes. Of course. I'll see what I can do."

She thought she heard him sigh in relief. "I love you, baby. And I'm sorry. I'll make it up to you. Just a minute. Rhys wants to talk to you."

She closed her eyes as Rhys' deep voice came over the line.

"Cat?"

"I'm here," she whispered.

"I'm sorry, sweetheart. This deal has us by the balls. We'll be back soon. I promise."

She couldn't even respond. She didn't want to hear yet one more promise she now knew wouldn't be kept. She murmured something appropriate, and then he said he had to go.

She eased the phone from her ear, sliding her thumb over the off button. Then she let it fall with a clank onto the table.

Not one word of their anniversary dinner that they'd blown off. They'd only called to cancel their vacation. The two-week trip she'd painstakingly planned, so excited that they'd agreed to go.

Her hands flew to her face, covering her eyes as tears seeped down her cheeks. Oh God, what had happened to them? She sank to the floor, the expensive wood hard against her stocking-clad knees.

It was time for her to face some hard facts. Her marriage was a mess. A disaster. And worse, she couldn't fix it. God knew she'd tried. The problem wasn't her, or lack of effort on her part. The problem was husbands who placed more importance on everything else in their lives but her. Husbands who took her complacence for granted.

She dragged herself to her feet and stumbled shakily toward the bedroom. When her gaze alighted on the trip itinerary on the nightstand, she closed her eyes and shook her head.

The trip was their last chance. One last effort on her part to put things right between them. To somehow capture something long missing in their relationship. She wanted so desperately to go back to the time when all that mattered was that they were together. In her mind, if she could just get them away for a few days, they would see how far off course they'd gone. And maybe they'd realize that they missed her as much as she missed them.

She went to the large walk-in closet and hauled out her packed suitcase, tossing it on the bed. She blinked and stared down at it. What was she doing?

I'll tell you what you're doing. You're going on that trip. Without Rhys and Logan. I doubt they'll even notice you're gone.

She glanced again at the itinerary. Maybe some time away was exactly what she needed.

She stepped over to the nightstand and picked up the sheet of paper with her flight and hotel reservations. With a sigh, she sank onto the bed, the words blurring in her vision.

She couldn't do this anymore. Pretend that everything was okay. When a wife didn't see her husband more than a few hours a week, when that husband never remembered important dates, cancelled every plan they had together, it was time to face the truth. Her marriage was over. It had been for a very long time.

The paper shook in her hand. She wasn't typically a hysterical ninny. She wasn't prone to overreaction. She'd spent the last five years sucking it up and smiling while on the inside she ached. She'd played the understanding wife to the hilt.

Now looking back, she realized what a huge mistake she'd made. She had no one to blame but herself. But damn it, that didn't mean she had to suffer any longer for it.

Galvanized to action, she stood and tugged her suitcase. She'd spend tonight in an airport hotel and catch her flight in the morning. Two weeks on a Jamaican beach sounded like a perfect amount of time to figure out what the hell she was going to do with the rest of her life.

Chapter Two

Logan boarded his jet, a smug smile curving his lips. One disaster averted. And it had only taken him two days to accomplish it. Two endless, excruciating days of meetings, phone calls and conference calls with Rhys and Montford. But it was over. The deal was sealed, and he and Rhys were poised to land the biggest contract their company had ever netted.

He wanted to call Catherine and share in the joy with her, but a quick check of his watch told him it was after midnight Eastern Time. Instead he flipped open his phone and called Paige.

Her sleepy voice came over the line a moment later, and he cringed guiltily. He didn't want to wake his wife, but he had no compunction about waking his assistant. A raise. She definitely deserved a raise.

"Paige, I'm on my way back. Rhys is flying in as well."

"Do you need your driver at the airport?" she asked.

"No, we'll take a cab to the apartment." He paused for a moment. "Did you talk to Catherine?"

There was a long silence. "I wasn't able to reach her either at home or her cell."

Logan sighed. "She probably let her cell run down again. She's forever forgetting to recharge it."

"I went by your apartment after I couldn't reach her," Paige continued, her voice tight. He could almost swear she sounded angry. "Your doorman said she hasn't been home in two days and that she left the same night you and Rhys flew out to San

Francisco and Atlanta. The night of your anniversary, by the way."

Fuck. Fuck, fuck, fuck! His hand tightened around the cell phone, and he closed his eyes as panic, sharp and unrelenting, flooded him.

Their anniversary. Their dinner date. He'd forgotten. And it wasn't the first time. His chest tightened as he imagined Catherine sitting in the restaurant by herself, waiting for him and Rhys to show up. And how she must have felt when she realized they weren't.

And then. God. He'd cancelled their trip.

How could he have forgotten? It wasn't as though it had completely slipped his mind. Her present sat in his desk drawer at work, wrapped and ready to go. But as soon as the deal had started to go south, everything else fled his mind. His only priority had been salvaging the biggest contract of his career.

"Are you still there?"

Paige's voice seeped into his consciousness. And then he realized what else she'd said. Alarm slammed into his chest.

"You said she's gone," he croaked. "That she hadn't been home in two days. What else did the doorman say? Where is she?"

"I don't know," Paige replied without an ounce of sympathy in her voice. "But I can't say I blame her."

His lips tightened. "What the hell are you talking about?"

"Catherine's a sweet girl, Logan, but she's not going to be so forgiving forever. You and Rhys take advantage of her. Horribly. One of these days you're going to look up, and she's going to be gone. Maybe she already is. Hopefully she'll end up with a man who'll show her a little more appreciation."

He couldn't breathe. Paige's words hit him like razor-sharp darts.

The phone went dead in his ear, but all he could process was the fact that Paige had said Catherine was gone.

He punched in the number to the apartment with shaky fingers. He waited as it rang. After the fourth time, the answering machine picked up, and he cursed.

"Catherine, baby, it's me, Logan. Pick up, baby. I know you're angry, but please, pick up the phone."

He hung up and called right back, frustrated when he got the same result. He was redialing again when the plane pulled away from the terminal to begin its taxi.

Frustrated, he slapped the phone shut and flung it across the seat.

Where was she? Had something happened to her? Had she left the apartment upset and been in an accident? Fear gripped him. Or had she simply walked out?

No, Paige was wrong. Catherine understood. She always understood.

Understood what? That her husband is an asshole who can't even remember their anniversary? He'd cancelled a trip he promised to take her on, hadn't been around in more months than he could count, and he hadn't made love to her in so long he ached.

He closed his eyes and banged his head against the back of the seat. Had she given up on him?

Rhys stepped off the plane and made his way up the exit corridor to the gate. He was tired as hell, but anticipation lightened his step as he imagined crawling into bed with Cat. God, he'd missed her. Right now a Jamaican beach and her in a thong sounded next to heaven.

A frown strained his lips as he tried to remember the last time he'd made love to Cat. The last months were all a blur of phone calls, business trips, endless meetings and negotiations. Uncertainty wedged its way into his chest. She had sounded so disappointed the night he and Logan had left. And now that he had a moment to breathe, he realized just how often he and Logan had been making excuses and apologies.

Suddenly he couldn't wait to get home. He was going to talk to Logan about rescheduling that vacation they'd promised Cat. Soon.

He checked his watch then fished for his cell phone to turn it back on. Logan landed a half hour before him, and they were supposed to hook up and ride together back to the apartment.

As soon as the phone powered up, it beeped to tell him he had a voicemail. Or ten. Damn, that was a lot of missed calls. He frowned as he scrolled through and saw they were all from Logan.

He put the phone to his ear and picked up his pace to baggage claim.

"Rhys, meet me at the apartment. We've got a problem."

He pulled the phone away with a frown. That was it? Goddamn Logan and his penchant for being short and providing no details. He punched in Logan's cell number and waited impatiently for him to answer. When it went straight to voicemail, Rhys swore and shoved the phone back into his pocket.

Adrenaline pounded through his veins. Shit, had something happened to Cat? Fuck the baggage. He broke into a run toward passenger pick-up and cut in front of at least three people waiting for a taxi. He thrust a wad of bills at the driver.

"I'm in a hurry."

The cabbie palmed the cash. "Yes sir."

An eternity later, he jumped out of the cab and bolted into the building. He cursed the elevator's slowness as he rode it to the top floor. When it opened, he stepped into the apartment and came up short when he saw Logan pacing the floor of the living room, phone to his ear.

"What do you mean you don't have a record of Catherine Wellesley at your hotel? She has to be there. I've called every goddamn hotel in Jamaica."

"What the fuck is going on?" Rhys demanded.

Logan swiveled around, hurled an expletive to whoever he was talking to on the phone then slapped it shut.

"Catherine is gone," he said hoarsely.

Rhys blinked as fear crawled up his spine. "Gone. What do you mean gone?"

"Haven't you tried to call her in the last two days?" Logan asked, his voice angry.

"Yes, I have. I assumed she'd let her cell phone go down again, and you know as well as I do she rarely answers the apartment phone."

"She's gone," Logan said again, and Rhys had to fight the urge to knock the hell out of him and demand that he get to the point.

"Where is she?" Rhys demanded.

"Hell if I know." Logan ran a hand through his hair then closed his eyes. "We forgot our anniversary," he said in a quieter voice. "Catherine made plans. Reservations. We were supposed to eat out, come home and spend the evening together then fly out to Jamaica the next morning. Only she ended up spending the night alone, and we cancelled the trip."

"Where. Is. She. Now," Rhys gritted out, afraid of what Logan would say next.

Logan rounded him, his eyes furious. "I don't know! I wish to hell I did. Paige informed me that Catherine left the same night we did and hasn't been home since. And then Paige told me what assholes we are."

Rhys shook his head. He didn't give a shit about Paige right now. He wanted to know where his wife was.

"The only thing missing is her luggage," Logan said.

Relief settled over Rhys. Maybe she hadn't left. As in walked out. Maybe she'd just gone on the trip. He couldn't blame her if she had. He and Logan had treated her like shit.

"I'm going to call the damn pilot," Logan muttered. "Have him fly us to Jamaica. If I have to personally go into every hotel on the island to find her, I will."

It was a sad testament that neither of them even had a clue what hotel she'd booked for them. They'd left all the details to her and never expressed any interest in the plans. They were both bastards of the first order.

Rhys sighed. "Let me get some clothes. I left my bags at the airport after I got your message."

"Make it quick. I'm calling down for the car now."

Yeah, quick. Suddenly they were fast on the uptake and going after Catherine. Something they should have done a long time ago. They never should have made her feel like she wasn't the most important thing in the world to them.

They. Hell. Fuck they. *He* shouldn't have let things get to this point. His relationship with Cat wasn't dependent on Logan's. Yes, they had an unusual arrangement, but it didn't mean that it gave him any free passes when it came to his responsibility to the woman he loved. It was time to dispense with the *they* in every statement and make Cat see how much she meant to *him*.

Chapter Three

Jamaica

Logan watched as his wife gyrated in time to the funky beat of the music. Torches lit the stretch of sand cordoned off into a dance floor. Their flames flickered and cast shadows, dancing in time with the throng of scantily clad partygoers.

God damn, he was tired, jet lagged, he hadn't slept in three days, and now his wife, *his woman*, damn it, was weaving in and out of his line of vision, strange men touching her, lusting after her.

She looked like a sea nymph, her long blond hair tumbling free over her shoulders. He didn't even remember the last time he'd seen it free of the loose knot she always shoved it into. Her usually pale skin glowed golden in the light of the torches. And her bikini. Where the fuck had she gotten the tiny scraps of material seemingly glued to strategic parts of her body?

The globes of her ass bounced provocatively, the thin string of her thong sliding seductively between the cheeks. His cock tightened and swelled at the memory of fucking her tight ass. A distant memory, since they hadn't had sex in months.

When she whirled around, her breasts bobbed and strained against the slight cups. His hands itched as he imagined plucking and strumming the nipples.

She glowed. Her smile lit the entire night. In that moment, he was struck by the fact that he hadn't seen her smile, hadn't seen her look this happy in months.

An uncomfortable tension settled in his stomach. Had he made her so unhappy? Was Paige right? Was he in danger of losing her?

She left you, dumbass. Without a word. No note. No phone call. Took the vacation you promised to take with her. What do you think?

Yeah, he was going to lose her.

His hand trembled as he raised it rub the back of his neck. No, he wouldn't lose her. Not without a damn fight.

Catherine smiled and laughed then raised her hands above her head and swayed to the frantic beat. The sand flew beneath her feet, and the cool ocean breeze whispered across her face.

Bodies flashed in and out of her vision in blurs of color. She closed her eyes and inhaled the salty air. For the space of a few minutes, she let her sadness go. She was here for a good time. A fresh start.

She danced closer to the incoming tide, and when she reached the perimeter of the crowd, she slipped away to walk down the beach.

The waves reached for her toes, and she playfully dodged the foamy water before finally allowing it to wash over her ankles.

When she'd walked far enough that the sound of the waves drowned out the distant music, she stopped and stared at the horizon. A blanket of stars draped itself over the water, brilliant diamonds twinkling against the black.

"It's beautiful, isn't it."

She spun around, shocked to see Logan standing there, hands shoved into his pockets. He looked as though he hadn't showered, shaved or changed in a week.

Rumpled pants, disheveled shirt. Work clothes.

She finally closed her mouth and tried to control the tremble of her muscles.

"What are you doing here?" she demanded.

He moved closer until she could see the anger outlined on his face. The moon cast a pale glow over both of them, and she backed hesitantly away until she was ankle-deep in the surf.

27

His fingers closed around her upper arm, and he pulled her forward until she was clear of the water.

"I came to find you," he said simply.

"But how did you know where I was?" she asked, still numb with the shock of seeing him. He was here. Not at work.

His expression darkened. "It wasn't easy. I had no idea where you'd gone. You left no note. Made no call. Just disappeared. I had to assume you'd gone on the trip you'd planned, but even then, I had no idea what arrangements you'd made. Jamaica isn't such a small place when you have no idea where to begin looking."

She crossed her arms over her chest and stared defiantly at him. Did the arrogant bastard actually expect her to feel badly after he'd stood her up on their anniversary then cancelled the trip he'd promised he'd take with her?

"Come here," he said quietly, pulling her into his strong arms.

She was a mass of conflicting emotions as she pressed against his chest. God, it had been so long since he'd held her, touched her. In the past, all it had taken was a simple caress, a few soft words, and she'd forget and forgive.

Not this time.

She started to pull away, but his hold on her tightened.

"Let's go back to the hotel room. I'm tired. I stink. I'm dirty. I've been in these clothes for three days. We can talk after I've had a shower."

"Where is Rhys?" she asked, afraid that maybe he hadn't come.

"Looking for you," he said darkly. "Now come on. Let's go back to the room."

"You should get your own," she said quietly.

He stared at her, his eyes blazing, and she looked away, swallowing the urge to run. He reached out, his fingers stroking over her wrist before curling around her palm.

"Come back to *our* room, Catherine. We've come a long way to find you. The least you can do is talk to us."

Tears brimmed in her eyes, and her nose burned from the effort of holding them back. "Talk? Now you want to talk? After months—years—of ignoring me, *now* you want to talk?"

She shook from head to toe, and she was fast losing the tenuous grip she had on her emotions.

"Come back with me."

It wasn't a request. It was a command. To her dismay, she started forward, allowing him to lead her down the beach toward the hotel.

His fingers remained tightly wrapped around her hand as if he feared she'd flee.

Through the crowd of dancers, up the steps to the veranda and past the live band. Into the cool interior of the hotel, down the hallway to the elevator. They walked, silently.

He pulled her into the elevator, pushed the button for the top floor then curled his arms around her, molding her back to his chest.

She closed her eyes, trembling in his arms. How long had it been since he'd held her? Touched her intimately? Looked at her like he'd done on the beach, like she was the only woman in the world, a woman he wanted badly.

His lips burrowed into her hair, nuzzling the back of her neck. A prickle of desire skittered down her spine. She craved him, needed him. God, she needed him.

She leaned back into him, cursing her weakness but loving the solid security she felt in his arms.

"Where did you get this outfit?" he murmured against her ear.

The elevator opened, and he curled a hand around her wrist once more, tugging her into the hallway.

"I bought it for our vacation," she said through tight lips.

He fumbled in his pocket as they neared the suite and pulled out the room card. He jammed the card into the slot and shoved the door open.

A blast of cool air raised goose bumps on her exposed skin, and she rubbed her arms as they walked further into the room.

His and Rhys' luggage was thrown carelessly on the floor as if they'd dumped it and left just as quickly. In their search for her? Her gaze slid sideways, gauging his mood.

He was looking intently at her even as he loosened his shirt and began pulling at his pants.

"What are you doing?" she asked faintly, heat surging to her cheeks.

The door opened and Rhys swept in, looking as haggard as Logan did. When his gaze alighted on her, relief poured over his face, lightening his green eyes.

"Cat, thank God," he whispered as he walked toward her.

He pulled her into his arms and held her tightly, his chest heaving against her. She tried to push him away, but he wouldn't let go. When he did finally relinquish her, it was only to tilt her head back and capture her lips in a demanding kiss.

Anger, need, sadness, passion. Love. It was too much. She yanked away, emotion nearly choking her. She turned, not wanting either man to see how upset, how indecisive, she was.

"Cat," Rhys said in his husky voice. "Look at me."

She shook her head and focused her watery stare at the opposite wall.

Logan reached out and touched her cheek, brushing at the trail of moisture. "Don't cry, Catherine. Please don't cry. Let us love you. Give us tonight. We'll talk tomorrow—I swear it."

She shook off his touch, immediately feeling bereft of the warmth of his fingers. She backed away, crossing her arms protectively over her chest.

"I don't want you here," she said in a shaky voice.

As she spoke, she lifted her chin and stared first at Rhys and then over at Logan. Hurt briefly flickered across Rhys' face, but Logan's dark eyes were unreadable.

"You don't want to be here, so why are you?" she challenged as anger bubbled free. She had to swallow and breathe deeply through her nose. The urge to scream at them, to make them bleed as she'd bled, was strong.

"Because you're here," Logan said quietly. "And you belong with us."

She couldn't control the flood of hurt as she yanked her gaze up to his. He actually flinched, and guilt crept into his expression.

Strong hands curled over her bare shoulders. Rhys moved in from behind, his lips pressing against the curve of her neck. Logan reached for her hand, and she pulled it away.

He ignored her rejection and closed the distance between them, reaching around to retrieve the hand she'd hidden behind her back.

Without saying another word, he tugged her away from Rhys and led her into the bedroom. His finger slid up her spine, eliciting a delicate shiver. He stopped when he reached the thin tie of her top. With a tug, the scrap of material fell away, baring her breasts.

The finger wandered back down her spine until it reached the small of her back. Then his hand caressed the bare skin of her bottom, cupping and kneading one cheek, then the other. He pulled the G-string from the cleft of her ass, running his finger down the length.

With a quick yank, he broke the strap and let the material fall down her legs.

"Logan, I don't think—"

He put a finger to her lips. "Shhhh."

She stared at him, praying she didn't look as vulnerable as she felt. With one hand splayed over her ass, he moved the other hand from her lips down to cup her breast in his palm. His thumb rubbed lightly over the nipple, causing it to tighten and pucker.

"Don't move," he commanded as he turned and walked out of the room.

He was back in seconds, one of her scarves in his hand. Her eyes widened as he quickly wrapped it around her wrists.

"Logan—"

"Shhhh," he said again. He finished restraining her wrists then nudged her toward the bed. The back of her knees met the mattress, and he pressed until she was forced to lie back. He raised her hands and secured them to the bedpost.

She stared at him with wide eyes, nervous as Rhys came to stand beside the bed. It had been so long. And she was weak. How could she welcome them back into her bed when they'd ignored her for so long? She closed her eyes, refusing to allow them to see the need and the longing.

"We both need a shower," Logan said in a low voice. "We've been traveling forever, haven't changed our clothes. And I want you to be here when we get back."

Beside her Rhys ran a finger over her shoulder, around the sensitive skin of her neck, into the hollow of her throat and then lower to her breast. He circled her nipple until it puckered and stood taut.

Need burned between her legs, tightening her pussy until she fidgeted and twisted restlessly. When was the last time either of them had touched her? Looked at her with lust in their eyes?

They'd sworn never to take advantage of her and that they'd always take care of her. Love her. Give her what she needed. Only they'd lied.

She turned her face away, not wanting them to see her pain. Rhys bent and kissed her softly on the temple. The simple gesture was nearly her undoing.

"I'll be right back," he whispered. "And then I'm going to love every inch of you."

She looked up to see them walk away, one into the bathroom adjoining the bedroom and the other back toward the living room and the other bathroom.

She tugged at the scarf binding her wrists, but it held firm. Closing her eyes, she heaved a heavy sigh. This is what she wanted. *Had* wanted, she corrected herself. It was what she'd spent the last months longing for.

It was too little, too late. Would they be here if she hadn't left them without a word? If they didn't fear she'd walked out on them?

It was a question she wasn't sure she was ready to hear the answer to. She still hadn't decided what exactly she wanted to do. She'd taken the trip to give her time to think about what her next step would be. She hadn't counted on them showing up. At least not so soon.

Chapter Four

Rhys leaned his forehead against the shower wall as water pelted his back. He'd seen something in Cat's eyes he never wanted to see again. Had never imagined seeing.

Pain. Pain that he'd caused. And worse, a loss of hope. As if she'd given up on him and their marriage.

He clenched his fist and pushed himself off the wall. How could he undo several years in a matter of a few days? How could he make her see that he loved her and didn't want to lose her? It wasn't as simple as apologizing. He could sense the difference in her. The resolve.

In a hurry to return to her, he washed and stepped out, dragging a towel over his body to dry it. His balls ached, and his cock was stiff as a board.

Naked, he walked back into the bedroom where Catherine still lay, her blond hair spread over the pillow. She looked at him as he approached, her expression wary, a mixture of sadness and desire in her eyes.

He sat down on the bed beside her and reached out a hand to touch her cheek.

"I know we need to talk," he said quietly. "But I'm no good with words. Let me show you, Cat. Let me love you. Then we'll talk. I promise."

Her eyes were shiny, brimming with moisture.

"I've missed you," she whispered.

The softly spoken words signaled her surrender, and he closed his eyes in relief. Then he reached up to untie her hands.

She turned fully on her back, watching him beneath her lashes. He could see her indecision, and he didn't want to give her a chance to change her mind.

He stood beside the bed and trailed his fingers over her breasts, stroked her puckered nipples then caressed his way over her soft belly.

"Spread your legs," he said.

She hesitated just a moment before relaxing her legs, allowing her thighs to part, giving him a tantalizing view of her pussy.

Silky blond curls guarded her tender pink flesh.

"Touch yourself," he said huskily. "Open yourself for me."

Her right hand glided slowly down her stomach until it hovered over the soft mound. After a brief pause, her fingers slid into the folds, spreading until he could see the opening to her pussy and her swollen clit.

Her middle finger stroked once then twice over the quivering bud. She moaned softly and closed her eyes. God, she was sexy. Head thrown back, hair streaming over the sheets, her lips parted as a sigh escaped them.

He crawled onto the bed, positioning himself at her feet. He bent down and pressed his lips to the inside of her ankle. Gently grasping her slender leg in his hand, he kissed a path upward, licking and nibbling.

When he reached the juncture of her thighs, he scooted down to her other foot and began again, giving this leg the same tender treatment.

Her breath caught when he nipped the inside of her thigh. His lips hovered over her pussy, and he smiled as he felt her hold herself in anticipation.

He moved instead to her belly and blazed a wet trail up her taut abdomen to the swells of her breasts.

"Oh..." The gasp escaped her lips as he sucked her nipple between his teeth.

Her hand left her pussy, and she dug her fingers into his hair, holding him to her breast.

He tugged himself away and moved his body up until his face hovered over hers. He kissed her, wanting to taste her, wanting to capture her sweet sounds into his mouth. He wanted to absorb every inch of her, make her forget everything but the fact that he was here with her.

Catherine broke away with a ragged breath. She sucked in mouthfuls of air before Rhys captured her mouth once again. He moved with urgency. He touched her, kissed her like he hadn't since they'd first been married.

Hot, wild, she wanted to crawl right out of her skin. Restless and aching, she could no longer remain still, no longer allow him control.

She pushed at him, rolling him off her. He looked at her with bewildered eyes as she rose over him, letting her hair spill onto his chest.

Placing both her hands on his shoulders, she lowered her head and consumed his lips in a hungry, carnal kiss. Too long had she gone without the close physical intimacy she craved, and now she wasn't content to lie back and allow him to call the shots.

When she pulled away to gasp for breath, she saw the surprise in his eyes, but she also saw something else. Want. Need. Curiosity. Desire.

A smile curved her lips. A wicked smile she hoped.

She straddled his body, shoving his arms upward. He arched one brow but allowed her to dictate his movements. When his hands were above his head, she trailed her fingers down the undersides of his arms until she reached his broad chest.

She shifted her body until she cradled his cock between her legs. Hard, thick, it brushed against her wetness, and she rubbed up and down, loving the electric currents that raced through her body every time her clit nudged the head of his penis.

"Tease," he gasped out.

"This is my show," she murmured as she continued to rock back and forth.

She leaned forward and nipped at his neck. Lightly at first, then she sank her teeth into the corded muscle behind his ear. He groaned and shifted underneath her. He started to lower his arms, but she sat up and put both hands on his chest in protest.

"Don't move."

He grinned and slowly let his hands fall back to the pillow. "I think I like you this way."

"Maybe I should have done it sooner, then," she whispered. "Maybe you'd want to spend more time with me if I had."

His eyes darkened into what looked like regret. "Cat—" he began.

She put a finger over his lips as he had done hers earlier. She reached between them with her other hand and grasped his swollen cock. With a twist of her hips, she positioned him at her entrance and slid down, engulfing him.

His entire body tensed and he moved his hands up, paused then let them fall back to the bed as if remembering her earlier dictate.

"Oh God," he groaned. "You feel so good."

"Tell me what you want," she said breathlessly. She stared down at him, stilling her movements. Then she arched, sliding nearly off of him.

"Cat..."

"Tell me," she commanded.

"I want you to fuck me," he growled. "I want your hands and lips on me. I want my dick so far in your pussy that I'm drowning."

She slid her palms over the hard muscles of his chest and slowly lowered her hips until he was fully within her again.

"Harder," he said.

"I want you to beg," she countered, her eyes locked with his once more.

A sound had her turning her head to see Logan standing in the doorway to the bathroom. Naked, his cock stiff and distended, his hand curled around it as he stroked back and forth.

He watched silently as she stared at him, her body still, Rhys buried deeply within her.

His fingers rolled over his engorged penis, coaxing the foreskin toward the head, pausing, then pulling downward again.

She knew he liked to watch. It aroused her too. There was something primal, forbidden, about belonging to two men, having one watch while the other pleasured her.

Slowly, she turned her attention back to Rhys. His hands were still above his head, and she leaned forward, gripping his shoulders as she lifted her hips, sliding up his cock with a leisure that contradicted the edgy need boiling just under the surface of her skin.

She trembled, shaking with the force of her desire. It had been too long, and she craved him. Craved them both with a desperation that frightened her. How was she supposed to survive the decision she must make? How was she supposed to exist away from them?

How could she remain with them when she was never a priority?

She let her chin fall to her chest in a gesture of defeat. She was fooling herself. Yes, she wanted them. Loved them with every breath. But it wasn't enough. They had to want and need her every bit as much.

Rhys reached up to touch her cheek, light and seeking, tentative almost as if he feared what he'd see in her eyes.

"Cat, I love you," he whispered. "Please believe that."

Warmth seeped through her veins, lighting hope in its path. She wanted to believe him. Wanted it more than anything.

One hand fell to her hip. The other hand crept to the opposite side, then down, cradling her buttocks in his firm grip.

No. This was her moment. She was in control. She wanted to hear him beg. She wanted him to feel the desperation she did. Wanted him to ache every bit as much as she did.

Pulling his hands away, she pushed them back up above his head. As she leaned forward, she purposely brushed the tips of her breasts across his mouth.

She felt his sigh blow over the taut peaks as she turned one way then the other, teasing him. He loved her breasts. Logan was more of an ass man. Her cheeks heated as she recalled how much he loved her ass. Rhys, on the other hand, spent a lot of time touching, licking and sucking her breasts.

When they did it at the same time? Heaven.

She nearly groaned aloud as the image of Logan fucking her ass while Rhys devoured her breasts came to mind.

She lowered herself another inch, fitting a puckered nipple to Rhys' lips. Her pregnancy had brought changes to her breasts, and she inhaled sharply as he took the nipple in his mouth. He sucked at it greedily, drawing it between his teeth. The sounds he made, like a man starving, drew in her stomach, clenching every muscle. Hot. Erotic.

She pulled away when the sensation became too much, locking her hands over his arms when he tried to move to hold her down. Remembering her plan, she rose and fell against him, taking him deeper into her pussy.

He closed his eyes, strain evident as his face creased in near agony. His breaths tore from his mouth, and he bucked upward with his hips.

"Beg," she whispered. "I won't end it until you beg."

When she felt him tense underneath her, she stopped completely, staving off his impending orgasm.

A tortured groan spilled from his mouth. "Cat," he gasped. "Please."

She leaned down and pressed her tongue to the center of his chest. She licked upward, leaving a warm, damp trail to his neck. When she nuzzled into the hollow of his throat, she clamped down with her teeth, nipping sharply.

His jaw went slack, and his pulse sped up. His heart pounded against her. One long delicious lick, up over his chin to his lips and then she took him, hard, in an aggressive kiss. All of the frustration came rushing out. Months of longing, painful need.

She dug her knees into his side and began to ride him. Her body undulated as she rose. She threw her head back, closed her eyes and concentrated on the pleasure rolling like the waves at the beach.

His hands skimmed over her belly, then up to cup her breasts, much more sensitive now. Her nipples were darker, and any stimulation was almost painful to bear.

She put her hands over his, holding them in place as she arched over him again and again.

Remembering that Logan was watching, she glanced over her shoulder. He met her gaze, his fist pumping at his swollen cock. But he wouldn't come.

She smiled. No, he'd find his release after he made her come. For a moment, she slowed, wanting to prolong Rhys' orgasm, thus making Logan wait longer.

"Finish it, Catherine," Logan growled.

She turned back to Rhys, a slight smile curving her lips.

"You're such a tease," Rhys said in a strained voice.

His thumbs brushed over her nipples, and she flinched. He frowned.

"Did I hurt you?"

She shook her head. Determined to distract him once more, she picked up her pace. Her fingers dug into his sides. He slid his hands down to cover hers. His fingers threaded through hers in a tender gesture, one that brought tears to her eyes.

Then he squeezed and his body bucked upward. "God, Cat, don't stop. Please don't stop."

She wasn't as close to her own orgasm yet, but that was okay. Logan would soon take care of that. A wicked smile worked at her mouth.

She rode. Hard and unrelenting. She writhed and twisted, coaxing him higher until his back bowed off the bed as he sought to get deeper inside her.

His cry split the room. His cock pulsed within her, and she clutched him to her, cradling him with her body, surrounding him as she milked his release.

Her breath caught when he placed his palm against her belly, almost as if he knew what secret she harbored. Emotion swelled, sharp and aching. How she'd always dreamed of giving them a child. Of having their loving devotion throughout her pregnancy. Of creating a perfect family.

His hand moved, sliding around to her back, and then he pulled her forward, enfolding her in his arms. He tucked her head underneath his chin and stroked her hair lovingly as he sought to catch his breath.

"I love you," he whispered, and for a moment she could forget past hurts. Focus on the present. Remembering would only ruin the moment, and it might be the last.

And yet she couldn't utter the words, no matter that she did love him. More than anything. Deeply, passionately, with every piece of her soul. Saying them hurt because it forced her to acknowledge that no matter how much she might love him—and Logan—in the end it wasn't enough.

Strong hands gripped her shoulders and flipped her over, rolling her off of Rhys. Logan stared down at her, his eyes glittering with desire.

A flutter started low in her abdomen and raced upward until tension coalesced in her chest and expanded into her throat. Her mouth went dry. She was about to be fucked and fucked hard.

Chapter Five

Catherine felt a brief moment of fear for her pregnancy. Logan was rough, animalistic almost. Their lovemaking was rarely gentle. Her doctor had assured her that she didn't need to exercise restraint in her sex life, but she wasn't so sure.

Logan's eyes flickered in confusion. "Catherine?" His voice came out questioning, but the tone wavered. For the first time, he sounded uncertain, and Logan was nothing if not self-assured.

He reached down and brushed gentle fingers across her rib cage, touching her, light and coaxing. It was a strange side to Logan. One she wasn't used to, and it battered her already ravaged senses.

Her nose drew up and stung, and she blinked furiously, determined not to give in. She'd spent far too long being weak and biddable. It had gained her nothing with her husbands but the idea that she'd take whatever they dished out, however they wanted to serve it up.

Logan leaned down and spread her legs, pulling her to the edge of the bed. Then he leaned over her, pressing his hard, muscled body to her chest.

She wrapped her arms around his neck and held him even closer, clinging and holding him tight. Emotion left her shaky and feeling needy. But then she needed this more than anything. More than breathing.

He framed her face with his elbows and stared down at her, his dark eyes fierce, smoldering with unsated lust and desire.

"Do you need me, Logan?" she whispered. "Do you need me like I need you? Do you think about me when you're not with me? When you're on all those trips, do you miss me?"

"God, baby," he said with a groan. "I've never not needed you, and I'm so goddamn sorry if I ever made you feel like I didn't."

"Take me, Logan," she said. "Like you used to. Don't treat me differently. I couldn't bear it. Tonight I want it to be like it's always been between us, when things were good. It's been so long since I was between you and Rhy. I want you both so much. I *need* you both."

His pupils flared, and for a moment he looked primal, all male, and she shivered as need exploded over her.

Without a word, he stalked toward the bathroom. A few seconds later, he returned, a tube in his hand.

"On your hands and knees," he said silkily. "I want to watch you suck Rhys' dick. Then I'm going to ride you hard, baby."

Rhys was there to help her roll over, and thank goodness, because she'd gone completely weak. Her hands shook as she rose to her knees. She stared at Rhys as he reached down to curl his fingers around his cock.

He stared back at her as be began rolling the length between his fingers, pausing at the head then pinching slightly.

Logan administered a sharp smack to her ass. She smiled. He was getting impatient.

She glanced at him over her shoulder, sending him a sultry stare. Slowly she ran her tongue over her top lip, watching as his jaw tightened in response. Then she turned back to Rhys, arching her ass invitingly in the air.

Rhys guided her down with his free hand, his fingers wrapping in her hair. The tip of his cock rubbed along her lips before she opened and allowed him to slide in.

"That's it, baby," Logan said in a passion-strained voice.

"You feel so good," Rhys breathed.

She took him all, sliding her lips down his cock until he came to rest at the back of her throat. She paused and swallowed, and he shuddered beneath her.

"God, I love it when you do that," Rhys choked out.

Logan reached around to cup her breasts, rolling the nipples between his fingers as she sucked up and down Rhys' erection. He played with the soft mounds for a few moments before moving his hands over her hips and to her ass.

She moaned softly when Logan positioned his cock at her entrance. She shifted back, trying to sheathe him, but he held her off with one hand.

Slowly, achingly slow, he slipped inside, stretching her, lighting fire to her pussy.

Rhys gripped her jaw, holding her as he fucked in and out of her mouth. Logan sank deep, his taut abdomen coming to rest against her ass.

Palms down, Logan ran his hands up her back and into her hair, gathering the strands then cupping the back of her head, pushing her down to meet Rhys' thrusts.

This...this was coming home. This is where she felt safe. Loved and cherished. Between the men she loved. She needed them. She needed their love. Her need was a jagged, double-edged knife, cutting both ways, deep and unrelenting.

She was only whole when she was with them.

Logan stroked deep, taking her hard. She lost herself in the taste of Rhys and the feel of Logan, of giving herself completely to their care.

Then Logan withdrew, and he eased his hands from her hair. Rhys pulled her away from his cock then took her arms and hoisted her up his body.

"Ride me, Cat," he instructed.

Her entire body clenched and tightened as he positioned her over his cock. Logan was still behind her, silent and waiting. She wanted to look but found the anticipation heightened by not knowing just when he'd step in and possess her.

Rhys eased her down, taking care as he came to rest deep inside her.

"Okay?" he asked.

She leaned forward to kiss him, her hair falling over his chest. "More than okay," she whispered.

Rhys' hands moved over her back and down to her buttocks. He held them in his firm grip as he thrust slowly into her. Then he spread her cheeks, baring her fully to Logan.

Cool liquid spilled over the seam of her ass, and she closed her eyes as Logan slid one finger inside.

Too long. It had been too long since they'd taken her, possessed her together. She missed it, craved it with a need that terrified her.

In and out, Logan carefully worked his finger, stretching her and preparing her.

"Are you ready for me, baby?" he asked.

"Please," she begged.

Rhys' hands spread her further open as Logan replaced his finger with his rigid cock. He probed delicately at her entrance, pushing inward with infinite patience.

For a long moment, her body denied him, but he persisted until finally she gave way, and he sank inside.

She went rigid in their arms as she fought the bombardment of physical sensations. She was stretched tight around both their cocks. Her ass burned as Logan started moving, but soon the pain seeped away, replaced by a coil of pleasure, one that bloomed and grew larger as he became more demanding in his movements.

Rhys moved his hands to her hips as Logan grasped her ass. In practiced rhythm, they moved, one forward, one back, filling her, thrusting, harder, deep.

Her breath caught in her throat when Logan withdrew with agonizing slowness. He paused at the rim, the head of his penis just inside her opening. Then he surged forward, burying himself to the hilt.

No work up, no long, slow build to orgasm. She came apart in their arms as the world exploded around her. They didn't stop, though, and instead of fading, her release continued, almost painful as it was prolonged.

On the fringed of her first, a second loomed, taking off where the first one ended.

"Rhys! Logan!"

"We've got you, baby," Logan said from above. "Never doubt that. We've got you."

She leaned into Rhys, panting for breath as her orgasm screamed through her body. His mouth latched onto her nipple, sucking avidly as a lightning storm blew through her veins.

Rhys trembled and then shouted hoarsely. He surged upward, and then she felt a rush of warmth.

Still, Logan pumped against her, his hips slapping against her ass.

He reached down, threaded his fingers through her hair and pulled upward, forcing her head back as he continued to thrust forcefully into her.

Rhys slipped from her pussy, and instead of moving, he reached down and slid his fingers across her clit. She jumped in reaction, his touch magnified by her orgasm.

"Come for us again, Cat," Rhys instructed as he stared up at her.

Logan tugged harder at her hair as Rhys pinched her clit between his fingers.

"I can't," she gasped. "Hurts."

Rhys put his other hand up to her jaw then moved his fingers to trace her lips. "It's the sweetest of hurts," he murmured.

"Give it to us," Logan growled. "I won't stop until you come for us again."

Rhys' hand moved from her face, down to her breasts. He twisted her nipples just enough to give the slightest hint of pain. Already ultrasensitive from her pregnancy, the added stimulation was gasoline on the fire. She shuddered violently, shaking and trembling like a tree in a windstorm.

The dual sensation of Rhys' fingers plucking her nipples and her clit and Logan thrusting furiously into her ass was more than she could take. She gave an inarticulate cry as her release flashed upon her with the speed and intensity of a freight train.

She lost all sense of time and place. She hovered on the verge of consciousness, Rhys' face swimming below her. Sharp, vivid colors burst in her vision. And then she was falling. Faster and harder.

She slumped forward. She was vaguely aware of Rhys catching her, of Logan's hands surrounding her. Her cheek met the warm skin of Rhys' chest, and her eyes fluttered closed.

Chapter Six

Catherine awoke in the still of the morning, when all was quiet and faint light shone around the curtains. She listened hard and could hear the roar of the ocean in the distance.

Hard arms lay over her body, and muscular legs twined with hers. And for a moment, she lay there, simply absorbing the warm contentment of waking in their arms. Their touch was possessive, determined, even in sleep. She gazed at Logan, his jaw dark with stubble. His hair was mussed, and he didn't so much as twitch in his sleep. He looked exhausted.

Carefully, she turned her head to look over her shoulder at Rhys, sprawled out beside her, his hand over her hip, her buttocks drawn into his groin.

When was the last time she'd awakened like this? An ache began in her chest, fierce and piercing. They stumbled into bed long after she went to sleep and got up with barely more than a brush of their lips across her forehead. There was no intimacy to their relationship anymore. They coexisted. There was no other word for it.

The longer she stared at them, the heavier her chest became. Quietly, so as not to awaken them, she extricated herself from their embrace and crawled from the bed. Not pausing to shower, she pulled on a pair of shorts and a T-shirt. She pulled her hair back into a ponytail, not wanting to be bothered by it.

She left the room, no clear path in mind other than she wanted to find a quiet place to be alone with her thoughts. There were many alcoves set amongst dense, strategically planted foliage. Single tables to allow for privacy were in the little niches, and each afforded a view of the beach.

She chose one as far away from the actual hotel as possible and settled into the chair facing the water. A waiter appeared promptly, and she ordered fruit juice, mourning the fact that she'd given up coffee since learning of her pregnancy.

She felt less anxious here. Calm settled over her as she enjoyed the quietness of the morning and the salty breeze off the ocean. Her life might be a wreck, but for the space of a few moments, she could pretend that she was on her dream vacation having the time of her life.

And it should be the time of her life. She should be celebrating her pregnancy, the five years of her marriage to the men she loved more than anything.

She glanced down at her wedding ring and idly twisted the band in circles around her finger. It wasn't a traditional ring. No simple band with a flashy engagement ring on top. They'd chosen a design with three twisting ropes intertwined. One continuous circle, no beginning or ending.

Two years ago, Logan and Rhys had tried to talk her into one of those ostentatious rocks. They felt she deserved something big and expensive now that their financial situation had improved so drastically, but she'd said no. She liked her ring. She didn't want or need bigger and better, not when her first ring held such a wealth of meaning.

So much had changed since their days of barebones existence living hand-to-mouth. But they'd been happy. God, those were the best days of her life. No, they didn't have much money, but it hadn't mattered to her. It never had. What she did have was their love and complete devotion.

The three of them had been together since their early days in college. Logan had come from a dirt-poor family and was only able to attend university via a scholarship. He'd always been the most determined to make something of himself.

Rhys' mother had worked two jobs to make sure he could go to college. When she died during his sophomore year, he'd vowed to see her dream of him graduating and becoming successful come true. Catherine and Logan had gone with him to her funeral, and Rhys had stood there at her grave, head bowed. Catherine had held his hand as he whispered his goodbye to his mother—and his vow to make her proud.

Catherine took another sip of her juice and stared over the water, lost in her memories. Looking back, she couldn't really pinpoint when things had changed from friendship between the three of them to something more. She'd been deeply conflicted about her feelings for both men and desperate not to lose either of them, even if it meant suppressing anything beyond friendship.

Logan, being Logan, had simply brought things to a head one night in their tiny apartment. He'd asked Rhys very bluntly if he loved Catherine. Rhys looked stunned—and guilty—as though he knew Logan loved her as well and that his admission would be a betrayal. But neither could he tell her to her face that he didn't love her.

Logan very matter-of-factly informed Rhys and Catherine that he also loved her. Then he calmly asked her how she felt about them. It had taken several moments for her to gather her courage and lay it on the line. She loved them both.

They hadn't immediately had all the answers. They already lived together, so embarking on a much deeper relationship had been easy. Logan and Rhys were extremely protective of her, not wanting the true nature of their relationship to become public. So outside the privacy of their apartment, they remained three best friends.

As they grew more secure in their relationship, they shed caution. Logan began to talk about a permanent arrangement. Marriage. More and more, he and Rhys didn't care that others knew they loved the same woman. And Catherine? As long as she had their love, nothing else mattered to her.

Wanting to show a visible connection to both men, she legally changed her last name to Cullen, and then she married Logan, taking his last name as well.

A shadow fell over her, obscuring the sun from her face. Dragged from her thoughts, she glanced up to see Rhys looking much as he had the night before. Haggard and tired. Worried.

"Can I sit?" he asked hesitantly.

She shrugged and gestured to the empty chair across from her. The waiter appeared, and Rhys ordered coffee and breakfast.

"You're not eating," he said as he stared at her simple glass of juice.

"I wasn't hungry."

He looked down then lifted his gaze to the distant waves. The breeze ruffled his dark hair, and she studied the lines around his eyes and firm mouth. Those lines weren't there five years ago. Back then he'd always had a ready smile, teasing and fun.

The light had gone out of his green eyes. She couldn't remember the last time she'd seen joy reflected in their depths.

She blinked when he caught her studying him.

"I was worried, Cat," he said quietly.

She shrugged again, unsure of how else to react.

Anger fired in his eyes, surprising her. Emotion. Apparently he was still capable of it, even if it was only anger.

"You didn't used to be so flip," he accused. "God, Cat, I thought you'd walked out on us."

She eyed him calmly, though beneath the surface she seethed like a cauldron. "What makes you think I haven't walked out?"

His eyes narrowed, and his lips tightened.

"Why should I stay, Rhy?" she asked quietly. "Give me one reason I shouldn't leave."

"I love you," he growled. "That should damn well be reason enough."

She smiled sadly then sat back, bringing the glass of juice to her lips. She took a small sip then pulled it away from her mouth, letting it dangle in front of her vision, something to focus on.

She glanced up at him. "Do you remember what it was like before we got married?"

His brows drew together in confusion. She ignored him and went on.

"Us three sharing a one-bedroom apartment, eating beans and franks, stocking up on ramen noodles because it was all we could afford. The foot rubs you used to give me when I came home from a double shift at the diner."

She stared dreamily off into the distance as those memories wrapped her in their warm embrace.

Rhys made a sound of impatience. "I try not to remember those days."

She jerked her gaze back to him to see a deep scowl marring his features. "Why?"

"Because we had nothing," he gritted out. "Logan and I couldn't take care of you. You worked too damn hard to support our start-up efforts."

She smiled gently. "And what do we have now?"

"We have money," he said bluntly. "We have a nice place to live, the best food to eat. You don't have to work yourself ragged."

"I'm not happy," she said, being equally blunt.

He looked at her in shock, his cheeks losing their color.

"I haven't been happy in a long time. Too long," she amended.

"Why?" he asked in a voice that cracked.

Her hand shook as she lowered the glass back to the table. "You don't love me," she said softly. "You don't even know I exist half the time unless it's to call me and say you can't make dinner or you're leaving on a last-minute business trip."

"We love you, Catherine, and we're not letting you go without a fight," Logan said in a grim voice.

She looked up to see him standing a few feet away, partially obscured by the greenery. He stepped forward, his face creased with determination. The waiter, ever solicitous, appeared with another chair that he hastily shoved up to the table. A second waiter appeared to deliver Rhys' food as Logan took his seat. He waved off a menu and ordered coffee.

"How much did you overhear?" she asked quietly.

"Everything," Logan bit out. "Every single ridiculous part."

She raised one eyebrow. "How like you to discount my feelings," she murmured. "God knows you've had enough practice."

Logan shifted impatiently. "Look, baby, I'm sorry we missed our anniversary dinner, and I'm sorry we cancelled the trip. Sorrier than you know. If there was any way I could have avoided it, believe me I would have."

She held her hand up, refusing to be swayed by those dark eyes caressing her, his tone low and beseeching.

"Once, I could understand. Hell, a dozen even. But you've made it your practice to put me second." She broke off with an indelicate snort, one that bordered precariously close to tears. "I doubt I rank anywhere as high as second. I've spent the last few years begging, craving your time, your love. I've been patient. I've been understanding. I've smiled and nodded when I was screaming on the inside. I accept that it's my fault. I let it go on way too long, but you know what? I don't have to do it any longer. You speak of an anniversary dinner and one cancelled trip, and God, I wish that was all it was. Would that it were that simple. You've made your lives without me, without regard to my feelings or my wants and needs. Well, it's time for me to step up and be responsible for my own happiness."

She stood, no longer able to remain still, to sit there calmly and rationally. She couldn't pretend to have a civil breakfast conversation when her entire life was falling apart.

"Cat, wait," Rhys called as she ducked out of the alcove and hurried down the winding paths.

"Catherine, damn it, stop."

Logan was close. She couldn't outrun him, but she wouldn't go meekly to the slaughter. Her spine stiff, she continued at a fast clip until his hand snagged her elbow and pulled her up short.

He yanked her around, pulling her close until she collided with his chest. His other hand cupped her face, and he slanted his lips over hers, drinking deep, tasting her, devouring her like a man starving.

"I won't let you go," he vowed. "You can say what you want. You can rail at me. You can hit me, hate me, but I'm never letting you go."

"You don't have a choice. You can't make me love you, Logan."

It was a sorry thing to say even as angry as she was. Hurt flashed in his eyes, and he looked...devastated. Her heart contracted as he stared at her.

"Are you saying you don't love me anymore?" he asked in a tight voice.

She closed her eyes as a tear slid down her cheek. "You know I love you."

"Prove it," he challenged.

She yanked her arm angrily away from him. "I don't have to prove anything to you," she spit out.

"Come back to the room with me and Rhys and listen to what we have to say, Catherine. Give us a chance. Let us try to make you happy again."

She glanced over his shoulder to see Rhys standing in the pathway, hands shoved into his pants pockets. He looked tired and defeated.

"Please, baby," Logan said softly. He reached for her hand, curling her fingers into his. His thumb stroked over her palm, and he brought her hand up to his mouth to kiss her knuckles.

"No sex," she said solemnly, knowing damn well they'd both use any means necessary to press their advantage. "Sex won't fix what's wrong."

Logan scowled.

"Talk. You're supposed to talk to me." As much as she wanted them to touch her again, to take her, to possess her—she'd spent the last months aching for them to do just that—they had to talk about the problem, not disguise it with sex.

Rhys chuckled in the background, and Logan only scowled harder.

"Jesus Christ, Catherine, when did you become one of those *let's talk about our feelings* girls?"

"When you stopped talking to me," she replied.

Not giving him a chance to respond or protest, she walked around him and back toward the hotel. Rhys fell into step beside her, but she ignored him as she made her way to the lobby.

She punched angrily at the elevator button, impatient when it didn't immediately respond. Rhys quietly took her hand and held it close to his body while they waited for the doors to open.

He couldn't know how much it hurt her to be this close, to feel him touch her so lovingly. If he did, surely he wouldn't do it.

He ushered her into the elevator, Logan crowding in behind them. She backed away as he closed in on her. His hands cupped her shoulders, and he kissed her deeply, hungrily.

"Do you remember, baby?" he asked huskily. "Remember when the elevator broke down in our old apartment?"

Fire bloomed in her cheeks. Oh yes, she remembered. Logan and Rhys had been insatiable. They'd taken her on the floor, against the doors, one holding her while the other fucked her in long delicious strokes. Then they held her between them, one fucking her ass while the other fucked her pussy. By the time the elevator was up and running again, she'd been thoroughly exhausted, and Logan had carried her back to the apartment.

"I remember," she whispered.

The elevator doors opened, and Logan reluctantly stepped away. He reached back for her hand as Rhys curled his fingers around her other. They pulled her toward their suite, and she followed, her heart lodged painfully in her throat.

Cooler air hit her, sending a shiver down her aching spine. Rhys turned and took her into his arms, his hands sliding up and down her back.

"What do you want, Cat? Tell me. I'll do anything for you."

"A long soaking bath," she mumbled against his chest. "You need to shave."

He chuckled. "Let me take care of you. I'll go draw you a bath and while you soak, I'll shave, and we'll talk. We used to do that a lot."

"Yeah, we did," she said with a smile.

"I'm going to hit the shower," Logan said. "I imagine we'll all feel better and *calmer* after a bath." He eyed her pointedly as he made his statement as though her hysteria could be blamed on the need for a bath. She almost laughed.

"Sit here," Rhys said as he eased her down on the bed. "I'll be right back."

With a sigh, she let him put her where he wanted and watched as he hurried to the bathroom. She slipped her flip-flops off and flexed her toes. She was tired. Weary to her bones. Just when she had her mind made up about the direction she wanted her life to take, Rhys and Logan stormed in and turned everything around.

She couldn't let them change her mind. Not when she'd finally grown a spine and decided to stop being the martyr in the relationship. On the other hand, was she being fair? How could she expect them to change, to make her happy, if she didn't tell them what she wanted, needed, and give them the chance to react?

A dull ache began at her temples. About the time she thought she'd taken a proactive stance, she realized that she'd reacted like a twit. Reactionary. Instead of standing up, fighting back and saying *no, it's not okay for you to ditch me again*, she'd stomped off like a sulky child.

Rhys returned and reached down for her hand. At first he just stroked it lightly with his fingertips, reawakening her to the pleasure she always found in his touch. She'd often told him that his fingers were the sweetest kind of magic.

Gently, he took her hand in his and pulled upward until she stood in front of him. Wordlessly, he undressed her, his palms and the pads of his fingertips brushing over her skin.

"Come," he said in a husky voice. "I've got your bath ready."

She followed him into the bathroom and gasped in surprise when she saw the beautiful arrangement he'd made. The tub was full of sudsy water, and lining the sides were scented, lit candles. Interspersed between the candles were red rose petals from the bouquet on the counter.

He kissed her once, lingeringly, before helping her over the side of the tub. She settled into the hot water with a blissful sigh. Oh, she needed this. Needed it badly.

She closed her eyes and leaned her head against the rim of the tub. The sound of the shower being turned on registered, and she heard Rhys get in.

A few minutes. It was all she needed. Just a few minutes to rest and relax.

Chapter Seven

"Sleeping in the tub isn't a good idea, baby."

Catherine's eyes fluttered open to see Logan sitting on the edge of the tub at her feet, studying her. She glanced over to where Rhys was shaving by the sink, his face still half-covered with shaving cream.

"I'm tired," she admitted.

She knew she had her pregnancy to blame for some of her fatigue. Honestly, there were days she couldn't even hold her head up, but she hadn't slept well at all since she'd left New York to come on vacation alone.

Logan's expression softened. "I think we could all use some rest. I know I'd sleep a lot better with you cuddled between us. What do you say we take a nap, order in some room service and spend the day together."

She was tempted. God, it sounded like heaven. Her indecision and temptation must have shone on her face because both men honed in.

"I'll give you a foot rub," Rhys said. "Logan can brush your hair. You always loved that."

Tears pricked her eyelids. It had been so long since they'd taken care of her. She missed them so much it was a physical ache. She longed for those much simpler days when they didn't have anything more than each other.

"We were supposed to talk," she said firmly.

"And we will," Logan interjected. "I can't think of a better way to spend the day. In bed, with you, talking."

"No sex?" she said with a raised eyebrow.

Logan uttered a soft hmmmph.

"No sex," Rhys said, and Logan shot him the evil eye.

She suppressed her smile and languidly began washing her body, raising one leg to run the cloth down then lowering it before raising the other.

Two sets of male eyes were glued to the motion of the cloth, and unable to resist teasing them a bit, she lifted her arm, making her breasts bob above the waterline. Carefully, she ran the cloth down the length of her arm and then over the taut tips of her breasts.

Logan's breath released in a hiss, and he changed his position on the tub's edge. His erection couldn't be disguised, however.

Feeling only a little guilty for inspiring lust she had no intention of sating, she tossed the washcloth aside and started to rise.

Logan reached for her hand, and after a brief moment of hesitation, she wrapped her fingers around his and let him pull her to stand in the tub.

Water and soapy bubbles cascaded down her body, and she hurriedly stepped out to wrap herself in the towel Rhys held. She let herself be enveloped, not only by the warmth of the towel, but by the heat of his embrace as he gathered her tightly to him.

"What would you like to eat?" Logan asked. "I noticed you didn't eat breakfast."

She shook her head. "Nothing yet. I'll wait and eat lunch with you and Rhys."

She tucked the end of the towel between her breasts and walked out of the bathroom, leaving the men to follow. The lushness of the bed called to her. Unable to resist, she shed the towel, crawled into the middle and collapsed facedown into the pillow.

Tired. She was so tired.

The bed dipped beside her, and gentle fingers tugged at her chin. "Sit up, baby, and I'll brush your hair."

She struggled to her knees, but her breast glanced over Logan's fingers. She nearly moaned when he tugged at one stiff nipple. He scooted against the headboard then turned her until her bottom was nestled between his thighs.

Rhys sat down at the end of the bed and cupped one of her feet in his palms. As Logan gathered the long strands of her hair, Rhys began massaging her instep. She sighed deeply as the men showered her with love and affection. She soaked it up like a rain-starved desert would a drop of water.

For several long minutes, they tended her, the only sounds being her sighs of pleasure. When she was nearly asleep sitting up, Logan leaned down and kissed the curve of her neck. A delicate shiver cascaded down her spine.

Rhys let her foot fall as Logan maneuvered from behind her. He plumped pillows and situated her in the middle as they took their places on either side of her.

Rhys reclined on his side, resting his cheek in his palm as he gazed at her. Logan adopted a similar position and let his fingers drift lazily over her hip and down her leg.

"Don't leave us, Catherine," Logan said abruptly. "I know you're hurt and angry, but we can work this out."

"Can we? And are you speaking for Rhys now?"

Both men looked startled at the bitterness in her voice.

"Of course he doesn't speak for me, Cat, but in this case, everything he says is true. We *can* work this out. I love you."

Her lips turned down into a resigned moue. "There's so much I want to say," she said in frustration. "So much that should have been said years ago."

"Then say it now," Logan said calmly. "We can't fix it if we don't know what's wrong, and damn it, Catherine, we—*I*—want to fix it."

She looked at her fingers clasped together in her lap. She pressed them together until the tips whitened. "Each of you has been handing me off to the other for a long time. Taking a team approach to our relationship."

Logan's protest was swift, but she silenced him with a look. "Let me finish. It's true. At first you both took your commitment to me very seriously. You took nothing for granted. Over time it became easier for the two of you to rely on each other instead of nurturing your relationship with me."

Logan made a strangled sound of irritation. He'd never been able to stomach touchy-feely emotional talk, and she knew it, but he couldn't avoid it this time. She would have her say. Rhys was more subdued. He wore an almost guilty expression as if she had touched on something he'd already realized.

"That's bullshit," Logan muttered.

She eyed him straight on. "You didn't have to be there all the time if Rhys was around. Rhys didn't have to feel bad about missing an event or special occasion if you were going to be there. You tag-teamed me instead of treating our relationship as one between the two of us instead of the three of us. You had it good. One of you was on standby at all times. Can't pay attention to poor ole Catherine? She has two husbands. She doesn't need but one around, right? Well, you were wrong."

She crossed her arms over her chest as her anger grew.

"Eventually you stopped even that, and both of you shut me out, placed everything ahead of me, your business, your colleagues, even your personal assistant got more of your attention than I did."

"We were busy making our business a success," Logan said tightly.

"At the expense of your marriage? Tell me, Logan, was it worth it? I've long thought money and success was more important to you than I was, but I want to hear it. Maybe I need to hear it, because imagining it is so much worse. Maybe I need to face it instead of wavering back and forth as I wonder if I'm overreacting."

Rhys sucked in his breath, and Logan's eyes widened in shock. For a long moment, there was complete silence as if both men were absorbing, finally, how dangerously close they were to a relationship that wasn't salvageable.

"We did it for you," Logan said, his voice strained and low. "We wanted the best for you."

"You and Rhys are...were what's best for me."

She uncurled her fingers and crossed her arms, trailing her hands up to her shoulders in an effort to instill comfort, anything to make the feeling of emptiness go away.

"I can't go on living like this," she whispered. "I deserve better."

Logan stared at Catherine. His wife. She looked utterly small and defeated and so damned sad. Worse, she looked resigned. She didn't see any other option other than leaving.

Panic knotted his stomach. He couldn't wrap his brain around a future without Catherine. No, he hadn't been around much. He and Rhys had been throwing themselves into their company. Making it a success. Never had he imagined that it could cost him the one person who'd loved him when he'd had nothing, been nobody.

He exchanged glances with Rhys, and Logan could see the same despair in his friend's eyes. Sex wouldn't fix this. Catherine was right about that much. Hell, he didn't even know what would fix this.

Or if it could be fixed at all.

He opened his mouth to speak. To say something, anything, but nothing came out. How could he possibly make up for years of hurt and neglect in a few days' time?

It seemed so simple now. He could have done so much differently, but she was right. He and Rhys had taken her for granted. She'd always stood by them, supported and loved them unconditionally. And now they faced losing her because they'd squandered her gift.

Rhys reached out and took Catherine's hand. She glanced at the other man, pain burning brightly in her eyes.

"Don't give up, Cat," Rhys said in a voice that sounded very close to pleading. But hell, right now Logan would beg if that's what it took, and he and Rhys had never begged for anything.

"We're here now. Give us the vacation we promised you. It's a starting point. We have a lot to work out, but we can't do that if you aren't with us."

"No cell phones, no email," Logan interjected. "Just you and us. Give us a chance to work this out, Catherine. I won't let you go without one hell of a fight."

Her eyes widened as she turned to stare at Logan. "Can you do that? Don't you have deals to work, people to stay in touch with?"

Logan cursed under his breath. Then he reached out to cup her chin. "You are more important than all of those things, baby. I know we haven't acted like it, and we have a lot to make up, to prove to you. But it starts now."

Indecision flickered in her expressive eyes, giving her a fragility that inspired every one of his protective instincts. And then he nearly laughed. Protective? When had he protected her? She'd been fending for herself for years.

"Give us a chance, Cat," Rhys asked softly. "Please."

"Answer me one question," Logan said, still holding her chin. His thumb stroked across her cheek and then over the fullness of her lips. "Do you still love us?"

Liquid emotion surged and welled in her eyes. Beneath his touch, her lips trembled and quaked.

"Because we love you, baby," he said softly. "That much hasn't changed. Will never change."

"I do love you," she whispered. "But sometimes...sometimes it just isn't enough."

"It will be," he said firmly. "I swear it will be."

Logan dropped his hand away from her face, and she glanced between him and Rhys. She drew in her bottom lip between her teeth, her brow creased in concentration. It bothered the hell out of him that she had to stop and consider for so long whether she was willing to stay with them.

"Catherine?" he prompted.

"All right," she said. "No cell phones, no emails, just us on vacation."

Chapter Eight

Rhys curled his arms tighter around Cat, but she didn't even stir. She was warm and soft against him, and he realized how long it had been since they'd lain like this. No hurry, no meetings to go to, no early a.m. flights or conference calls.

She was right. He and Logan had dropped the ball in their relationship with her, and it sickened him that he hadn't seen it until it was too late. Too late to prevent her hurt and sadness.

He wouldn't allow that it was too late for their marriage.

He glanced up at Logan, who was preparing to phone in the room service order. "She's exhausted," he murmured.

Logan frowned as he held the phone to his ear. "She looks different. I can't put my finger on it. Somehow she seems more fragile. I don't know, like she could break at any time. I don't like it."

Rhys didn't respond because Logan broke off to place the food order. He was right, though. Cat looked fragile. Dark shadows rested in the hollows beneath her eyes. Hollows that didn't used to be there. She was thinner too. There was a sadness that hung over her, one that suggested it wasn't a recent unhappiness but one that had resided for a length of time.

His jaw tightened as his teeth came together. They would change this. He would change it. He couldn't remember not loving Catherine. Yeah, he'd taken her for granted in a huge way, but never because he didn't love her or want her with every breath he took.

Logan hung up the phone and glanced toward Rhys. "Food will be here in twenty minutes. We'll let her sleep until then."

Rhys lightly touched her cheek with his finger. He wanted to kiss her. He ached to love her, to make love to her, just the two of them. He looked back up at Logan. "I want some time with her," he said in a quiet voice.

Logan nodded and ran a weary hand through his hair. "We both need time with her. She booked two weeks at this resort, but it's going to take longer than that to make this right."

"What are we going to do about work?" Rhys asked.

As much as they were willing to do whatever it took to get Catherine back, as important as she was to them, they couldn't just blow off their commitments. It would ruin them.

Logan slouched down into a chair several feet from the bed. "I'm going to make some phone calls in the morning, iron out as much as I can, streamline things so they can run as long without us as possible. I don't think Catherine means for us to do anything drastic in regards to the company. Her point is we've cut her completely out of the picture."

He sighed and tilted his head up to stare at the ceiling.

"And she's right. That's what we've done. Here we are poised to land the biggest deal of our lives, and at the same time, we figure out what utter fuck-ups we are."

His chin came to rest on his chest as he refocused his attention on Rhys. "What the fuck are we going to do, Rhy? We can't lose her. We can't lose our business. I feel like everything is slipping away, and it scares the shit out of me."

It was unusual to see a chink in Logan's armor. He was always controlled and methodical. Now he looked defeated.

"We win her back," Rhys said simply. "We give her a vacation to remember, but more importantly, we make her remember how much we love her."

Logan nodded. "Yeah, I know. I'm just...worried."

Rhys looked down at Cat, the soft rise and fall of her chest. "So am I," he admitted.

*
**

Catherine awoke to the smell of food. Seafood. Rhys was propped on an elbow at her side, and Logan was busy setting food on the bed. She glanced down at the selection, and her stomach promptly revolted.

Saliva pooled in her mouth, and her stomach heaved. She took in several short breaths, praying she wouldn't need to make a run for the bathroom.

She closed her eyes as the knot grew bigger inside her belly. A flush of heat billowed over her body, and then she went cold just as quickly.

Throwing off the covers, she lunged out of bed.

"Cat, what the hell?" Rhys demanded.

Her bare feet hit the tile of the bathroom floor, and her knees quickly followed as she gripped the toilet seat with her hands to steady herself.

Stomach lurching, she painfully heaved, nothing coming up as her belly clenched and spasmed. Still, she couldn't stop the dry retches, and moaned when her body convulsed again.

"Cat, honey, are you okay?"

Rhys put his hands on her shoulders then slid his fingers over her hair to pull it out of the way.

"What the hell is wrong?" Logan demanded from the doorway. "Do I need to get a doctor?"

She shook her head sharply even as another dry heave seized her.

"Easy now," Rhys said soothingly. "Do you want something to drink? Would that help?"

She leaned into his shoulder, feeling like a wet noodle. She'd gone too long without eating, but the idea of the seafood waiting for her made her stomach protest all the more.

"I just need something to eat," she said as she pushed away from Rhys. She looked apologetically up at Logan. "Something besides seafood?"

"There's soup and a pasta starter," Logan replied. "That okay?"

She smiled and tried to stand. Rhys caught her in his arms and hoisted her upward. "I'm fine, Rhys," she said. Then she turned back to Logan. "Soup and pasta sound wonderful."

They sat on the bed, cross-legged, her naked except for the sheet draped across her lap and Logan and Rhys in shorts. The soup soothed her stomach and allowed her to eat the pasta. She was hungrier than she'd thought and finished not only her portion but the men's as well.

"No more skipping meals," Logan said darkly. "You haven't been sleeping either."

She eyed him levelly. "I haven't been sleeping well in ages, Logan. I never sleep well when you and Rhys aren't there."

Dark color flooded his cheeks, and she felt a twinge of guilt. She hadn't really meant it as a dart, but as an honest statement of fact.

"What would you like to do tomorrow?" Rhys asked.

She turned to him and pursed her lips. "Honestly? I'd like to have breakfast at a little shack I found while surfing the internet. It's down the beach, and they're supposed to have wonderful food. Then I'd like to do some sunbathing and maybe a little swimming."

She shifted her gaze to Logan to see him staring intently at her. "Then I'd like to come back and take a long, hot bath, maybe schedule a massage in the spa and then go out to dinner and dancing."

Logan scowled. "I don't want another man's hands on my wife. I'll give you a damn massage."

She laughed. "Who says it would be a man?"

"Don't want us to rub you down?" Rhys asked with a wicked grin.

"I'd love it," she said honestly.

She stared at the both of them, their relaxed postures, the easy smile on Rhys' face.

"I've missed this," she said. "I've missed you."

Logan leaned forward, his hand cupping her chin with a firm grip. His lips brushed across hers, lightly at first then coming back, firmer, more demanding.

"I've missed you, baby. So damn much."

She brought her hand up to his cheek. Her lips parted as his tongue probed and pushed inward. To her surprise, as she pulled away, Rhys was gone.

She blinked in surprise and surveyed the room. "Rhys?" she called.

"He'll be back, baby. He's leaving us alone for a while. A favor I intend to repay as soon as possible."

She turned her stare back to him. "Oh."

"You're right," he said reluctantly. "Rhys and I haven't treated this relationship as one between you and me and him and you. It's not fair to you, and we want that to change."

"No more passing me off to the free man?" she asked with a slight lift to the corner of her mouth.

"I have a feeling, before long, you're going to be very, very sick of seeing us," he said as he pulled her to him again.

She melted against him, absorbing his warmth. "Not a chance," she murmured against his mouth, just before she kissed him. Hard.

"Uh, baby? I thought you said no sex."

"I lied."

Chapter Nine

Catherine pushed at Logan, sending him sprawling onto the pillows.

"Tell me you're planning to have your wicked way with me," he said in a tone so hopeful she had to laugh.

On hands and knees, she crawled up his body, letting her breasts slide over the tops of his legs and then his abdomen. The shorts he wore bulged at the crotch, the material tight and straining.

"Is that for me?" she asked sweetly as she gave his cock a gentle pat.

He grabbed her hand and cupped it over his erection until she could feel the length of him in her palm.

"Oh, it's for you all right," he said with a grunt.

She leaned down and grazed her teeth across the material of his shorts. He cursed and flinched, his legs trembling beneath her.

Repositioning her hands, she put them palms down across the tops of his thighs. His skin was warm and hair-roughened beneath her touch. She slid her palms upward, underneath the legs of his shorts, inward until she boldly cupped his hardness.

Her fingers flexed and skimmed down to the base and below to his sac. She fondled and rolled it in her hand until he arched his hips, straining for more.

"Take them off, Catherine," he rasped.

She smiled and removed her hands. She tugged at the waistband of his shorts, pulling them down around his hips as he bowed upward so she could remove them.

When she had them around his knees, he growled with impatience, reached down and yanked them off before throwing them across the room.

"Come here," he ordered as he reached for her.

She went willingly, pressing her body to his. She sighed in complete and utter pleasure as his body cradled hers. They fit so perfectly, blended together, her soft curves to his harder planes.

She twined her arms around him and just laid her head on his chest for a long moment. He kissed the top of her head and ran his hands lovingly up and down her back, petting, caressing, feathering light touches across her skin.

"I've missed you so much, baby."

She turned her face into his chest and kissed his skin.

"I want you to ride me," he said as he lifted her upward. "Just like you did Rhys. You looked so damn sexy. I've never wanted to be him so bad in my life."

She barely had time to grasp his cock and position him before he lowered her down. He held her for a moment to give her time to adjust and then pulled her until she sheathed him completely.

Her hands flew out to brace against his chest as she twitched around his cock. She felt impossibly stretched, deliciously so. She was slick around him, and she slid up and down with ease.

There was comfort in their familiarity, that after so long, they could come back together, remembering every touch of the past. Her chest tightened, her heart seizing with love.

"I love you," she whispered, echoing what filled her.

"Oh baby, I love you," he returned.

He reached up, cupped her face and pulled her down to meet his kiss. He rolled his hips upward, thrusting into her even as his tongue thrust between her lips.

She met his tongue with her own, tasting him, absorbing his strength, his scent.

"I'll never let you go," he whispered. "You have to know that."

A fist clutched at her throat. Her nose stung, and she fought the swell of emotion. She wanted to believe him. She wanted to reach out and hold his words close to her heart. More than anything she wanted to be with him and Rhys. Always.

"I don't want to go," she said in a broken voice. "I never wanted to go anywhere. But I couldn't stay, Logan."

He kissed her again, swallowing her distress. His arms encircled her, his hands splaying out over her back, cupping her tenderly. They slid down to her ass, and he lifted then lowered her, aiding his thrusts.

"Ride me, baby. Sit up and take your man. Take him hard."

She rose, feeling like a goddess, power flowing through her when she saw the feral light in his eyes. He wanted her desperately. No matter the past, right here and right now, he only saw her. Only wanted her. He was hers to command, his body her playground.

Her hands trailed up the midline of his chest, then parted as her fingers circled his nipples. She played in the fine hairs on his upper chest, then chased them down his firm belly to his navel.

The muscles in his abdomen clenched and rippled as she picked up her pace. She squeezed her knees against his sides, threw back her head and raised her hands to her breasts.

He trembled and shook as she rose and fell above him. She cupped her breasts in her palms and pinched the nipples between her fingers, elongating them into taut peaks.

His fingers dug into her hips as she continued to tease him. "I'm close, baby. So close," he groaned. "Come with me. I want you with me."

She paused for the merest of moments. Leaning down, she swept her lips across his in a tender kiss. "I've never wanted to be without you, Logan."

Clutching him to her, she undulated her hips, closing her eyes as her orgasm blew like wind, the most gentle of breezes, through her groin.

Warm, sweet, and spreading like honey, pleasure...love. She shook, and he held her. His cry sounded in her ears as he flooded into her.

Suddenly she was swept into the grip of yet another orgasm, sharper this time, the first merely a prelude.

"Logan!" she gasped.

He fused his mouth to hers, gasping for breath even as he took hers. He devoured her, ravenous, hungry. His teeth grazed her lips, nipped then sucked avidly.

His hands gripped her buttocks, pressing her against him as he bucked underneath her. Finally he slowed, his thrusts more gentle, long and easy.

She came to rest on top of him, her body limp and satisfied, draped across him like a rag. His hands caressed her, moving over her curves with tenderness that made her ache.

"Can you reach the covers?" he asked faintly. "Because I'm not sure I can move."

She chuckled softly and reached blindly down, groping for the sheets. She made a halfhearted kick then pulled them over her body to cover them both.

"Another nap sounds pretty damn good," he murmured in her ear.

"Want me to move?" she asked in a sleepy voice, though she had no desire to go anywhere.

"Don't move a muscle. You feel good."

"Love you," she whispered.

"I love you too, baby."

He squeezed her close to him, and for the first time in a long time, she felt like things would actually be all right.

Chapter Ten

Logan got up the next morning, the pale light of dawn filtering through the drapes. Rhys was sprawled on the couch across the suite, and Logan winced at how uncomfortable he looked.

He pulled on a pair of shorts then walked over to Rhys and shook him awake.

"You look like hell, man," Logan said in amusement.

"Gee thanks," Rhys said around a yawn.

"Look, I wanted to say thanks for yesterday."

Rhys sat up and wiped the sleep from his eyes. "Not a problem."

"I'd like to return the favor this morning. I need to make phone calls so we can kick-start this vacation. I know we were supposed to all have breakfast together, but why don't I leave you with Catherine, and I'll catch up to you later on the beach."

Rhys nodded and looked over at the bed. Longing flickered in his eyes.

"I'll hop in the shower and be out of here in ten minutes," Logan promised.

Rhys hauled himself up and headed for the bed. He crawled up next to Catherine and pulled her into his arms.

She muttered a sleepy "Rhys", and Logan smiled. He felt lighter today. He felt hope. The mind-numbing panic was, for the moment, gone.

He and Rhys were getting another chance, and he was determined they wouldn't fuck it up.

*
**

Catherine woke to Rhys' lips pressing tender kisses over her shoulder.

"Morning, sleeping beauty," he murmured.

She turned over and cuddled into his chest. "Where were you?" she asked.

"I was here. I slept on the couch. Miss me?"

She put her hand to his chest, content to touch him. "Very much. Where's Logan?"

"He's making phone calls."

She stiffened, and Rhys cupped her chin, forcing her gaze upward. "It's not what you think, Cat. When we flew down here, we weren't sure if we'd find you or if you were even here. We left abruptly, and no one knows where the hell we are. He needs to smooth some things with the company and make it so we can spend the rest of our vacation here with you."

Shame crowded her mind. "I'm sorry. I know I'm oversensitive. I don't expect you to drop everything."

"No, but you should be able to expect our attention. Our love and our regard. From now on, you'll have those things. I swear it."

She smiled and reached up to kiss him. "So is it just you and me for breakfast?"

"Hmm, well I know what I want," he murmured.

She gasped as he began to make his way down her body with those sinful lips. When he reached her belly, she felt a flutter, a warm sensation as he kissed where his child was cradled.

She should tell them now. No, the announcement hadn't gone the way she'd planned, but that was the way the cookie crumbled sometimes. But then again, if she told them now, it would change the entire dynamic of their vacation.

Ten more days wouldn't matter, and then she could give them the two EPT sticks she'd wrapped for their anniversary present as soon as they returned home.

She smiled as she imagined their reactions. And then they could spend the evening making love as they dreamed about the future.

Rhys rolled over her and situated himself between her legs as he pressed a kiss to her navel. Then he worked lower, spreading her thighs as he moved down.

She held her breath as his finger gently delved between her folds, parting the delicate skin. His warm breath blew over the highly sensitized flesh, and then his tongue rasped over her clitoris.

"Rhys!"

He chuckled and continued to nuzzle her. Each brush of his tongue sent a shockwave through her belly. Her pussy clenched and she strained upward, wanting more.

"I'm going to make you come," he growled. "All over my mouth. I want to taste it."

She shuddered and closed her eyes. She reached up to grasp the headboard, holding tight as she writhed beneath him. His hands slid underneath her ass, cupping the globes as he raised her to his mouth.

His tongue plunged deep, warm and wet, rough and yet exquisitely tender. Her legs fell open wider, and he sucked her straining clit between his teeth.

"Come for me, love." He flicked his teeth over her clit, barely grazing the peak, but it sent spasms racing straight to her core.

"I love you," she whispered. "I need you so much, Rhys."

His mouth, whisper-sweet, soft and fluttering, pressed against her quivering flesh. He kissed her, just one gentle kiss.

She shattered, there in his arms, against his mouth. A sob spilled from her lips. The ceiling blurred, and she closed her eyes as sweet bliss descended, filling her, lifting her high then floating downward like a leaf riding the wind.

Her hands left the headboard, and she reached blindly down, wanting to touch him, to connect. He moved up her body, pulling her close then sweeping down to claim her lips.

"I love you too, Cat, and I'm never letting you go."

He rolled to the side, bringing her with him. He tucked her head under his chin as she nestled into his body. It felt so good to be back in his arms.

"Let's shower together then go eat breakfast," Rhys murmured close to her ear. "Logan said he'd meet us on the beach."

"That means I have to move," she said on a blissful sigh. "I don't want to move."

He chuckled and stroked a hand through her hair. "I'd love nothing better than to keep you naked and in bed all day, but you need to eat. I don't want any more episodes like last night. While we're here, Logan and I are going to take very good care of you, which means you'll eat and sleep well."

She smiled and turned her face up to his. "I love you," she repeated, because she just couldn't say it enough.

He leaned down to kiss the tip of her nose. "And I love you. Now let's go get cleaned up. I'm starving."

Chapter Eleven

Catherine laughed and did a twirl on the beach, her head thrown back, her blond hair streaming down her back. The power her laughter had on Logan was phenomenal. He hadn't realized just how long she'd been so unhappy. How long *he'd* been unhappy.

The last week had been nothing short of magical as he and Rhys had done everything they could to put back together their tattered relationship with their wife. She was smiling again, and lightness reflected in her eyes.

They teased and played, and it brought back the old days with startling clarity. Catherine had been right. They had been happier then. Even with nothing. They'd had each other, and he and Rhys had damn sure had her love.

It was humbling that his quest to make it big, to provide for Catherine, to be a success, had nearly brought him his greatest failure.

She ran for him, Rhys chasing behind her. He grinned as she launched herself into his arms.

Logan gathered her close and whirled her around, placing his back between her and Rhys.

"This is a switch," he said with a laugh. "Usually it's you running for Rhys."

She shrieked when Rhys ducked around him and made a grab for her waist. Logan hoisted her over his shoulder and playfully shoved at Rhys.

He headed for the water, his hand cupped possessively over her ass.

"Logan, no!" she exclaimed when she figured out his intent. "Rhys, help!"

Rhys died laughing. "Oh, now you want my help. Weren't you running from me a minute ago? Sorry, sweetheart. You're on your own."

Logan smacked her on the behind and waded into the water. She wiggled and squirmed as she tried to extricate herself from his grip. Finally she stopped fighting and started pleading.

"I can't believe you'd be so mean," she said in exasperation. "I ran to you for help!"

He allowed her body to slide down his until her lips were in line with his own, but still he held her, her toes just dipping into the surf. He waded deeper as he kissed her.

"Yes, you did, and I helped. Do you see Rhys anywhere?"

"Beast," she muttered.

He nipped at her bottom lip just before he launched himself forward like a tree toppling in the forest. They landed in the water, his arms curled protectively around her body.

She came up with him, sputtering for air, her frown murderous even as laughter gleamed in her eyes.

"Oh darn, now we both need a shower," he said innocently.

She wiped her hair from her eyes then laughed. "You are so pathetic."

"No, I just really, really love what you do to me in the shower." He nearly groaned when his entire body tightened.

"Well, you're carrying me back, because I'm not getting all that sand caked on my wet body."

He reached down and plucked her out of the water. She landed with a thump against his chest, and he grinned down at her. "I think Rhys has a good idea what I'm up to. Seems he's disappeared. Maybe he's warming up the shower."

"And maybe he wants what you've been getting," she said in a teasing voice.

"Oh, there's no doubt about that, baby. He'd be a damn fool not to."

Logan picked up his pace, hurrying across the sand and to the pathway leading to the hotel. The little tease had taken to joining him in the shower and giving certain portions of his anatomy very personal attention. It almost made him want to start taking three or four a day for that very reason.

He also made it a point to pay her back in very creative fashion.

A few minutes later, he burst into their suite, and sure enough, the shower was running. Only Rhys, the bastard, was already in it. He started to turn and go into the other bathroom with Catherine, but she grinned and slid out of his arms.

She leaned up on tiptoe to kiss him. "Give me five minutes. Poor Rhys is probably feeling neglected. He'll be out shortly and then you can come wash me."

She sashayed toward the shower, her ass swaying, that tiny little string of her thong rubbing erotically between those delectable cheeks.

"Goddamn Rhys," he groaned as his cock grew even harder.

Catherine opened the shower door to find Rhys standing under the spray, eyes closed, his hand curled around his engorged cock.

"Expecting me?" she asked huskily.

He opened his eyes and stared at her, lust tightening his features. She stepped forward, leaving the stall open so Logan could see the two of them and anticipate the fact that he was next.

There was a degree of naughtiness in what she planned. The idea of sucking off both men in the shower filled her with evil glee. But more enticing than that was the knowledge of what they'd do to her afterwards.

When Rhys reached to turn off the water, she put a hand on his wrist.

"Leave it," she murmured.

She stripped off her bikini then shook out her hair before ducking her head under the spray. Knowing that both men were watching her, she ran her hands seductively up her body, over her curves. Her breasts, taut and aching, felt heavy in her palms.

They tingled as she slowly caressed and teased the nipples until they puckered and stood painfully erect.

Rhys groaned and curled his hand around his cock, the head dark and swollen above his fist. As he watched her, he stroked until he was hard and straining.

She placed her hands on his chest, loving the feel of all that masculine muscle and hair-roughened skin. Her fingers glided easily over the surface, clinging to all the dips and valleys.

She followed the wet, dark trail of hair down to his navel, lowering herself as she went. When her knees met the bottom of the shower, the tile hard and cool against her skin, she moved his hand from his cock and replaced it with her own.

Squeezing lightly, she worked her hand up and down the length. She loved the feel of him. Firm. Thick. Delicious.

Rising up, she eased the blunt crown past her lips, pausing to lick a circle around the rim. She explored the difference in textures, from the velvety softness of the foreskin, to the slightly rougher feel of the head.

She licked at the vertical slit, smiling when he flinched and moaned. Finally, she took mercy and swallowed him deep.

His hands flew to her head, holding her as he rocked up on his toes.

She let him take over. Let him fuck her mouth. She loved that about him and Logan both. They were never afraid to take what they wanted.

Her hands fell away as his thrusts became more urgent. She braced herself against his muscled thighs and let fingers wander down his legs then back up again, around to his firm ass that coiled and flexed with each forward motion.

She closed her eyes and tilted her head back to allow him to slide deeper into her throat.

"Oh yeah," Logan growled from across the bathroom.

She tried to turn her head to see him, knowing he was watching, but Rhys yanked her chin back with his hand.

"Oh no, Cat. Right now you and that pretty mouth are all mine. Logan's just going to have to wait his turn."

She shivered at the raw ownership in his voice. She also knew the impact it would have on Logan. He would be more turned on. More eager to possess her.

Rhys' hand curled underneath her jaw and forced it upward, angling her to take him even deeper. He slid all the way in and held himself there as she sucked in air through her nose.

"Beautiful," he said with a growl. "I love the way your lips look stretched around my dick." He pulled back, allowing the tip to dance over her tongue before rocking forward again.

"Stick your tongue out, Cat. That's it," he said as he slid out. "Use your hand. Make me come all over your tongue."

"Shit," Logan breathed.

She curled her fingers around the thick base of his cock and worked it up and down. She rocked up on her knees to give herself a better position.

He touched her face, glanced his fingers over her ears and to the back of her head in eager desperation. His movements became more erratic, and his cock jerked and pulsed in her hand.

The first hot rope splashed onto her tongue quickly followed by another and then another. It hit the back of her throat, some falling forward onto her tongue then running over her lips, and some going down as she swallowed.

Her movements became more gentle, and she licked at the crown as the last of his come erupted into her mouth.

Almost before Rhys could step away, Logan moved in, his movements urgent. He was hard and straining, and Catherine knew he was already close to orgasm.

She stared up at him, knowing he was hugely turned on by watching another man fuck her mouth, by seeing the evidence on her lips and tongue. She let the remainder of Rhys' come slide over her lips then licked over her mouth to remove it.

"God," Logan whispered.

He grasped her jaw and held her firm as he impatiently thrust into her mouth. There was no finesse to his movements but rather the hard urgency of a man pushed way beyond his limit.

He reached down, grasped her arms in his hands and hauled her back until her head bumped against the wall of the shower. Both hands framing her face, he positioned her and then thrust deep.

The water stopped, and Catherine dimly registered that Rhys had turned it off. But he didn't leave, which surprised her. Logan was much more of a voyeur than Rhys.

A blowjob didn't adequately describe what she was doing. But then *she* wasn't doing anything. Logan was fucking her mouth as hard and as ruthlessly as he fucked her pussy. Long, deep strokes, filling her until he stole her breath.

His fingers dug into her skull, scraped through her hair, and his harsh breathing echoed off the marble walls.

There was no warning, no slow work-up to his release. He exploded in her mouth. Warm fluid splashed onto her tongue, and she was forced to swallow it all as he pumped harder and faster.

His agonized groan filled her ears even as he filled her mouth.

Then his thrusts became slower and more gentle. His hands relaxed against her head, and with a shudder, he finally pulled away.

Two sets of hands reached for her, cupping her elbows and helping her to her feet. She wobbled between them, faltering to put one foot in front of the other.

"Easy, love," Rhys soothed as he helped her out of the shower.

She shivered, and Logan quickly wrapped a towel around her. She clutched at the ends as the two men dried themselves with quick swipes of their towels. Then they turned their attention back on her.

Caught between them, she sighed in contentment as Logan dried her hair, and Rhys ran the other towel down her body, absorbing every droplet of water from her skin.

He ventured close to her pussy, and she trembled. On edge. Sharp and wanting. It was the only way to describe the tension coiling through her veins. She needed to come. Wanted it badly.

"We're going to take turns fucking you, baby," Logan whispered silkily in her ear. "Long and hard until you beg for mercy. Then we're going to fuck you together."

Her knees buckled, and she had to grab for Rhys' shoulder to steady herself.

Rhys took her wrist and pulled her until she fell against him. He wrapped his arms around her, hoisted her up until she was eye-level with him and kissed her hard and long.

Never taking his mouth from hers, he took off for the bedroom, her dangling legs bumping against his.

When he reached the bed, he lowered her to the mattress. Not giving her any time to adjust or react, he reached down, spread her legs and dove into her, filling her in one heated thrust.

Her nerve endings short-circuited. It was as though someone set off an entire package of firecrackers in her groin.

Hard and fast he rode her, rocking endlessly against her hips. His weight pressed her into the bed, and not an inch of her flesh was left uncovered by his.

Flush against each other, heated and only getting hotter, their bodies undulated in perfect rhythm. His mouth worked over her neck, ravenous, carnal and utterly demanding. He nipped and bit, sucked and licked, and still he fucked her harder.

She gasped for air. Her lungs screamed. Her body screamed louder, demanding release.

Harsh, almost angry, her orgasm rose, tearing through her abdomen with savage intensity. She threw her arms around Rhys and yelled his name hoarsely.

Her body was still alive with sharp tingles when Rhys rolled off her. Logan was over her immediately, thrusting inside her.

She was sensitive, too sensitive, and each thrust sent a shaft of nearly painful pleasure rocketing through her pussy. Instead of lying over her as Rhys had done, Logan dragged her body until her ass rested on the edge of the bed.

He curled his arms around her knees, spreading her wide to receive him. Rhys climbed onto the bed beside her, his cock in his hand.

"Over here, Cat," he said, tapping her jaw with his free hand.

She turned her head so that her cheek rested against the mattress and Rhys had easy access to her mouth. With no preliminaries, he thrust inside as Logan continued to pound into her pussy.

A ragged moan worked from deep inside her chest, fluttering around Rhys' cock and escaping her lips in a long, sensual breath.

Then Logan withdrew and turned her entire body on her side so that she faced Rhys. Logan's hands moved over her ass, and he lifted her just enough that he could slide back inside her pussy in the new position.

His cock hit new places, angling differently than before. He lifted her leg high, bending it at the knee so that her pussy was completely open to him.

"I want your ass, baby," he rasped out. "I want it bad. Just like this, you lying on your side sucking Rhys' dick while I watch."

He pulled out then reached down, coating his fingers in her wetness. He spread it over the tight ring of her anus, dipping inward, stretching and lubricating the opening. Then he positioned his cock back at her pussy, driving in once more, covering his erection in her fluids.

Withdrawing, he moved over and pushed against her anus.

Her ass parted for him, sucking him in. The resistance was there, deliciously edgy and sharp. The brief moment in which she wanted to cry out and tell him to stop disappeared as her body surrendered, and he surged forward, locking her into sweet, overwhelming pleasure.

This was what she craved with a force that frightened her at times. Connected to both men, loving them with her body, mind and heart.

Logan cupped her breast, rubbing his thumb over her nipple as he fucked in and out of her ass with slow, deep thrusts. He slid inward then stopped, resting balls-deep for a long moment before withdrawing, the head rimming her entrance.

He stroked lightly, shallow, teasing her opening before ramming forward again.

Rhys stroked her hair, tucking the strands behind her ears then touching her cheek tenderly as he eased back and forth over her lips.

Then he withdrew, backed away and bent down to capture her lips in a savage kiss. His hands pulled at her hair, straining her neck backward as he ravished her mouth.

Their tongues met and tangled, clashed and retreated. She lost her breath. He took it and gave it back.

"I want your ass next," he whispered into her mouth.

She shuddered against Logan's thrusts, her eyes closing in bliss.

But Logan heard Rhys, and he pulled away from her. Rhys turned her over onto her stomach and pulled her legs until she was positioned beneath him.

"Go get cleaned up," Rhys told Logan. "We'll take her together."

She was already arching up to accept Rhys when he covered her ass and slid deep. She dug her hands into the covers, clenching her fingers tight. Her eyes closed, and she turned her face to the side so she could breathe as Rhys began fucking her, riding her hard, pressing her firmly into the mattress.

He settled into an easy rhythm, his cock working in and out of her ass with delicious friction. He nudged her thighs wider apart with his knees then leaned harder onto her back, allowing more of his weight to rest against her.

She was blanketed by him. He filled her over and over, plunging deep. His possession thrilled her.

The slow, steady slaps filled the room. Her ass jiggled, and her body rocked into the bed. He whispered loving words into her ear. They wafted lazily around her, comforting her, stroking deeper than his thrusts ever could.

The endearments pierced a part of her soul that had lain cold for a long time. As if stepping into the sun after a long, hard winter, she warmed and began to bloom.

"I love you," she whispered as she opened herself fully to him.

He kissed the arch of her neck and then her shoulder. "I love you too," he whispered back. "I'll always love you, Cat. I'll always need you."

She moaned, helpless against the cascade of feeling he unleashed.

Another hand brushed across her face, the finger tracing a line around her lips. Logan.

"I'm going to turn over with you," Rhys said as he reached underneath her with his arms.

Still embedded deep in her ass, he rolled sharply, bringing her on top of him. Now she stared up at the ceiling, her body angled back, Rhys wedged tightly inside her.

Logan loomed over her, his eyes glittering with want. Lust. He looked so powerful. All male. Dominant. Fierce.

Rhys spread his legs, and it sent him deeper until she whimpered against the fullness. Her ass burned and stretched, and still she wanted more.

Logan smiled, then grabbed her knees, pulling them wider apart until she was bare and helpless against whatever he wanted to do. How he would even manage to fit inside her pussy with Rhys filling her ass so full was a mystery, but they always managed, much to her exquisite delight.

He fitted his cock to her opening, and Rhys stilled his movements to allow Logan to gain entry. There was a moment of tension as her body fought the reality of two cocks, and then they were both lodged deep inside.

"Oh God," she said weakly.

Rhys cupped her breasts, plumping and caressing the supple flesh as he waited for Logan to set the pace. He plucked at her stiff nipples, rolling them between his fingers as she squirmed between them.

"Baby, you have to stop that," Logan groaned. "Give me a minute or I'm going to come."

She smiled, confident in her power. She loved that she could drive them both so crazy. They were thick and hard inside her, two powerful men. Sexy and rugged.

To entice him further, she gave another tiny wiggle then clamped down on his cock as hard as she could.

"Oh hell," he grunted.

Logan started driving in and out of her. His movements rocked her against Rhys, and she loved the way he cradled her body, absorbed Logan's power.

She was protected and cherished between them, their hands gentle even when their cocks weren't. And she loved that too.

Rhys' hands slipped down to her waist, and his fingers dug into her skin as he too began to thrust into her body. Logan's hands replaced Rhys' at her breasts, and he gently pulled at her nipples as both men moved against her.

"I want you to come with me," she gasped.

"Are you close?" Logan growled.

His face was strained, and she knew it wouldn't be long.

"Yes, oh God, yes."

"Give me a minute to catch up," Rhys said as he pushed harder.

Logan halted and leaned over her, panting to catch his breath. He sucked one nipple into his mouth and bit down gently, grazing the tip with his teeth.

Rhys moaned, and his grip tightened at her waist.

"Now," she whispered to Logan as she wrapped her arms around his shoulders.

He took off, fucking her, almost brutally. The two cocks stabbed deep, and she started to unravel. Faster and harder, she unwound until she lost all focus. Logan blurred in her vision as lightning seized her, sizzled through her.

She cried out, part in pleasure, part in the unending agony of such unbearable tension. Warm liquid eased their way, and she went slick around them.

Their shouts filled her ears, their come filled her body.

She went completely limp, no longer to maintain any sort of muscle tone. She was theirs to fuck, to hold.

Logan jerked against her, once, twice, held himself tight against her for a long moment before finally easing gently from the tight clasp of her pussy.

As soon as he was off, Rhys rolled them on their sides, and he too withdrew from her aching body. She lay there, unable to form a coherent thought, too exhausted to move. It was almost too much effort to breathe.

They gently cleaned her, taking care with her tender areas. Then Logan pulled her upward and looped her arms around his neck. She went willingly, a limp rag doll against his chest as he carried her further up the bed to lay her down.

Rhys crawled in behind her and spooned against her back. His hand swept down her side and over her hip even as he murmured sweet words in her ear.

Logan leaned in to kiss her lips. Then he pulled the covers up over them and told her to sleep.

Chapter Twelve

A brisk knock at their door woke Catherine. She stirred and started to climb from between Logan and Rhys when Logan put a hand out to stop her.

"You stay here, baby. I'll see who it is."

He rose and hurriedly yanked on some clothes before walking to the door. Catherine sat up, and Rhys leaned up beside her as she strained to see who was there.

"My apologies for disturbing you, but I have an urgent message for Logan Wellesley and Rhys Cullen."

"I'm Logan."

Catherine saw him reach out, and then he stepped back into the room, closing the door behind him. She studied his face as he opened the piece of folded paper the messenger had delivered.

And then her heart sank when she saw his expression darken.

"What is it?" Rhys demanded.

"Maybe nothing," Logan muttered. "It's a message from Kingston. Wants me to call him as soon as possible."

Rhys frowned. "What the hell could he want?"

"That's what I need to find out." He cast an apologetic look at Catherine. "I won't be long, baby. You and Rhys get dressed and head to the restaurant. I'll meet you there as soon as I'm done."

She swallowed and nodded, though she couldn't get rid of the dread tightening her chest. Whatever it was, she had the feeling it had just ended their vacation.

Logan disappeared out the door, and she sat there for a moment, worry nagging at her. Rhys cupped her shoulder and pressed a kiss to the side of her head.

"Don't look like that, sweetheart. Whatever it is, Logan will fix it."

"Yes, he's good at fixing things," she said faintly.

She slid out of bed and went into the bathroom to take a quick shower. When she came out, Rhys was sitting on the bed, fully dressed, waiting on her.

"I'll just be a minute," she said. "Why don't you go ahead so we aren't late for our reservation."

"You sure?" he asked.

She nodded and smiled. "I'm hungry, and I've been looking forward to dinner all day. I'd hate to lose out because we were five minutes late."

He stood and pulled her into his arms. "Okay, but don't be long."

After he left, she selected her clothing and took care with her hair and makeup. Why all of a sudden it was so important for her to look nice, she wasn't sure, but it made her feel better, more secure. As if painting on a mask made her better prepared to deal with what was to come.

Ten minutes later, she left the hotel room and walked toward the lobby. After stopping at the desk to find out exactly where in the hotel the restaurant was located, she started back on her way.

As she walked down the corridor branching off from the lobby, she heard Logan's angry voice. She halted abruptly outside one of the conference rooms. The door was ajar, and it was obvious that Logan was spitting mad.

She leaned in, standing as close to the door as she could without pushing it open.

"There is nothing more important to me than this deal," Logan said tersely. "*Nothing.* Whatever I have to do to secure your confidence will be done."

There was a pause.

"Yes, I'm out of town, but I can leave at a moment's notice. No, nothing important. Just some downtime, and that's not as important as this deal."

She sucked in her breath. Surely he didn't mean it. He couldn't.

"Rhys and I will be out as soon as I can get our pilot down here. I'll call you when we land in San Francisco, and we can set up a time to meet."

Knowing he was about to end the call, Catherine stumbled away from the doorway and hurried toward the restaurant. She felt ill.

In a desperate attempt to calm herself, she ducked into the ladies' room. She braced herself against the sink, her stomach in one gigantic knot.

No, she wasn't going to get upset over this. It was business. He didn't mean it. He couldn't have meant it. When it came to his company, Logan was wound tighter than a watch. Whatever it was, he was reacting to it out of anger.

She looked at herself in the mirror and knew she was seriously deluding herself. A leopard didn't change his spots, and if he did, it certainly wasn't overnight. She was a fool to think that everything wrong in their relationship could be fixed in a week's time.

She blew out her breath and tried to regain her composure. One thing she was sure of, no matter what Logan may have spouted on the phone, he'd never hurt her like that to her face. He'd been angry and obviously trying to salvage a business deal. She wouldn't hold that against him. What mattered was how he planned to deal with what happened next.

After dabbing at her makeup and smoothing her hair, she walked out of the bathroom and made her way into the restaurant. She was quickly ushered to a table in the back, and when she looked up, she saw that Logan had arrived ahead of her.

He and Rhys were engaged in tense conversation, but they immediately went silent when they looked up and saw her walking toward them.

They stood as she was seated then retook their own seats.

"What is it?" she asked softly.

Logan and Rhys exchanged uneasy glances. The both looked like they'd rather be taken out and shot rather than tell her anything.

Finally Rhys broke the silence. "We have to go back, Cat."

She flinched even though she knew it was coming. "Why?" she asked. "What happened?"

Logan looked at her, his lips tight. "Kingston wants us in San Francisco at eight a.m. tomorrow. He's entertaining a last-minute bid and wants to meet with us to discuss our project."

"I thought it was a done deal," she said. "I thought that was the purpose of your trips to San Francisco and Atlanta on the night of our anniversary."

Both men winced.

"He could tie it up in litigation forever, and he knows we can't afford that," Logan bit out. "We'd spend more time and money making him honor the agreement than we'd get out of the original deal. He has us by the balls, and he goddamn well knows it."

"So you have to go meet with him," she said quietly.

Logan sighed. "Yes, baby, we do. It's important."

"Cat," Rhys said in a strained voice.

Reluctantly, she brought her gaze up to meet his. Regret burned brightly in his eyes.

"I'm sorry, and I know that's a useless word right now. This won't take long, I swear it. We want you to stay here and enjoy the last two days. Get a massage, pamper yourself. We'll try to get back here so we can fly home together. If nothing else, we'll send the jet for you and meet you in New York as soon as we can."

Massage. Pamper. God, was she supposed to forget that until now they'd given her all her massages, that they'd done all the pampering?

Resentment billowed in her chest, rose in her throat, and she swallowed hard, holding it back, knowing they didn't deserve her rage.

"When do you leave?" she asked calmly.

"I've already called the pilot," Logan said in a low voice. "He'll be here around midnight."

She nodded, proud of herself for not losing her composure.

The waiter appeared, and she recited her order in a controlled voice. They only had a few hours and then she'd sleep alone. Something that she'd grown accustomed to not doing for the last week.

"Baby, look at me," Logan said when the waiter left. "Please."

She stared down for a long moment, trying to hold back the tears. He reached over and gently nudged at her chin, forcing her gaze upward.

"Listen to me. We'll meet with Kingston tomorrow morning, and I'll call you just as soon as we finish. I promise. I know you have no reason to trust what I'm saying, but Rhys and I *will* make this up to you."

She nodded again, not trusting herself to speak. She knew she wasn't being fair, but it was hard to put her trust in them after only a week. After so long of being brushed aside, of never coming first, it frightened her to think that after having a brief moment of bliss, it could all slide away again.

They ate in uncomfortable silence. A couple of times, Rhys or Logan brought up business, and she could tell they were dying to discuss strategy, but each time, they glanced over at her and the conversation died.

Her food didn't set well, and an uncomfortable ache nagged at her side. She twisted in her seat, ready to go back to the room as the men were obviously impatient to return as well.

Though they still had a few hours yet when they got back to the room, the mood was tense. She hated it. Hated the breach that had opened up with one simple phone call. And she had no idea what to do to fix it, or if she even could.

She watched as they packed their clothes and toiletries. Unable to stand the silence any longer, she went to Rhys and wrapped her arms around his waist. She laid her cheek against his back and just held on.

She felt him sigh, a deep sound of regret, and she knew he hated leaving as much as she did. He gathered her hands in his and pulled them upward until they rested over his heart. Then he let them go and slowly turned until she faced him.

He drew her into his arms and hugged her tightly. "I love you."

"I love you too," she whispered.

When he finally relinquished his hold on her, she glanced over at Logan.

"Come here, baby," he said when she hesitated.

She went into his arms, and he buried his face in her hair.

"I know the timing on this sucks, and I know you're upset."

"Thank you for this week," she said, not wanting him to go without knowing how much it had meant to her.

He stiffened, and she could feel anger build within him. Puzzled by his reaction, she pulled away and stared at him in confusion.

He touched her face, cupping her cheek and rubbing his thumb over her skin. "It pisses me off that you feel you had to thank me for spending time with you. God. You're my wife, and if anyone is entitled to my time, it's you."

She tried to smile but gave up before she broke down and cried. How could she tell him that she hadn't felt entitled to anything in a long time? Now that he said it, it pissed her off too, that she'd thanked her own husband for something she should be able to take for granted.

With a shake of her head, she warded off her anger and resentment. She wouldn't ruin their last moments together, nor would she send them off to San Francisco worried that she was going to divorce them. If this week had taught her anything, it was that she wasn't prepared to walk away without a fight.

Chapter Thirteen

Catherine shifted uncomfortably in the lounger overlooking the beach and stared down at the silent cell phone. The sun had long since set, and the moon had risen over the water, but she had no desire to go back to the room alone.

The ache intensified in her side, and she turned again, curling her knees to her chest. She was miserable. Felt miserable, and she wasn't sure if she'd caught a bug, eaten bad food or was just down in the dumps because Logan and Rhys had gone.

They'd been gone nearly twenty-four hours, and she was waiting for them to call. Logan had said he'd phone as soon as their meeting was over. At one point, she considered calling him, but she hated to pile on him if he was stressed and trying to salvage his contract.

The phone rang in her hand, and she snatched it up, opening it without looking to see who was calling.

"Logan?"

"Hey, baby."

He sounded tired, but she felt a thrill that he'd called like he'd promised.

"How are you? How did it go? Are you finished?" she asked in a rush.

He chuckled. "One at a time. I'm good. Rhys is good. It went okay, and yes, we're done."

She breathed a sigh of relief.

"Listen, baby. I called Paige and asked her to make flight arrangements for you if that's okay. Rhys and I will take the jet back. It will save us some time if you don't wait on it to return to Jamaica and we aren't stuck trying to make reservations. She'll be calling you shortly, but I asked her to get you on the first flight out in the morning. Rhys and I are going to crash here at a hotel and fly home in the morning as well. We'll pick you up at the airport and ride home together. That sound good?"

She smiled. "It sounds perfect."

"We want a do-over for our anniversary. Dinner, dancing and then we're going to make love to you all night long."

A light shiver prickled her skin. "I can't wait," she said huskily.

"Okay then, baby, let me go. You get some rest and we'll see you tomorrow."

"I love you. Tell Rhy I love him."

"Love you too," he said.

She hung up and hugged herself in satisfaction, ignoring the twinge in her side. She carefully got out of the lounger and trudged toward the hotel. Fatigue rippled through her body, but then she hadn't slept worth a damn after Rhys and Logan had left the night before.

What she really needed was some Tylenol and a good long sleep. She stopped by the gift shop in the lobby and purchased the tablets and a bottle of water then headed up to her room. As she was walking in, her phone rang.

"Mrs. Cullen-Wellesley?"

"Hi Paige," Catherine said warmly. "And it's Catherine for the hundredth time."

"I've made reservations for you to fly out at eight-twenty in the morning. You'll have a brief layover in Miami and will arrive in New York at four-ten in the afternoon. Mr. Cullen and Mr. Wellesley will meet you at the airport."

"Thank you, Paige. I appreciate it."

"Is everything all right...Catherine? Is there anything else I can do for you?"

"I'm fine, and thank you for making the arrangements."

Catherine hung up and stared at her suitcase she hadn't yet packed. She was slightly ashamed of the fact she hadn't been convinced that Logan would call or that he would wrap up when he said he would. She'd been prepared to stay on for another few days.

After stuffing her suitcase halfheartedly, she dragged herself into bed after calling the front desk for a wake-up call and also to have a car waiting to take her to the airport.

It would be okay. Things were going to be okay this time.

Things were not okay.

Catherine dragged tiredly from the boarding ramp into the terminal, clutching her side. What had brewed for a day and a half as a dull ache had rapidly escalated into fiery pain.

The flight had been long and miserable, and she'd spent the entire time sipping water and praying she wouldn't lose the contents of her stomach all over the seat.

She turned on her cell phone, hoping to find a message from Rhys or Logan. This wasn't the way she'd wanted to tell them about her pregnancy, but she was scared something was wrong.

Trying not to panic, she quickened her stride then slowed down when each step sent a new wave of pain through her abdomen. Okay, nice and slow. Rhys and Logan would be waiting for her in baggage claim or maybe even at the security checkpoint.

She exited the checkpoint and stared around at the people milling about. Not wanting to stand for long, she picked up her phone and started the walk to baggage claim.

She was punching speed dial for Logan's number when the LCD flashed that she had an incoming call. Relief came swift.

"Logan, where are you?" she asked as she brought the phone to her ear.

"Ah, it's me, Paige."

Catherine frowned. "Oh, sorry, Paige, I just assumed it would be Logan."

"About Mr. Wellesley," Paige said after a brief hesitation.

No. No, no, not again. Catherine stopped and leaned against the wall with her free hand.

"He and Mr. Cullen were delayed in San Francisco. They won't be able to meet you at the airport."

"Was their flight delayed? Are they catching another one?" Catherine asked.

"No, not immediately and no, it wasn't delayed. They stayed on another day to meet with Mr. Kingston again and are surveying the construction site. I'm not entirely sure when they're going to fly in."

"I see," Catherine said faintly.

"I'm having a car meet you. If you'll wait inside baggage claim, I'll have the driver come in to collect you," Paige hurried to say.

Catherine closed her eyes and leaned heavily against the wall. "No, I'll take a cab. I'd prefer not to wait."

"If you're sure..."

Paige didn't sound convinced.

"Tell me something, Paige. When did this change of plans take place?"

There was a long silence, and Catherine shook her head.

"When I called them back last night to tell them I'd made your flight arrangements, they told me that Kingston wanted to meet with them again."

Catherine pressed her lips together and her grip tightened around the phone. "Okay well, you can tell Mr. Cullen and Mr. Wellesley, should they call to get a report, that I made it in just fine, and that for the record, my flight was perfectly miserable, and I would have much preferred to remain in Jamaica since it's clear they aren't coming home anytime soon."

She slapped the phone shut and took in several gasps as the pain in her side became nearly unbearable. She bent over to try and steady herself, sucking in air through her nose.

A chill worked up her spine, and she shivered. A bug. She must have caught a bug in Jamaica. She was tired and achy, and a chill had set in. She needed more Tylenol for the fever, and then she needed to call her obstetrician.

After waiting impatiently for her baggage, she hauled it toward the taxi rank outside and waited her turn for a cab. After twenty minutes, she climbed into the backseat and wearily supplied her address.

On the way home, she phoned her obstetrician and got his answering service. She left a message for him to call her as soon as possible then leaned her head against the seat and closed her eyes.

The next thing she knew, the cabbie had reached back to touch her shoulder.

"Sorry," she mumbled.

The doorman to their apartment building opened her door.

"Mrs. Wellesley, welcome home. I'll get your baggage."

She reached gratefully for his hand as he helped her out. She stumbled as she stepped onto the curb, and Stuart put a hand to her elbow.

"Are you all right, Mrs. Wellesley?"

"I'm fine," she said. "Long trip."

"Why don't you go on up. I'll bring your bags up in a moment."

She smiled. "Thank you."

She walked as quickly as she could to the elevator and was grateful when it opened and someone got off just as she approached. She stepped inside, inserted her keycard then punched the button for the top floor.

As the elevator soared upward, she wavered and reached out to brace herself. A searing bolt of pain speared through her side, and she doubled over in agony.

She gasped as wave upon wave splintered through her body. She cried out in pain and then again in fear. Her baby. She couldn't lose her baby.

Her knees buckled, and she grabbed at the railing. Her vision dimmed, and she couldn't breathe for the horrific, burning pain.

She was vaguely aware of hitting the floor, and then mercifully, blackness enfolded her.

Chapter Fourteen

Logan let the phone ring until the answering machine picked up then he hung up for the fortieth time. Then he dialed Catherine's cell phone. Again. He swore when it went straight to voicemail.

He and Rhys stood outside the door of passenger pickup waiting for their driver, and both men wore extremely grim expressions.

Rhys, too, was on the phone, talking to Paige. When he slapped the phone shut, jaw clenched, Logan knew he hadn't been any more successful gaining information about Catherine.

"What did she say?" Logan asked.

"The same as the last time," Rhys said tersely. "She talked to Catherine right after she got off the plane. She took a cab home, and she was pissed."

Logan blew out his breath. Hard to do around the sick feeling in his stomach.

"We blew it," Rhys said. "All we had to goddamn do was come home when we said we were, and we fucking blew it. Goddamn Kingston."

Logan silently agreed. Even though he'd finally told Kingston to take his fucking deal and shove it up his ass, it had been too little too late. Kingston had dicked them around from the beginning, high on a power trip and goaded by his ego.

He'd loved jacking him and Rhys around, having them at his beck and call. He'd dangled the hotel deal in front of their noses then watched with glee when they jumped when he said jump.

Logan and Rhys had gone through the motions. One more hour. A few more hours. One more meeting until it added up to two fucking days, and they'd stood there knowing that once again, they'd shit on Catherine and for what? A few more million dollars?

In a moment of complete and utter clarity, Logan realized that it would never be enough. And in the end, he'd be left standing with everything and nothing all at the same time.

Telling Kingston to go fuck himself was freeing. Realizing that it was in all likelihood too late had thrust a knife into Logan's gut that he still hadn't been able to remove.

When the car pulled around, he and Rhys threw their bags in and jumped in after them. All the way home, Logan relived those last moments in Jamaica with Catherine. The worry and sadness on her face as she contemplated being shoved aside once more.

He'd assured her. He'd promised her. And once again, he'd failed her.

Would she be there? God, he hoped so. He couldn't face being without her. They were going to need a lot of time to mend their relationship and to regain her trust.

When they pulled up to the apartment, he and Rhys jumped out. Before they made it to the entrance, Stuart nearly ran them over.

"Mr. Cullen, Mr. Wellesley, I'm so glad to see you. How is Mrs. Wellesley? Will she be released from the hospital soon?"

The older man was clearly agitated, and he wrung his hands in rapid fashion. Rhys stared at Stuart with an open mouth, and fear lodged solidly in Logan's throat. He tried to speak, to demand to know what Stuart was talking about, but all that came out was a garbled exclamation.

"What the hell are you talking about?" Rhys asked.

Stuart paled and then stared down at their bags as if just realizing that they'd come back into town. "You don't know."

"Know what?" Logan snarled, finally finding his voice.

"Mrs. Wellesley arrived home two days ago. I met her at the door and sent her up to the apartment. She clearly wasn't feeling well. I collected her bags, and when I went to bring them up, I found her in the elevator unconscious. I summoned an ambulance, and she was rushed to the hospital."

A buzz began in Logan's ears, loud, incessant, swarming like a hoard of angry bees.

"What hospital?" Rhys demanded.

Logan barely waited for the answer before he bolted back to the car. Rhys piled in beside him as Logan told the driver to get them to the hospital.

"What could be wrong?" Rhys asked in a shaky voice. "She seemed fine when we left her. She was quiet, not exactly herself, but I chalked that up to her disappointment over our leaving."

Logan closed his eyes. Disappointment. Yeah, that was one way to put it.

"I don't know," he said. "I don't fucking know. But we should have been here. Goddamn it, if we'd met her plane, we would have been here when she needed us."

Rhys closed his eyes and leaned his head back against the seat. He was fighting for control, and Logan could certainly sympathize. He was ready to explode in a hundred different directions. Only the thought that Catherine was in a hospital, that she needed him and Rhys, kept him from losing his cool.

When the driver pulled around to the hospital, both men jumped out and ran inside to the information desk. The receptionist eyed them warily but looked up the information they asked for without comment.

"Hmm, yes, we have a Mrs. Cullen-Wellesley. Room 811."

Logan and Rhys both turned to go but she stopped them.

"I'm sorry, but she isn't allowed visitors."

Logan rounded furiously. "What?"

She visibly blanched. "I'm sorry, sir. It says right on her file. No visitors. Doctor's orders."

"The doctor can go to hell," Logan said icily. "I will see my wife."

Even as he turned back to Rhys, the receptionist was hurriedly picking up the phone. Logan ran for the elevator then cursed when it took too damn long. Giving up, he bolted for the stairs, Rhys on his heels.

They took the stairs two at a time, bursting out of the stairwell on the eighth floor. A quick check of the signs above the hallway told him that room 811 was in the corridor to the right.

They took off, and as they counted down the numbers to the rooms, Logan glanced ahead and saw two security officers standing outside a room.

Ignoring them, Logan and Rhys both reached for the door only for the two men to step in front of them.

"I'm sorry, but you can't go in there."

"That is my *wife* in there," Logan seethed. "I just got back into town. I have no idea what's wrong with her or if she's okay. I only just found out where she was, and you're telling me I can't go in there?"

The security officer's expression eased into one of sympathy. "Sir, if you'll wait at the nurse's station, the doctor is on his way up to see you now. He'll give you a full report on her condition."

"I don't need a goddamn report," Rhys interjected. "I want to see how she is doing with my own eyes."

The guard eyed him curiously but didn't question why if she was Logan's wife, Rhys was breathing fire as well.

"I understand your frustration," the other guard said calmly. "I would appreciate it if you waited at the nurse's station. You're causing a disruption, and we don't want any of the patients, including your...wife," he said, looking at Logan, "to be disturbed."

Logan sucked in a deep breath. He wanted to hit something. Catherine was lying in a bed just on the other side of that door, and he couldn't go in. Couldn't see her. Couldn't hold her. Couldn't touch her and couldn't tell her he loved her. Couldn't find out what the hell was wrong with her.

"Let's go, Logan," Rhys said in a low voice. "The sooner we talk to the doctor, the sooner we can see Cat."

Reluctantly, Logan backed off and followed Rhys down the hall toward the nurse's station. When they arrived, Rhys barked out a question to the nearest nurse and was directed into a small lounge adjoining the station.

They paced the interior until Logan thought he'd go mad. When an elderly man in a lab coat walked in, Logan all but pounced on him.

"Are you Catherine's doctor?" he demanded.

"You must be Mr. Wellesley," the doctor said, extending his hand. "I'm Doctor Morgan."

Logan bit his lip in frustration and returned the man's gesture. Rhys stepped forward. "How is Catherine? What happened to her?"

"Acute appendicitis," the doctor returned. "Unfortunately, it ruptured as she arrived in the emergency room. I performed immediate surgery to remove the appendix but it was complicated by her pregnancy and the high risk of infection."

Logan felt all the blood drain from his face. Rhys went chalk white and swayed. "Did you say pregnancy?" Rhys choked out.

The doctor blinked in surprise. "You didn't know?" He cleared his throat. "I assumed given the nature of your relationship to the patient that you would be aware of her pregnancy." He directed his statement to Logan. "She was quite clear that she was married to Logan Wellesley. That is you, correct?"

Logan nodded, still numb to his toes. "Catherine. Is she okay? The baby?"

The doctor blew out his breath. "Why don't you both sit down, and I'll bring you up to speed on her condition."

He and Rhys both sank into nearby chairs. Rhys looked as shocked as he felt. Pregnant. How pregnant? She couldn't be very far along.

"Why can't we see her?" Rhys demanded. "We were told no visitors on your orders."

"Not my orders," the doctor said with a shake of his head. "Those were Mrs. Wellesley's wishes."

Logan looked at the doctor in shock. "*What?*"

"After she came out of surgery, she was quite distraught. She asked for you and Rhys Cullen." He looked up at Rhys. "I assume that's you?"

Rhys nodded.

"She was convinced she'd miscarried the baby, and it took us quite a while to make her understand what had happened to her, and that at least for now, she was still pregnant."

"What do you mean *for now?*" Logan asked as cold fear snaked up his spine.

"Just that she underwent surgery for a ruptured appendix, which is a risky enough endeavor and when you factor in that the patient is pregnant, it gets trickier. Plus, she runs a high risk of infection which could cause problems with the pregnancy. So far she's responded well to antibiotics, but she's not beyond the risk of losing the child. It's very much a wait-and-see situation.

That first day, she asked continually for you. The nurses tried to phone the number she provided but were unable to reach you. The second day, however, she went silent, and well, she retreated. She directed me not to allow any visitors, and she stopped trying to phone you. She hasn't asked for anything. Not even when she can return home."

Logan cursed, and Rhys' eyes glittered with unshed tears.

"I cautioned her about the need to remain calm, and apparently she feels that seeing you would upset her and potentially cause risk to the baby."

Logan dropped his face into his hands. He wanted to goddamn cry like a baby.

"When can she go home?" Rhys asked, his voice thick with emotion.

"If all goes well? In a couple of days. I'm watching her closely to make sure she doesn't spike a temp and that she's recovering as she should. I want her to have a full round of antibiotics to kill off all the infection in her system."

"And we're supposed to just sit around and not see her for several days?" Logan ground out.

Compassion softened the doctor's gaze. "What I'm saying is that Mrs. Wellesley has been through an ordeal both physically and emotionally. She's terrified of losing her child, and she's been in considerable pain. As difficult as it may be for you not to see her, consider how difficult the situation is for her."

Rhys dropped his hands helplessly at his sides.

"Leave your contact numbers with the nurses. If anything at all changes with her condition or if she relents and agrees to visitors, they'll call you immediately. In the meantime, I suggest you go home and get some rest. I'll let you know when she'll be discharged."

Just like that. As though she were having some routine checkup that they should worry nothing about.

Logan watched the doctor go, shock still trickling through his system. Trickling. Hell. More like a dam bursting.

Rhys stalked out of the small room and over to the nurses' desk. Logan rose to follow him, surprised his feet were obeying his brain's commands. Or maybe they weren't, since his mind was screaming at him to go see Catherine.

Rhys snatched up a pad and a pen and scribbled for several long moments. Then he tore the top piece off, folded it and thrust it at the nurse.

"Give this to Catherine Cullen. Make sure she gets it."

The nurse took the paper and nodded. "Go home now," she said gently. "I'll make sure she gets it. I promise."

They walked back out of the hospital in silence. Logan was convinced that it was all one really bad dream. That he'd wake up in Jamaica with Catherine in his arms.

Neither of them spoke until they stepped into the apartment. It seemed empty without Catherine. Ominous.

Rhys dropped onto the couch, tilted his head up and closed his eyes. "She's pregnant," he said, and he sounded awed.

Logan was trying to do the math. It was too soon for them to have gotten her pregnant in Jamaica. And to his enduring shame, it had been at least three months before the trip since they'd made love to her. Unless...

He frowned and looked over at Rhys. It was odd, really. In a relationship such as theirs, they'd certainly considered the eventuality of Catherine having their child and that it might be his or Rhys'.

But if Rhys had made love to her in the past couple of months, when Logan wasn't there, the child was most certainly his. It shouldn't bother him, but he preferred a scenario where the child could be either of theirs. He preferred not knowing. At least then he could imagine it was his.

He shook his head and glanced away from Rhys. Stupid. The child was theirs. It would be raised by the three of them. He wouldn't entertain any alternative. Petty jealousies, especially right now, were just boneheaded and completely selfish.

"What's wrong?" Rhys demanded.

Logan looked back up at him. "When was the last time you made love to Catherine? Before Jamaica, I mean."

Rhys' eyes dulled. "Probably three months ago. It was the same night...I mean we both made love to her. I hadn't since then."

Relief made Logan breathe easier. So there was no way to know whose baby it was. Then he shook his head again. Did it matter? Did it really goddamn matter? He'd thought he was beyond all that.

"That means she has to be over three months pregnant then," Logan said grimly.

"Which means she knew," Rhys said.

Logan sighed. "It doesn't take a rocket scientist to figure out why she hadn't told us yet." He rubbed a tired hand through his hair. "Who could blame her?"

"I don't want to lose her," Rhys said in a quiet voice. "Or our child."

"Then maybe it's time we put as much time and effort into our relationship with Catherine as we do our business," Logan said. "Starting now. It's going to take all we've got to get her back, Rhy. I feel that. I think it's gone beyond disappointment or even anger. But she's going to need us when she's discharged from the hospital. She won't even be able to think about leaving until she's completely healed. We can use that time to show her she comes first and that she always will."

Rhys looked up at him, hope flaring in his eyes. "Then let's do it."

Chapter Fifteen

Catherine stared down at the note now wrinkled and worn from its constant place in her hand over the last three days. She smoothed the edges and let her gaze travel over the ink.

Cat,

I love you. God, I want to see you so badly, but I understand why you don't want to see me. I'll wait. No matter how long it takes. I'll be here when you're ready to go home. Take care of yourself and our baby.

Rhy

Over and over she read those words, wrapped them around her. She'd never felt so alone in her life, and yet she knew they were just outside. The nurses had told her that they'd come every day and just sat. Waiting.

She smoothed a hand over her belly, careful of her healing incisions. The doctor had assured her that all looked well with her pregnancy, but lingering fear gripped her. She didn't have words for the terror of waking in a strange bed, of faint, drug-masked pain in her abdomen, and the thought that in one terrible moment, her child had been taken.

Mindful of the doctor's caution about getting upset, she tempered her thoughts and settled on more bland images. No, she wouldn't allow them to risk her child by upsetting her.

They'd taken far too much already. Her love. Her hopes. Her happiness.

They wouldn't get an outburst from her. No emotion. No pain. She was through begging for something they couldn't give.

She looked up when the door opened, almost fearful that Logan and Rhys would disregard her wishes and come inside. Relief came quickly when she saw the nurse enter.

"The doctor says you can go home today. Are you ready for that?" she asked softly.

Catherine held her breath. Was she? She knew she'd have to face them when she was discharged. She didn't have another place to go and couldn't do so even if she did. Whether she liked it or not, she was going to have to allow them to take her home and take care of her until she was completely well.

Slowly, she nodded.

The nurse squeezed her hand comfortingly. "Your obstetrician will be up to see you one more time before you go. He'll want to see you regularly in the next few weeks to monitor the baby's progress. You'll have a follow-up with your surgeon in two weeks. In the meantime, you're to get plenty of rest, drink plenty of fluids, eat and take it easy. No stress."

No stress. She was one big ball of stress even if she was working damn hard to radiate calm.

"Okay then, I'll take out your IV and help you shower if you like, or you can wait until you get home. Completely up to you. After your OB sees you, I'll be back to give you your paperwork and prescriptions, and then you're free to go."

"Thank you," Catherine said.

"You're welcome," the nurse said with a smile. "Now, let's get you ready to go, shall we?"

Rhys paced the hallway as he waited for Catherine to come out. The nurse had pushed a wheelchair in her room fifteen minutes ago, and still he and Logan waited.

Logan was no better off than he was. He stood opposite Catherine's door, his stance tense with expectation.

Then the door opened and the nurse backed out of the room, pulling Catherine in the wheelchair. When she turned Catherine around, Rhys' breath left his chest.

She looked small, huddled in the wheelchair, deep shadows under her eyes. Her hands were clenched in her lap, and she stared up at him, no emotion reflected.

"Cat," he whispered as he fell to one knee beside the wheelchair.

He reached out and touched her cheek. She didn't react, but her gaze followed him.

"Are you okay? Are you hurting? How is the baby?"

There. The tiniest flicker of feeling.

"The baby is fine," she said huskily.

He took her hand in his, uncurled her fingers and kissed her palm. "Thank God." He looked back up at her. "Are you ready to go home? The car is waiting downstairs."

She gave a small nod, and Rhys stood. She turned her head to look at Logan, who still hadn't said anything. His eyes were haunted. There was so much regret for the world to see that it made Rhys uncomfortable.

"I'll take her from here," Logan said politely to the nurse.

As he walked behind the wheelchair to grasp the handles, his hand brushed over Catherine's shoulder and lingered there for a moment before he started forward.

The entire way down, the silence was heavy. Stifling. A thousand questions stampeded Rhys' mind. But he held back. Talk was cheap. The time for talking was past. It was up to him and Logan to show her that they couldn't—wouldn't—live without her.

When they arrived at the car, the driver hurried out to open the door. Rhys bent over Catherine.

"Do you want me to help you into the car or would you prefer I carry you? I don't want to hurt you, so you tell me what you need me to do."

"Don't pull me," she murmured. "Let me pull against you. I'll walk."

As Logan held the wheelchair still, Rhys stretched his arm out and held it rigid as her small hand circled his wrist. Her face tightened, and she paled as she strained upward. Logan cursed and put one hand to her back to hold her steady.

When she was upright, Rhys stood there for a moment to let her catch her breath.

"Hurts," she gritted out.

"I know, love. I'm sorry. As soon as we get you home, we'll make you comfortable, I promise."

He smoothed her hair away from her face, a face that seemed so much thinner than it had just a few days ago. With slow, small steps, she headed for the open door.

Logan hurried around to the other side and slid into the backseat. He leaned forward as Catherine ducked into the car and eased down with a groan.

Logan reached over, lifted her and moved her closer to him. After making sure she was comfortable, Rhys climbed in next to her.

"Okay?" Rhys asked as he regarded her shallow breathing.

She nodded, and Logan curled his arm around her shoulders, tugging her gently into his chest. He was shaking from head to toe.

"God, baby, I was so scared."

The words came out choked, and Rhys had to look away as he was reminded of just how afraid he'd been as well. He reached for her hand, wanting to touch her even as Logan held her.

She was quiet. Too damn quiet, and it scared him. The light had gone out of her eyes. He'd been prepared for anger. Fear. Hurt. But what he wasn't prepared for was her indifference.

They drove home, Catherine limp against Logan, her eyes closed. Rhys kept his hand curled around hers. He suspected she kept her eyes closed to keep him and Logan from seeing too deeply within. Which meant that despite her façade, she wasn't as indifferent as she appeared.

He'd take hope where he could get it. He wouldn't let her and their child go without a fight.

They pulled up to the building, and she stirred, opening her eyes as the car stopped.

"Just stay where you are," Logan murmured. "I'll carry you so you won't have to move."

She tensed for a moment as if expecting his actions to cause her pain, but he moved slowly, inching her out of the car with extreme care.

Stuart held the door open and was uncharacteristically silent as Rhys passed through followed by Logan carrying Catherine.

On the way up, Rhys stared at Catherine as she leaned her head against Logan's shoulder. It was killing him, this silence. He wanted her to yell at him, to hit him, do something other than shut him out. But she couldn't afford that kind of emotional outburst, and he wouldn't drive her to it.

The elevator doors opened, and Rhys started out ahead of Logan. Unable to resist, he stopped and lowered his head, pressing his lips to her hair.

He inhaled her sweet scent, wanting to hold it, and her, close to him. Never let her go.

She turned slightly, her gaze meeting his. For that moment, her barriers fell, and he saw raw, aching emotion entrenched in her eyes.

"Cat," he whispered. "I love you."

She closed her eyes again and turned away into Logan's neck. Rhys' shoulders slumped, and he walked into the apartment. Logan carried Catherine inside.

"Not to bed," she murmured when Logan headed toward the bedroom.

"Baby, you should be resting," Logan protested in a gruff voice.

"Please, I want to sit up for a while. And eat. I'm hungry."

"Couch okay? I don't think a chair would be very comfortable."

Rhys busied himself making her something to eat while Logan fussed over her on the couch. A few minutes later, he carried a tray and set on the couch beside her before settling down next to it.

They watched her eat, and only when she was finished did Rhys ask what was uppermost on his mind.

"Why didn't you tell us you were pregnant?" he asked.

Her hand fluttered down to her abdomen. He wanted to put his hand there too, but he didn't want to hurt her or bump her incisions.

She stared down at her hand, refusing to look at either him or Logan. "I had planned to tell you the night of our anniversary," she said quietly.

Rhys' chest caved in just a little more, and Logan cursed under his breath.

"Later...later I wasn't sure what I was going to do, what I wanted. I knew if I told you in Jamaica that it would change everything, and I wanted that time with you and Logan. I wanted things like they used to be."

"And what about now?" Logan asked. "Do you want to be with us now? Do you want to stay with us?"

Her eyes became troubled. She licked her lips, and fatigue swamped her face. "I-I don't know. I can't answer that now. Right now I hurt too much."

Rhys knew she didn't refer to physical pain, and it knotted his gut.

"What I want is for you to rest and get better," Rhys said. "Logan and I aren't going anywhere. We have a lot to make up to you, and words aren't going to convey that. It'll take time, and fortunately for us, you aren't in any shape right now to go anywhere. We're taking total advantage of that."

A half-smile fluttered across her lips. Then she glanced between him and Logan, concern crowding her features.

"Are you happy? About the baby?"

Logan went soft about the same time Rhys felt himself unfold. They both reached for her. Logan's hand slid up her arm as Rhys' tucked around her neck.

"I couldn't be happier," Logan said. "I was so damn worried when you were in the hospital. I still am. I want this baby, Catherine. As much as I want you."

She turned her head to Rhys, and he slid his hand around to cup her cheek.

"I'd love a girl," he said with a smile. "Who looks just like her mother. Logan and I can spoil her rotten. Of course I'm happy, love. But I'm happier that you're okay and that you're home with us where you belong."

She looked away, and Rhys had to hold back his sigh. He exchanged worried glances with Logan. The two of them had expected a battle, an argument, and then they'd planned to throw down the challenge. They'd show her, prove to her, that they were through putting her last.

Only she hadn't responded how they'd thought. Now they were faced with not only proving themselves to her, but they were also faced with tearing down the protective barrier she'd created around herself.

Chapter Sixteen

Catherine walked into the kitchen to pour herself a glass of juice. As she moved into the living room, she was surprised to see both Logan and Rhys. They had laptops open on the coffee table. Cell phones were out. Logan was talking to someone on one of them. There was even a fax machine on the floor with an extension cord leading to the wall plug.

"Good morning, beautiful," Rhys said as he looked up and saw her.

She glanced self-consciously down at her rumpled knee-length T-shirt and bare legs and grimaced. She didn't feel beautiful, even if she was feeling a lot better since she'd left the hospital several weeks ago.

"What's Logan doing?" she asked as a way to put the focus off her bedraggled appearance. He was talking on the phone, but he looked at ease, not at all tense like he did in ninety percent of the phone calls he made.

"He's talking with our new director of operations."

Her brows furrowed. "Your what?"

He grinned. "Thought that might trip you up."

She walked over and sat down in the chair across from the couch. Though she slept between both men each night, she still wasn't comfortable overtly seeking out their attention or affection. She wanted nothing more than to snuggle into Rhys' arms on the couch, but she didn't like what the action implied.

"What's going on?" she asked. "Who's your new director of operations, and what the hell is that anyway?"

"Paige is," Rhys replied.

Catherine raised her eyebrows in surprise. "Paige? Not that she doesn't deserve the promotion. I hope you gave her a hefty raise as well."

"Oh, we did," Rhys muttered. "It was the only way she'd take the job."

She grinned and realized it felt good to let go and smile. It felt strange, and then it hit her that she hadn't smiled—really smiled—since Jamaica.

Poor Rhys was looking at her like a desperate man. It couldn't have been easy living like this for the last several weeks. Always on tiptoe.

Neither he nor Logan had pressed her. Hadn't made demands or tried to persuade her to stay. In fact, they hadn't done a lot of talking at all beyond idle everyday chitchat, asking how she was doing, if she needed anything, that sort of thing.

But what they had done was show her that she was all-important. Yes, they worked, but astonishingly, they were home by five every day, six at the latest. There had been one overnight business trip that only Logan had gone on, and he'd returned early the next day.

They ate dinner every night together, usually ordered in, but the guys also took turns cooking. Evenings in the kitchen had turned out to be the highlight of her day as they talked about everything and nothing.

At night, they crawled in beside her, always close to her, touching and snuggling. It was so much like the early days in their relationship that it made her physically ache.

How much longer would they keep it up? They were relentless in their quest to make her stay. She certainly couldn't dispute that, but was it real? If she gave in, would things go back to the way they'd been before?

Logan bent over her chair, startling her from her thoughts. She hadn't realized he'd gotten off the phone. He leaned in close and kissed her gently on the lips. She sucked in her breath in surprise.

"Good morning," he murmured.

Then he very lightly put a hand on her belly, splaying his fingers over her shirt.

"How is the little one today?"

A sudden wash of emotion hit her hard in the chest. This was how it was *supposed* to be. She stared down at his hand and imagined a larger swell. She was only just now starting to pooch the slightest bit, but in a few months, she'd round out quite nicely.

She had fantasies about lying between him and Rhys, their hands on her belly feeling the baby move. Gentle kisses and late night conversations with their son or daughter.

"Why do you look so sad, baby?" Logan whispered.

She shook her head, refusing to voice aloud her innermost wants and dreams. As long as she kept them closely guarded, they remained hers. The moment she let them go, they entered the realm of harsh reality.

He stroked her cheek, light and loving. Then he kissed her eyelids before backing away.

"Are you not going into the office today?" she croaked.

He smiled. "Nope. Rhys and I are working from home. Paige is more than capable of running the office along with her new staff. I think she's loving her new digs."

"Staff?" she echoed in disbelief.

Logan and Rhys didn't have a staff. They had Paige who they piled way too much work on. They had a secretary who worked on an as-needed basis, and they had one or two temps who filled in during busy times, but a staff? Logan was too much of a control freak to relinquish the running of their business to staff members.

"She's on quite a power trip," Rhys said in amusement. "It's why Logan and I are hiding at home today. She's holding orientation and letting her new worker bees know exactly what she expects from them."

Catherine laughed. Rhys froze and stared at her with a fierce expression.

"That is the most beautiful sound," he murmured.

Her chest caught, and her heart fluttered uncomfortably.

"So what's with the decision to hire a staff?" she asked casually, afraid to read too much into their action.

"It was way past time," Logan said. "Rhys and I have been too set on doing everything ourselves. It wasn't fair to you, and it wasn't fair to Paige, who we also took advantage of. We've made it up to her. We're still making it up to you and will be for a long while."

He spoke with such seriousness and determination. Against her will, excitement rose, unfurled like a budding flower.

"Are you ready to talk about us?" Rhys asked quietly.

She froze. No, they hadn't pushed her. In fact they'd been nothing but patient. But the issue had still taken up residence. The gigantic elephant in the room, always watching.

"I need to call and confirm my appointment with the obstetrician for tomorrow," she said as she hastily rose from her seat. "I'm getting an ultrasound."

"We know," Rhys said, his gaze directed on her. "We've made arrangements to go. We wouldn't miss it for the world."

She held her breath, trying not to hope, yet grabbing on to his promise with sick excitement. On some level she felt like a complete idiot for placing that kind of faith squarely back in their hands when they'd let her down time after time.

Despite the effort they'd put into spending more time with her, she still couldn't keep the doubt from creeping in. All it would take was one little problem. Some deal going south. An issue with the new staff, and they'd quickly drop her to go fix it.

"We'll be there," Logan said calmly. "You'll be riding with us."

The next morning, Rhys got up and dressed for work, but to Catherine's shock, Logan stayed in bed, his arm draped possessively over her body.

She was debating whether or not to wake Logan when Rhys returned to the bed and bent over and kissed her.

"I have to run in for a few minutes and sign a few documents for Paige, but I'll be back in time for your appointment."

"Rhys, what about Logan?" she whispered.

Rhys smiled. "What about him?"

"Would you two please be quiet," Logan said in irritation. "It's damn hard to sleep with you carrying on a conversation in my ear."

Rhys chuckled, kissed Catherine one more time and headed for the door.

She turned as best she could under Logan's arm so she could face him. "Are you sick?" she asked. "Are you feeling okay?"

He pried one eye open and stared balefully at her. "I'm fine."

"Logan, you've never slept this late in your life. You never miss work."

"I do today." He leaned into her and kissed her. His hand glided up her body until his palm cradled the side of her neck. "And I plan to do a lot more of it. Is that going to be a problem for you, Mrs. Wellesley?"

Her mouth widened in shock, and he took swift advantage. His tongue licked deliciously over her lips and slid inside, warm and slightly rough.

"We've got a couple hours before your appointment. Why don't we sleep a little longer, take a shower together and then I'll make you breakfast," he murmured as he stole little kisses.

She burrowed into his arms, forgetting her reserve and that she was valiantly trying to guard herself from further hurt. She laid her cheek against his bare chest and closed her eyes, just enjoying the perfection of one simple moment.

Chapter Seventeen

Her stomach in knots, Catherine sat between Logan and Rhys in the waiting room. They sensed her anxiety, because they touched her frequently—gentle, reassuring caresses meant to alleviate her concerns.

There hadn't been anything to suggest there was a problem with her pregnancy. Her recovery from her surgery had been uncomplicated and swift. But she could still taste the fear, heavy on her tongue, still remember that one terrible moment waking up and knowing without a doubt she'd lost her child.

Her stomach gave a violent twist when her name was announced. Clutching at Logan's and Rhys' hands, she made her way toward the door on unsteady feet.

She went through the preliminaries mechanically. Peed in a cup, let the nurse take vitals and answered questions in a monotone. Logan and Rhys both looked at her in concern, but her single-minded focus was on seeing her baby.

She half-feared that when they did the ultrasound, they'd find something horrible. A shudder worked over her shoulders.

Several agonizing minutes—what seemed like hours—later, the doctor came in, pushing a portable ultrasound. He smiled and greeted her then nodded at Logan and Rhys.

"Are you ready to see your baby, Mrs. Wellesley?" the doctor asked.

She nodded, unable to speak for fear she'd throw up.

Logan helped her lie back, and the doctor tucked a sheet in the waistband of her pants and pulled downward to expose the slight swell of her belly. Then he arranged her shirt just below her breasts.

Rhys stood at the head of the exam table, and she reached upward, finding his hand. Logan watched from her feet, both his hands curled around her ankles as his fingers worked in nervous patterns.

They were as worried as she was.

The doctor worked in silence. He squirted warm gel on her belly then took the probe and worked it in a tight circle, spreading the goo.

Everything else faded away but the screen and the black blurs working in and out of focus. She wasn't conscious of holding her breath until she grew lightheaded. She blew it out in a long stream then sucked in deeply.

"There we are," the doctor said as he pointed at the monitor.

Catherine stared in wonder at the screen. She could make out a head and a body. She could see arms and legs. The baby was moving.

She listened in a daze as the doctor pointed out features. He showed her the heart rate, eyes, nose, the mouth.

It was a *miracle.*

"Do you want to know what you're having?" the doctor asked.

She opened her mouth, and it hung there. Did she want to know? God, it didn't matter. Her baby was okay.

"Cat, do you want to know if it's a boy or girl?" Rhys whispered close to her ear.

"Y-yes, please." Excitement buzzed through her veins. It was real. She hadn't lost her baby.

The doctor hummed as he probed around. He murmured once or twice, presumably to the baby, and then he smiled.

"Congratulations, Mama. You're having a beautiful baby girl."

It was too much. Completely and utterly overwhelmed, Catherine burst into tears. Big, gulping sobs wracked her body. The doctor looked at her in concern, but she couldn't stop. It was as if a floodgate had burst wide open.

She heard the men talk around her, but didn't process what was being said. And then she was alone with Rhys and Logan. Logan pulled her up and crushed her in his arms. Behind her, Rhys sat on the edge of the exam table and rubbed her back soothingly as he murmured in her ear.

Relief, achingly sweet, flowed through her veins. Warm, powerful, the healer of all things. *Hope.*

All the things she'd turned off in the past few weeks came storming back. Sharp, painful yet welcome. She *wanted* to feel again.

But still the tears came. Cleansing, like rain.

Logan and Rhys said nothing through it all. They just held her as her body shook with her sobs.

When they slowed enough that she could speak, she formed the one prevailing thought that echoed through her mind.

"Home," she said, her throat raw. "I want to go home."

Logan picked her up and held her protectively in his arms. "We'll take you, baby. Just lie there. We'll get you home."

The trip home was a blur. She kept her face buried in Logan's chest, drawing comfort and strength from his firm embrace.

When they walked into the apartment, he settled her on the couch. Rhys positioned pillows around her back and tugged a blanket over her lap. They were treating her as though she was fragile, but for the first time in a long while, she finally felt strong.

Rhys sat on the edge of the couch, concern burning brightly in his eyes. Logan sat at her feet, his hand stroking her leg.

"Are you all right?" Rhys asked anxiously.

"I was so afraid," she said, and tears flooded her eyes again. She wiped them away in irritation. Her eyes were already swollen, hot and scratchy. Her nose felt like it was twice its normal size, and her head ached.

"I mean, I know the doctor said the baby was okay, but I didn't believe him. I was so worried that we'd get there today and do the sonogram, and they'd find out that the baby was…"

She couldn't even complete the horrible thought.

"Oh honey," Rhys said as he pulled her into his arms. "I'm so sorry."

"I've been so stupid about everything," she said against his chest.

He pulled away from her in shock. Logan shook his head, a deep frown engraved on his face.

"Baby, if anyone's been stupid, it's me and Rhys. God, when I think of what could have happened to you because we weren't where we were supposed to be—"

He broke off, shaking his head, but she could see the residual fear in his eyes.

She wiped at her face again with her palms. "I won't lie to you. I was—am—angry. I was hurt. But I could have told you. Yes, I planned to tell you the night of our anniversary. I had it all planned out, how I'd tell you, and I imagined your reactions. I'd hoped that you'd want to spend more time with me, that somehow we could go back and recapture the way it used to be.

"But then in Jamaica, I didn't want to tell you until we got back because I knew it would change the entire tone of the vacation. I was selfish because I wanted it to be just us. I wanted you to want to be with me because you loved me, not because I was pregnant."

Logan leaned forward, his entire body tense, like a coiled spring. There was urgency in his expression, a keen edge of desperation she wasn't used to. "Baby, we do love you, and we do want to be with you, child or no child. Do I want our baby? More than you could possibly know. This was our dream. To one day have a family. To be a family. You, me, Rhys. And our child."

"I should have told you," she said softly. "Don't you see? If I had told you, I don't think you would have left even for the deal with Kingston. You would have taken me back to New York, fussed over me and made me see a doctor. I would have never gone so long until my appendix ruptured, and I wouldn't have almost lost our child. Instead I played stupid games, wanting something from you that seems so unimportant in the face of our child's life."

Rhys touched her hair, and she could see love brimming in his eyes. Soft and melting. She also realized it had always been there. She just hadn't looked. She hadn't dug far enough, hadn't challenged him or Logan enough.

Her meek acceptance of the status quo of their marriage put her as much at fault as it did them.

"We could play the blame game for infinity," Rhys said gently. "What if Logan and I hadn't been such bastards? What if we'd shown up for our anniversary dinner and you'd told us like you'd planned? What if we'd been with you when you started feeling unwell? What if we hadn't put our business before you?"

"What if I hadn't let you?" she challenged.

Logan's hand tightened around her leg and she looked down at him. The same love, beautiful and untarnished, shone in his dark eyes.

"I think it's safe to say that we all have our share of what-ifs. But baby, it won't change the past. We can damn sure change the future, though."

She licked her lips and drew up her courage to ask him what had weighed on her mind and heart since that last night in Jamaica.

"Logan, there's something I need to ask you."

He stared unflinchingly back at her. "Anything."

His calm bolstered her, gave her such hope.

"That last day in Jamaica, when you called Kingston. I-I overheard part of your phone conversation when I was on my way to the restaurant."

He cocked his head as though trying to remember as well.

"You said that there was nothing more important to you than the deal, that there was nothing you wouldn't do to secure it. You said the vacation wasn't important, that it was just downtime."

His face grayed, and his lips tightened. Then he leaned forward until his chin rested on her knee. His arm snaked around her drawn-up legs.

"Listen to me, baby. I won't deny saying just that. I was furious. I was trying to impress upon Kingston how important the contract was to our business. In that moment, I would have said anything at all. I didn't *mean* it."

"I believe you," she said softly. And she did. She just had to know, to get it out of her mind so it wouldn't take root, dark and insidious.

Rhys touched her chin, his fingers gentle yet firm as he turned her toward him.

"Do you believe we love you, Cat? Do you believe that there's nothing we want more than you and our baby, here with us, always?"

She dipped her head until her mouth slid across his fingertips. She kissed each one then peeked back up at him. "I do," she said.

"And will you stay?" Logan asked, his voice shaken and a little unsure.

She reached for his hand then took Rhys' and pulled them to her heart. "I love you both so much. I've made mistakes too. I want the chance to make things right between us again. I've never wanted anything other than a life with the two of you. I want to stay. I never want to be anywhere but where you are."

She savored the connection, the symbolism of holding their hands over her heart. Then she slid them slowly down until they covered her belly. Their family. Their connection to each other. Love. Perfect and true.

Rhys wrapped his other arm around her shoulders and pulled her close. He trembled against her, his body shaking as he gripped her arm fiercely.

Logan rubbed lightly over her belly, his large hand molding to the curvature. Then he leaned down and pressed his lips to the mound before turning his head to rest his cheek against her stomach.

She smiled and let go of his hand, lowering her fingers to run through his hair. It was a picture she'd carry with her always. That one moment of discovery, that love, despite all its imperfections, was glorious above all else.

What else could make past wrongs and hurts pale, slide silently away, forgotten and forgiven?

Here, in her hands, her heart, pressed close to her body and soul, was all that mattered.

Epilogue

She loved Saturdays. Sundays too. But Saturdays seemed more special because after a long week of work, Logan and Rhys slept in.

Today was no exception. Catherine awoke to gentle hands exploring the bulging mass of her stomach. The baby rolled beneath their fingertips, and both men grinned.

"Good morning, princess," Rhys said, pressing his mouth to Catherine's belly. "You sure did keep your mama up a long time last night."

Catherine laughed softly. That she had. In turn, Catherine kept Rhys and Logan awake with all her flopping around.

Logan swept his palm across one particularly noticeable protrusion. A delighted smile crossed his face when what Catherine suspected was the baby's foot moved in response.

"Does she ever slow down?" Logan asked in awe.

"No," Catherine said darkly.

Rhys rubbed along her tightly drawn stomach. "How's your back this morning?"

"I haven't moved yet, so it's doing fine," she said with a grimace.

"It won't be long now," Logan soothed.

She let out an unhappy sigh. "I know."

Rhys and Logan both cocked their head in question.

"You don't sound happy about that," Rhys commented.

She grinned ruefully. "Isn't it ridiculous? As much bitching as I've done about swollen feet, aching back, leaking breasts and insane hormonal swings, I wouldn't have traded this for the world."

She glanced between the two men and reached out to touch their cheeks.

"I've loved being pregnant. I've loved having you both with me every step of the way. You'll never know how much this has meant to me."

Logan's expression darkened. "You say that as if everything will change as soon as you're no longer pregnant."

She smiled and shook her head. No, she knew better. Whatever doubts she may have harbored before, the last months had proven to her that she could count on Logan and Rhys to keep their promises this time around.

They'd worked hard to keep their business viable and thriving, but they'd worked harder to make sure she knew how important she was to them.

"Besides, there will be other babies," Rhys pointed out.

Her chest tightened. Other babies. A dreamy smile poured over her lips.

"Let's have this one before we start thinking about knocking her up again," Logan muttered.

Rhys grinned, and Catherine laughed. It was a well-known fact that her pregnancy thrilled and terrified Logan in equal parts. The closer she came to her due date, the more brooding he became, and the more psychotic he got about their plan for when she went into labor.

He'd nearly driven her and Rhys insane when he made them do a test run. He'd almost fired their driver for getting them to the hospital two minutes behind what Logan perceived to be a reasonable time.

Never mind the harried driver would have made it with ten minutes to spare if they hadn't been pulled over by a NYC police officer.

"Which one of you is making breakfast?" she asked as her stomach protested the fact she hadn't eaten dinner the night before.

"Finally hungry?" Rhys asked.

"You shouldn't skip meals," Logan said tightly.

She rolled her eyes and shoved at Logan so she could get out of bed. A graceful departure it wasn't. By the time she heaved her cumbersome body over the edge, with much assistance from Logan and Rhys, she was already out of breath. And despite her hopes that her back would feel better, the nagging ache hit her as soon as she took a step.

Refusing to give in to the urge to wince and maybe whine a little, she walked slowly toward the bathroom. A long, warm bath sounded as close to orgasmic bliss as she'd come for weeks. Not that the guys wouldn't have been more than happy to accommodate her desire for orgasms or bliss, but hell, did anyone even think of sex when they were as big as a house and grouchy as a rattlesnake?

She closed the bathroom door, her desire for some peace and solitude, not to mention time away from their prying, over-concerned eyes, outweighing her usual joy in them fussing over her.

When the water was drawn, she stepped in and gingerly lowered herself down into the bath. Oh sweet Jesus, had anything ever felt so good?

She lay there, her head tilted back, eyes closed, until the water started to cool around her. Unwilling to give up the comfort of the bath yet, she flipped the stopper with her toe to allow the water to run down. Then she reached up with her other foot to start the hot water running again.

Ahhh. Much better.

She settled back down and grimaced as a tight pain constricted her belly. At least the baby wasn't doing her usual kung fu moves.

A knock on the door interrupted her absolute zero train of thought, and she frowned.

"Honey, breakfast is almost ready, and if you don't get out soon, you're going to look like a prune for a week."

She growled and heard Rhys chuckle in response. With a contented sigh, she relaxed back into the water only to tense up as another odd ripple tightened across her belly. This one was harder than the last and it started low in her back then reached around her lower belly into her groin.

Hell. Surely not now. She still had two weeks to go. She didn't have a watch, so she couldn't time them, but there was a clock by the sink.

All lazy dullness gone, she took notice of the time on the clock and then tried to make herself relax as she waited to see if there was any regularity to her pains.

A half hour later, she'd timed three contractions, all precisely ten minutes apart.

Okay, nothing to panic over, and she damn sure wasn't going to rouse Logan's freak-out tendencies. Not yet anyway. She gripped the tub to try and haul herself upward just as another contraction hit. Damn it.

"Logan," she called out, knowing damn well he was lurking outside the bathroom.

Sure enough, almost before she could get his name out, the door opened, and he burst in, a scowl on his face.

"Are you okay?" he asked. "What's with closing the bathroom door? You could have fallen, and we wouldn't hear you."

She smiled and kept her tone purposely light. "Help me up?" she asked, extending her hand.

His expression eased as he bent over the tub. He gripped her hand and put his arm behind her back to help her stand. Keeping his fingers curled tight around her hand, he helped her over the side then handed her a towel.

"Thanks," she said, even as another contraction centered in her abdomen. Damn, that one came out of sync with the others. Her gaze crept to the clock. Three minutes. That didn't make a lot of sense.

"You can go now," she said to Logan, trying not to sound too hopeful. "I just need to do girly stuff, and then I'll be out to eat. Tell Rhys to keep it warm for me, please."

He brushed his lips across her cheek and then headed out of the bathroom. She grinned at the obvious way he swung the door wide open and left it.

She took her time brushing out her hair and securing it in a ponytail. When the next pain hit, she looked at the clock.

Seven minutes. Her face scrunched into a frown. Well hell. Ten minutes, three minutes then seven minutes.

Real labor was supposed to be regular with the time between contractions gradually lessening. Which meant she was probably just having...what? Fake ones? She almost laughed. There wasn't anything fake about the pain.

With a grumble, she finished dressing. Now after making such a big deal out of eating, she was going to have to figure out a reason why she'd suddenly lost her appetite.

She'd taken a step into the bedroom when liquid seeped down her leg, soaking the maternity pants she'd pulled on. She stopped in her tracks and stared down as more liquid pooled on the floor.

Her first thought amused her. Or maybe she was just a babbling fool in shock because the only reaction she could muster was one of extreme aggravation because now she'd have to get dressed all over again. The second thought was that she hadn't bothered to shave her legs, and now she was most definitely going to the hospital. With hairy legs.

"Cat, what the hell is taking you so long?" Rhys asked from the doorway. "Breakfast was on the table a half hour ago."

She turned to look at him. Her fear and uncertainty must have shone on her face because Rhys went from teasing aggravation to utter seriousness in two seconds flat.

He strode across the room and cupped her elbow with his hand. "What's wrong?" he demanded.

She stared down at the puddle of water on the floor then tried to pry the wet material from the inside of her leg.

"Oh shit. Honey, did your water break?"

Stupid question. But she nodded anyway.

"Oh boy," he breathed. "Logan is going to freak."

She giggled and relaxed just a bit. Things were going to be fine. Rhys wouldn't flip out on her, and between the two of them, they could handle Logan and get her to the hospital.

"Let's get you changed," he said in a calm voice. "I'll call for the driver, and I'll send Logan down with the bag. It'll give him something to do."

Twenty minutes later, Rhys helped Catherine out of the elevator and toward the door where the car was waiting. Logan was pacing outside the entrance, and when Catherine and Rhys walked out, he all but pounced on Catherine.

She smiled as he went a bit, okay a lot, overboard as he ushered her inside the car, but she couldn't fault how loving he was toward her and their baby. Even if he was a little overzealous.

At the hospital, Rhys took care of checking in and the paperwork, which was just as well since he was the only calm one despite the appearance Catherine gave to the contrary.

Inside she was a mess. A complete and utter mess. She wasn't ready for motherhood. What the hell did she know about babies? Other than she wanted this one so badly she ached.

Hours later as she panted between contractions and Logan and Rhys hovered nearby, she wondered why any woman ever wanted children.

"It won't be long now," the doctor said as he positioned himself between her legs.

Logan and Rhys stood on either side of her head, their hands laced with hers. They squeezed reassuringly even as she caught her breath and bore down with the next contraction.

All the air escaped her lungs and she sagged against the pillows, her strength nearly gone.

"I can't do this," she whispered.

Rhys leaned down and brushed her hair from her face. He kissed her tenderly. "Yes, you can. You can do anything, Cat."

Logan also leaned down, her hand clasped tight in his. "I know you're tired, baby. I know you hurt. But hold on a little longer. Do what the doctor says. Think of how wonderful it will be to finally hold our daughter in your arms."

Her body stirred as the next contraction began low in her back. Burning, growing, and with it the undeniable urge to push.

She gripped their hands, sucked in her breath and pulled against them as she pushed with everything she had.

"That's it, baby," Logan urged.

"You're doing it!" Rhys said excitedly.

The doctor's words faded away. Even Logan and Rhys became a blur as she focused on her body's urgings. Just when she was sure she couldn't take a minute more, she felt the most exquisite relief, as if her stomach caved in. The pressure was gone, the pain relief immediate.

"The head's out," the doctor announced. "Give me just a minute and then one more push and your daughter will be here."

Both Logan and Rhys peered over her legs, craning for a view of the baby.

"Push with your next contraction," the doctor said.

She put her chin down and pushed. The sensation of her daughter sliding free was one she'd never forget as long as she lived.

She collapsed back against the bed as she heard a small cry from her newborn baby. And then she was placed on Catherine's stomach, wrapped in a loose blanket.

With trembling hands, Catherine gathered her in her arms and pulled her close. Tears blurred her vision as she looked down at the blinking eyes of her baby.

Logan and Rhys bent down so they too could get a good look at their daughter. Catherine opened the blanket so they could all peek at the fingers and toes of the squirming bundle.

"She's perfect," Rhys said in a choked voice.

Logan reached out with a shaking hand to touch the side of the baby's face. "Beautiful," he whispered. Then he turned to look at Catherine. Her breath caught as she saw the emotion in his eyes. Love. So much love and tenderness. "Thank you," he said in a voice clogged with tears. "Thank you for my daughter."

"Lauren," Catherine said in a quiet voice.

"Lauren. I like it," Rhys said as he traced each of the ten tiny toes.

"Lauren Cullen-Wellesley," Logan echoed in deep satisfaction.

The three of them huddled close around their daughter and then Catherine lifted her to her breast. Catherine laughed in delight when Lauren began rooting and nuzzling in her attempt to latch on.

Logan cupped his hand behind Lauren's tiny head as she suckled at her mother's breast. Rhys cradled her bottom while Catherine touched the dark hair at Lauren's crown.

Then she stared up at her husbands and let her sheer joy in this moment shine in her smile. They smiled back.

"I love you, Cat," Rhys said.

Logan leaned in close and kissed her gently. "I love you, baby."

"And I love you," she told them both. "So much. I don't think we'll ever have a day more perfect than this."

Rhys smiled then looked back down at their daughter. "I don't know, Cat. I think the days will only get better."

Songbird

Dedication

To Jamie for all her knitted love.

Chapter One

Emily Donovan woke with stinging eyes, her body shuddering in the throes of a nightmare. The same nightmare she had every night.

She closed her eyes against the unbearable ache in her chest and tried to fall back into oblivion, but the memories were too vivid, too alive in her mind.

Sean.

How she missed him. He hadn't deserved to die. He'd been too young, so full of life. He'd loved her unreservedly, picked up the pieces of her shattered heart and helped put her back together.

As always when she thought of Sean, images of his two older brothers, Taggert and Greer, haunted her. It angered her that she couldn't separate her memories of Sean from the other two Donovan brothers, but they were as much a part of her soul as Sean had been. But Sean had accepted her. Loved her. Taggert and Greer had shoved her away.

The ache in her chest stole her breath, and she opened her eyes to stare at the blurred ceiling. The lamp at the side of her bed cast elongated shadows, sometimes frightening, but the dark was scarier, so she always left it on.

The days had gotten a little easier. She managed to perform normal activities. Eating. Sleeping—finally. But her sleep was still tortured by images of that night. By Sean's blood covering her hands. By his whispered *I love you* and his warm smile before he took his last breath.

"It's not fair," she whispered fiercely. "It should have been me, not you."

Her breath stuttered out in a sob that clawed at her throat. It hurt to inhale. It hurt to exhale. It hurt to *live*.

Giving up on sleep, she crawled out of bed, feeling much older than her twenty-five years. She'd *always* been so much older than her years. Quieter, more mature. Only the Donovan brothers had been able to bring her out of her shell, and she'd give anything to go back to those days in the Montana mountains where only the skies were bigger than their dreams.

She'd lived hers. Just for a little while. Just as Tagg had always predicted. Their little songbird was destined for bigger and better things than the Mountain Pass Ranch. But she hadn't wanted fame and fortune. She'd only wanted their love.

With a weary sigh, she walked into the kitchen clad in only her silky pajama top. Sean had bought it for her, and when she'd laughingly informed him he got ripped off because only the top was there, he smugly told her he preferred easy access and had thrown away the bottoms.

Mechanically she performed the rituals of morning. Preparing coffee that she didn't even like, toasting a bagel she wouldn't taste. All the things that made her life feel normal.

The chair was cool on her bare legs, and she scooted up to the small, two-person table where she'd placed her saucer and cup. She drank, barely wincing when the hot liquid hit her tongue. Chewing the bagel took effort. Swallowing took more.

What was she supposed to do today? The question filtered calmly through her mind, and she stared at the half-empty cup in her hand in bemusement. She had no job to go to. No appointments. No schedule. She only had one goal. To survive another day.

Maybe she'd take a walk. Challenge herself to face the city she'd fled to. Its size and people would swallow her up. Offer her the anonymity she desperately craved.

The mere idea of leaving her apartment without a specific destination in mind sent a wave of nausea through her belly. The coffee bubbled like a volcano about to erupt, and she swallowed rapidly.

She couldn't go on like this, living in the shadows, afraid to step into the light. Sean would hate the life she led. He'd look at her with those intense blue eyes, and his lips would thin in disapproval.

She looked down, studying her fingers, and wondered how long it would take before she didn't feel so flayed alive when she thought of Sean. When she couldn't *feel* the knife that had ended his life.

A firm knock sounded at the door. Her head whipped up, and panic hit her like a sledgehammer. Each breath squeezed from her lungs, crushing her chest.

Stop being stupid.

No one knew she was here. She knew none of her neighbors. She was safe.

Who the hell could be at her door at five in the morning?

Renewed fear gripped her by the throat.

Maybe it was just her apartment manager. Or a neighbor.

At five in the morning?

Her gaze flickered over the four deadbolts she'd had installed. No one was getting in unless she let them.

The knock sounded again. Harder this time.

She flinched and hastily stood, her heart beating in a vicious cadence.

She didn't have to answer. She could pretend to be asleep. Or not at home.

Hesitating, she turned away from the door only to yank back around when the knocking persisted.

Whoever it was wasn't going away.

Damp palms wiped nervously on her pajama top. She glanced down, realizing she wasn't dressed for company, and then she laughed—a harsh, dry sound that assaulted her ears.

She wasn't entertaining guests. The sooner she answered the door and sent them on their way, the better.

It took everything she had to make that walk across the living room to the door. She put her palm on the surface and leaned forward to peer out the peephole.

She gasped, blinked, stepped back then surged forward again, straining to see. Her stomach plummeted.

Oh God.

Greer and Taggert Donovan stood in the hallway, their expressions grim—and determined.

How had they found her?

Stupid question.

She closed her eyes and leaned her forehead on the door. Not now. She couldn't face them right now. Maybe never. How was she to look at them knowing how much they reminded her of Sean? Of how much she loved Sean?

Of how much she loved Greer and Taggert.

Her fingers splayed out over the wood as if she could touch them through the barrier. She turned her head so that her cheek pressed against the surface and then reached for the top lock, letting her hand rest on it without moving it.

Another knock jarred her face and then she heard Taggert's voice, low and entreating.

"Emmy, open the door."

She swallowed once and slowly pulled away until she was an arm's length from the locks, her hand still on the top one. As she turned it, the click echoed harshly.

With shaking fingers, she worked down until she reached the last. She grasped the knob and turned, cracking the door and bracing her free hand on the frame.

Her gaze met and locked first with Taggert and then Greer. They filled the doorway, the entire hallway, and God, they looked just as she remembered. Stetsons, faded jeans and boots.

For the longest time she stared and they stared back. Then Greer stepped forward but halted when she retreated a step.

"Open the door, Emmy," he said softly.

Her knees trembling, she eased the door wider until there was a gaping space, more space than she'd allowed in a year. Greer's expression softened, his leaf green eyes filled with regret. Then he simply opened his arms.

The first step was the hardest, but suddenly she found herself in his warm embrace. She buried her face in his chest, inhaling the faint smells of tobacco and horses, two scents that seemed permanently branded on him.

She shook against him, but the tears wouldn't come. Her eyes were so dry they hurt.

He lifted her and walked with her into the apartment. Taggert closed the door behind them, and she turned to see him fingering the locks, a scowl on his face.

"Have you cried even once, Emmy?" Greer asked quietly as he held her.

It made her sound so heartless. She hadn't cried. Not at the hospital when they told her Sean was gone. Not at his funeral or afterward when they buried him in the family plot on Mountain Pass land. Not in the many months since. Crying made it all so...final.

She wrapped her arms around his waist and squeezed. It felt so good to be back in his arms.

"I missed you," she whispered.

"Aww Em, we missed you too," Greer said in a low voice.

Taggert made an impatient sound, and she pulled away from Greer to stare at the oldest Donovan brother.

"Why the hell did you disappear on us, Emmy?" Taggert demanded. "You were Sean's wife. We would have taken care of you. The MPR is your home. It's always been your home. Long before you married Sean. Frank's going crazy. No one's seen you. And now we find you holed up like a prisoner in an apartment in the city. You hate the city."

Her hand flew to her throat, her pulse pounding against her fingers.

"I told Frank I couldn't do it anymore," she cracked out. "He knows. I told him not to look for me. I can't—won't—sing."

"You think that's all he cares about?" Taggert asked. "He's your manager, but that doesn't mean he's a complete mercenary asshole. He's worried sick over you. We all are."

"Tagg, enough," Greer warned.

Taggert threw up one hand and turned away, his entire body simmering with frustration. Then he turned back around and pinned her with the force of his stare. Warm, liquid chocolate. She'd always loved his eyes. They made his already dark looks even darker, but she'd never been afraid of him. He'd always been her Tagg, and she'd always loved him.

"Come here, damn it," he said gruffly.

She only hesitated a moment before she walked into his arms. He hugged her fiercely, stealing her breath with the force of his grip. But God, for the first time in a year, she felt safe.

His breath whispered roughly over her hair, her only signal of the turmoil that rolled beneath his tough exterior.

"Goddamn it, Emmy, what were you thinking?"

She couldn't answer. The words were lodged in her throat, so thick and swollen she feared choking. She concentrated on breathing, taking in his solid strength and the crisp, clean smell of his shirt. He still used the same detergent, the same plain deodorant. No frills, no aftershave, no cologne.

He pried her away from him, holding her shoulders as he stared down at her.

"You're coming home with us."

She opened her mouth, to say what, she wasn't sure, but he silenced her with one hard stare.

"No arguments. Greer and I aren't taking no for an answer. You belong at home. Sean would want you there. Not locked away here in some strange city, afraid to leave your apartment. You aren't living. You're barely existing."

Oh no, she wouldn't lose her composure now. Would not give in to the grief slicing her insides up. It had been a year. She could hear Sean's name without reacting as though she'd been slapped.

"He's right, Songbird," Greer said in a soft, soothing voice.

He couldn't know how much the endearment hurt. It, more than Sean's name, sent splinters of agony washing through her body.

She closed her eyes and swayed in Taggert's grip, biting her lip, welcoming the pain as a distraction.

"Don't call me that," she rasped. "Never again."

Taggert caught her chin in his fingers and feathered his thumb across her jaw. "You will sing again, Emmy. In time. When you're ready."

She shook her head mutely, but he just held firm and stared back at her as if infusing her with his will.

"Yes, you will. You're coming home. You'll heal. You'll live again. You'll sing."

Chapter Two

"We should have driven," Taggert muttered. He sank lower in his seat as the plane began its taxi.

"Why didn't you?" Emily asked curiously as she glanced over at him. Taggert's dislike of flying was hardly secret. In fact, she couldn't remember the last time he'd willingly got on a plane.

"We were in a hurry to get to you," Greer said.

She looked down at her hands, surprised at how numb she still was even after being dragged out of her apartment by the two brothers. It was all a little surreal, and at any moment she expected to wake up staring at her plain white ceiling just like every other day.

Taggert reached over and folded his hand over hers, his thumb rubbing over the side of her wrist.

"You had to know we'd come, Emmy."

She swallowed but couldn't say anything. She hadn't known they'd come. They'd made their feelings and wishes perfectly clear four years ago. They couldn't have *been* any clearer.

Greer sighed and shifted uncomfortably, his knees pressing into the seat in front of him.

"Lean over on me and get some sleep," he directed. "You look like you could use some rest, and it's a long-ass flight."

With the armrests up on either side of her, leaning into either man was easy. Greer shifted his arm up and over her, and she nestled into the crook of his shoulder.

Taggert kept hold of her hand, and it struck her that this was the only time in years either man had allowed himself to touch her. Oh, there'd been casual, quick hugs. Perfunctory kisses on the cheek when she and Sean made the trip back, but the trips became fewer when she could no longer bear the strain and Sean couldn't bear to see her unhappy.

Because of her, he'd left the only place he'd ever called home, and he'd never gotten the chance to go back until they brought him to Mountain Pass in a casket.

Why now? Why were they changing their approach with her? Now, when it was too late. Four years ago she would have given her soul for them to understand, for them to accept her love—for all of them. Sean had understood. Why hadn't Taggert and Greer?

Her anger surprised her, sudden like a flashflood. For so long she'd felt nothing but overwhelming sorrow and regret, and now the red-hot glow of rage simmered within.

"We never meant to hurt you, Emmy," Greer whispered close to her ear.

Had he felt her anger? Could he sense it boiling?

Not now. Not here. Maybe never, but definitely not here, trapped with all these people.

"Rest," Taggert ordered. "Lay off, Greer. There'll be plenty of time to hash it out when we get home."

Instead of being irritated at his dictate, she sighed in relief and closed her eyes against Greer's chest. She willed herself to go to sleep, if for no other reason than to avoid meaningless chitchat, or worse, a conversation that had the potential to reopen old wounds.

She slept deep and dreamlessly, and when she woke to Taggert's gentle shaking, she had to orient herself to her surroundings. The plane was nearly empty, and Taggert pulled himself out of his seat and into the aisle before reaching a hand back for her.

Still fighting the heavy veil of sleep, she allowed him to pull her from her seat. She stumbled a little, and Tagg caught her with a firm hand to her elbow.

"Easy," he murmured. "Don't try to take it too fast."

She hadn't slept that hard in a year, and she wondered why now, on an uncomfortable flight? She didn't have to look too hard for her answer. Taggert and Greer made her feel safe. They always had. Maybe they were right to make her come home, even if it would be the most difficult thing she'd ever done.

Barely aware of her surroundings, she managed to walk dazedly off the plane. She stood at the gate, confused by where to go next. Greer slipped an arm around her waist and urged her forward.

There were no suitcases to collect. Everything she'd taken was shoved into a small overnight bag. She'd opted to just walk away, and maybe that's what she did best. Run. Tagg and Greer had said they'd take care of her apartment and her belongings, and she let them, too emotionally wrung out to focus on anything more than taking her next breath.

She accepted long ago that she was weak. A strong person would never have existed as she had for the last year. She was a coward who took the path of least resistance, but she recognized her limitations and knew that even if she wanted to be more resilient, she'd fail. She'd died with Sean, only her body was too stupid to realize it.

Greer and Taggert herded her toward the parking area and into a new-looking blue SUV.

"Where's the Dooley?" she asked faintly. The red, extended cab diesel truck was as much a fixture of the MPR as the Donovan brothers.

Tagg threw the luggage in the back while Greer opened the passenger door for Emily.

"It's still there. Relegated to the work truck now. She's seen better days."

He waited patiently for her to climb in, and then he reached for a pillow lying on the floor behind the driver's seat. He plumped it and tossed it on the seat.

"Lay down, sweet pea. Get some sleep. You look like you're in another world. I'll wake you up when we get home."

Her eyes were so heavy, she wasn't sure she could keep them open if she tried, so she settled down on the seat, snuggling her face into the soft pillow.

She dimly registered doors shutting, the engine starting and the SUV rocking into motion. Tagg's and Greer's low voices buzzed warmly in her ears, but she couldn't decipher what they were saying.

Home.

She was going home.

It terrified her and offered her sweet comfort all at the same time.

"I hope we're doing the right thing," Greer murmured as he turned to look over his shoulder at a sleeping Emily.

"We are," Taggert said grimly. "You saw her. Hell, Greer, how much longer was she going to last like that? Did you see the locks she had on the door?"

"Well at least she was smart about her safety," Greer said.

Taggert scowled. "She should have damn well come home a long time ago. She should have never left."

"You and I both know why she did," Greer muttered.

Taggert glanced away, his fingers tight around the steering wheel. Yeah, he knew why she'd left. Why she couldn't stay. Why she and Sean made a life away from the ranch. Why she'd ended up Sean's wife in the first place.

He'd made mistakes. No question. But that didn't mean Emily was going to keep paying for them. Four years was a long time. The last year had been hell on all of them, but especially Emily. Sweet, delicate Emily with the voice of an angel and a heart to match.

Goddamn, it hurt him to see her so defeated. She wouldn't even sing, and she'd always sung. Always. He couldn't remember a time when she wasn't weaving words into beautiful music.

"We shouldn't have let this go on for so long," Taggert said. "We should have dragged her ass home months ago."

Greer nodded. "Agreed. But we can't change the past." He rubbed a tired hand over his face. "God, if we could. All we can do is make damn sure Emily feels safe with us, that she knows the ranch is her home."

"And that this time we aren't going to give her up like we did before," Taggert vowed.

"She may not want us now," Greer said carefully. "Time changes things. She married Sean. She's a different woman now."

Taggert turned fiercely to Greer, slowing down as he did. "You look at that girl back there and you tell me she's a different woman. She's hurting like hell. She's grieving. She's tried to stop living, but she's still the same sweet, giving girl we've known all our lives. She loved us, Greer. We shit on that love, but she loved us, and I don't believe for a minute she gave that love lightly. We can get her back. I didn't say it would be easy, and it shouldn't be after we turned her away, but I won't give up."

"I hear you, man. She needs time, and she'll have all the time in the world at the ranch where we can take care of her and end this path to self destruction she's on."

Grief and regret, so much regret, swirled in Taggert's stomach. Sean shouldn't have died protecting Emily. His older brothers let him down—let him and Emily both down. Taggert would have to live with that for the rest of his life. But he wouldn't surrender Emily the same way. She was alive, damn it, and she was going to start acting like it.

Chapter Three

Emily woke in Taggert's arms as he strode from the SUV toward the front porch of the two-story frame house. She'd always loved this house. Whitewashed, it could have existed a hundred years before, a farm house on a fledgling cattle spread. And it did, she reminded herself ruefully. This land had been in the Donovan family for over a century, built when the west was still new, when people with big dreams came to settle the raw, untamed land.

The sun was sliding over the mountains, and the chill of the spring air elicited a trail of goose bumps over her arms.

Tagg looked down at her as he mounted the steps, and his eyes softened. "We're home, Emmy."

He set her down, almost as if he knew how important it was that she walk inside on her own. Greer opened the door, and Emily stepped into the living room.

The first thing that hit her was the smell. It was hard to put a name on the smell of home. It was older, musty but not unpleasant, just the reality of an aged house. There was a hint of tobacco, the scent of leather and a faint whisper of daffodils.

Nothing had changed. The furniture was the same down to Taggert's favorite threadbare armchair with ottoman. The old television had been replaced and a flatscreen was mounted on the wall catty-corner to the stone fireplace.

Through the adjacent door, she knew she'd find the kitchen the same as she'd left it, its large open floor plan inviting and homey, the wraparound bar that hugged the entire kitchen a place for people to gather, talk and eat at the end of a long day.

She could almost hear the laughter echoing through the hallways.

"Emily, my dear! It's so good to see you."

She blinked in shock to see Doc Summerston stand from his perch on the couch. She'd been so busy remembering that she hadn't even noticed him in the room. What on earth was he doing here?

"Hello, Doc," she said a little nervously.

Greer wrapped his arm around her shoulders and gave her a light squeeze. "We asked Doc to come out and look you over."

She inhaled in surprise and glanced sharply up at him and then over to Taggert who looked none too apologetic.

"Is that all right with you, Emily?" Doc asked in a gentle voice.

Her shoulders went down in defeat. It didn't really matter. The sooner she got it over with, the sooner she could go to bed.

"Where am I sleeping?" she murmured.

"In your room," Taggert said.

She nodded and started for the stairs, Doc following behind her. Was there a diagnosis for dead-and-don't-know-it? She almost laughed. Doc would think her terribly fatalistic.

"Well, we got her here, now what the hell are we going to do?" Greer demanded after Emily and Doc disappeared up the stairs.

"That's a loaded question," Taggert said with a sigh. "We take it one day at a time."

"It scares me to see her this way. It's like she's given up."

Taggert scowled. "I think she gave up a long time ago."

The two men paced the living room, and fifteen minutes later, Doc came down the stairs, a grim look on his face.

"Well?" Taggert asked impatiently.

Doc sighed. "It hurts my heart to see her like this. I watched that girl grow up, so happy and sunny. No one could look at her without smiling."

"Is she okay? I mean physically?" Greer interjected.

"Well, yes and no. The problem is, she just doesn't care. She's weary to her bones. I doubt she's slept for more than a few hours at a time in the last year. She's only eating enough to get by. She's given up. There's so much hurt in that little girl's eyes, it makes me ache."

"That makes two of us," Greer muttered.

Taggert shoved an impatient hand through his hair. "So what can we do?"

Doc pinned them both with a resigned look. "I hate to say it, but you're going to have to get tough with her."

Taggert frowned. Greer winced a little, but he knew Doc was right. As tempting as it was to coddle and baby her, it wasn't going to help her rejoin the land of the living.

"She has a routine of not having a routine. She eats, she sleeps—or tries to, and then she does it all over again. She's on autopilot and a crash is inevitable. Give her a day or two to rest. I gave her something to help her sleep through the night tonight. Make sure she gets plenty to eat. But then, you're going to have to make her break out of her comfort zone."

Taggert swore long and low. "Christ, she'll hate us."

"Maybe at first," Doc said. "She'll come around, though, and then she'll understand."

Greer sighed. He and Taggert wanted nothing more than to bring her home so they could protect and love her. Making her hate them again...

"We appreciate you coming by, Doc," Greer said.

"Anytime. I'm just glad Emily is home where she belongs. It's been a tough road for her, but she's young and resilient. She'll bounce back."

"I hope to hell you're right," Taggert said.

Emily woke to a stream of sunlight piercing the white ruffled curtains. For a moment she lay there soaking in the warmth, and then she turned to look at the old alarm clock on the nightstand. Eight o'clock.

Taggert and Greer would have been up several hours already. Work started early and ended late on a ranch. They and the hands put in long hours every day.

Sundays though...Sunday had always been their day. In the summers they snuck down to the watering hole, one of the Donovan brothers keeping watch for Emily's dad. A few times he'd shown up, but by the time he had, they'd gotten Emily out of the creek and headed home.

Emily's mother had died when she was young, and her father was the epitome of old-time conservative strict. Spare the rod, spoil the child. A motto that should have been his family crest.

She'd gotten more beatings over spending time with the Donovan boys than anything else. She wasn't a rebellious child, and she was usually obedient. Except when it came to Taggert, Greer and Sean. Spending time with them had been worth every lash of her father's belt.

They'd hated her father, but he was her father, and she owed him as much respect as she could give. He'd been proud of her singing. He loved to hear her sing in church. Every Sunday she sang with the choir, her clear, radiant voice rising above the others.

He'd hit the roof when her attention turned to more commercial songs, and he'd forbidden her from seeking any sort of a career outside the church.

One night she'd snuck out, and Sean drove her to the neighboring town where the honkeytonk was having talent night. She'd sung her heart out and garnered the attention of Frank, an agent to several already established singers in the business.

Her father was waiting—with his belt—when she returned home. It had been the worst beating she'd suffered, and she didn't go anywhere for three days for fear Taggert, Greer or Sean would find out.

The two things she loved most in the world—the Donovan brothers and singing—were the things forbidden to her by her father.

She'd taken her courage in her hands and gone to the ranch, determined to make the brothers see how she felt about them. In her youth and inexperience, she hadn't considered how ludicrous her wants were. She only knew how desperately she loved them all.

It was the worst night of her life. Far worse than any beating she'd ever suffered. Sean hadn't been there, but Taggert and Greer had gently but candidly told her that what she wanted wasn't possible.

Then she'd gone home to face her father and his wrath.

Sean came for her two days later, furious with his brothers and ready to kill her father for what he'd done. Sean had refused to leave her there one minute longer. They eloped, but that hadn't been the final nail in the coffin of her nonexistent relationship with her father.

He'd seemed willing to forgive her marriage to Sean, but when she told him she had a record deal, he'd disowned her.

It seemed everyone but Sean had turned his back on her, and now Sean was gone. All because of her.

He loved her, put her first—her career, her wants and needs—and she hadn't been able to save him.

She waited for the tears to come, even welcomed them, because anything was better than this barren wasteland that resided in her chest. But she simply stared at the window, her grief sealed behind an impenetrable wall of ice.

With a heavy sigh, she slid her legs toward the edge of the bed and struggled upward. Funny, she didn't remember getting undressed last night, but she supposed she had after Doc gave her a sleeping pill.

Normally she wouldn't bother with a shower, because there was only her to put up with her appearance, but she wasn't in her apartment anymore. Aside from Greer and Taggert, there were a number of ranch hands who lived here.

Grimacing over the effort it took to dig in her bag for clothes and the basic toiletries, she trudged off to the shower and without waiting for it to warm, stepped underneath the spray.

The cold shocked some of the lethargy from her system, and by the time she washed and rinsed her hair, it didn't quite feel like sludge ran through her veins.

After drying off and dressing, she looked at herself in the mirror and winced. She looked...well, dead. There was no life, no spark in her eyes, and her lips were drawn, not in a frown, but in a flat line of indifference. Even a frown denoted some sort of emotion.

To her surprise, her stomach growled, and she took it as a promising sign. Maybe the mountain air was good for her. Or maybe it had just been too long since she had a decent meal.

Leaving her still-damp hair hanging to her shoulders, she picked up her mess and went back into her bedroom. She pulled up short when she saw Taggert standing in the doorway.

"Oh good, there you are. I was coming up to see if you wanted to eat. Buck left breakfast for you."

"I thought it was against his religion to hold a meal for anyone," she said dryly. "'Either be there when it's put on the table or go without'."

Taggert chuckled, and she watched the dimple in his cheek deepen. It always amazed her how something so innocuous as a dimple could transform his hardness.

He reached out his hand. "Come on, Emmy. Come eat with me. Afterward I'll take you out to see the new colts."

A flicker of interest stirred for a moment, but the thought of walking so far exhausted her.

"Maybe I'll just eat and hang out here," she murmured.

His eyes hardened for a moment, but he didn't argue. Instead he motioned for her hand again, and when she finally extended it, he pulled her out into the hallway.

"You've lost weight," he said bluntly as they descended the stairs. "You need to start eating again."

Her cheeks tightened, but she remained silent.

When they got to the kitchen she was surprised to see Buck puttering around and even more surprised to see that he still wore the same apron he had years ago. It was worn, had holes and was so thin she could see through it.

"What are you staring at, girly?" he asked rudely.

She felt her lips going upward in a smile, and it shocked her. But it grew even larger as she stared at the cantankerous man who'd been the Donovans' cook since before she was born.

"Well, now, that's better. Come here so I can hug you."

Mechanically, she went forward, still enjoying the sensation of smiling. He hugged her tightly, and she smelled the faint mint of his snuff.

"Still chewing," she said with a sigh. "Buck, your mouth is going to rot and fall off."

He drew away and glared at her. "Still nagging, I see. Greer hasn't given up his smokes, so nag him if you feel the need, but leave me be. I've been chewing for forty years, and I don't aim to quit anytime soon."

She rolled her eyes as she stepped back. "Pardon me for not wanting you both to die of cancer."

"The good Lord will take me when he's ready and not a minute sooner."

Her smile disappeared and the heavy weight descended on her chest again.

"Ah sheeit," Buck said. "That was a damn fool thing of me to say, Emmy. I wouldn't hurt you for the world."

"I know," she said, trying valiantly to resummon her smile.

Giving up, she took a seat at the bar beside Taggert and avoided both their gazes. When Buck put a plate in front of her, she ate without tasting. She knew they watched her and also knew they were measuring every bite, so she made herself eat all of it.

When she pushed the plate away, Buck gave a grunt of satisfaction and picked it up to put it in the sink.

"So how about that walk out to the stable?" Taggert asked.

There was a challenge in his voice that made her groan inwardly. What she really wanted to do was go back to bed or even curl up on the couch and absorb the familiar smells of the Donovan house.

But she was embarrassed to tell him no, to explain that she didn't have the energy to do much more than brush her hair. It was still damp, and if she went outside, she'd need to comb it and dry it.

She raised trembling fingers to press against her forehead.

"Are you okay?"

Taggert's concerned voice brushed over her ears. She tried to nod, but all she managed was a clipped half motion that could either be deciphered as a yes or a no.

"The walk can wait," he said after a pause. "You should get some more rest. When you're feeling more up to it, I'll take you out to see the horses."

Relief made her weak. She put her hands on the edge of the bar to push herself off the stool, and then she made her way toward the living room. Did the closet still hold all those wonderful old afghans that Maria Donovan had made?

She stopped just outside the living room and opened the hallway closet to see a pile of blankets residing on the same shelf they'd always rested on.

She pulled one down and briefly held it to her nose, savoring the smell. Home. It smelled like home.

Carrying it into the living room, she sank onto the couch with something akin to bliss. Haphazardly, she arranged the blanket around her body and drew it up to her chin before closing her heavy lids.

Chapter Four

"You shouldn't have caved so goddamn easy," Greer said in disgust.

He took one last drag of his cigarette then tossed it down and ground it under his boot heel.

"That's easy for you to say," Taggert growled. "You weren't looking at her. She was about to collapse. I honest to God think it took everything she had to get up, shower and eat. Besides, I'm done with being the older brother and bully in this shit. I can't forget it was me doing all the talking when we sent her away. Like it was my decision as head of the fucking household."

Greer held up his hand in surrender. "I understand. I just can't stand this. I feel like we're losing her all over again, and there's not a damned thing we can do."

"I know what *I'm* going to do," Taggert gritted out. "I'm going to be there every step of the way. I'm never going to give her a chance to think I don't want her—that I don't...love her," he ended in a nearly silent exhale.

"Work?" Greer asked.

"Fuck work. Our hands are more than capable of running the show for a while. Rand will keep things going smoothly."

"Okay."

"Look man, if you don't want this—"

"Shut the fuck up," Greer said coldly. "That's a stupid-ass thing to say. We made a decision. We made a mistake. There's nothing more to discuss."

Taggert held both hands up. "All right, then stop second-guessing *my* decisions. You handle Emmy your way. I'll handle her mine."

Greer nodded. He watched as Tagg turned and stalked inside the house. Tagg might be the older brother, but he was definitely the impatient hothead of the family. Neither of them liked his judgment questioned even if they had monumentally fucked up in the past.

Greer sighed. It wouldn't be the first time they'd locked heads, and it sure as hell wouldn't be the last.

He walked toward the house, the need to see Emily again eating at him. He'd talk with Rand later.

Emily sat in the dark, her hands covered with sticky warmth. She couldn't move, couldn't breathe.

Sean.

Where was Sean?

She knew something terrible had happened, but she couldn't *see*. The dark suffocated her like some cloak of doom wrapping around her neck.

"Sean," she whispered.

Some of the dark faded. Distant laughter sounded, raising the hairs at her nape. Slowly, she lifted her hands, staring in horror at the bright red blood dripping from her palms.

Then she looked down to see Sean lying on the ground, a gaping knife wound in his chest.

Blood. So much blood. Sean's blood.

A scream rose from the depths of her soul, clawing a path up her throat, raw and scraping.

"Emmy. Emmy, wake up, love. Baby, shhh. You're all right, I swear it. Come on. Open those pretty eyes for me."

Taggert's voice sounded urgently, close to her, and she turned frantically to him, seeking escape from the horrific image of Sean awash in his own blood.

Her eyes fluttered open to see Taggert on his knees beside the couch, Greer standing behind him. Worry creased their brows. Had she screamed aloud?

She couldn't catch her breath. The more she sucked in, the tighter her chest became.

Taggert stroked her face with a gentle hand. "Breathe, baby. With me. Look at me."

She focused on those dark eyes, trying to mimic the slow rise and fall of his chest.

"That's it, Emmy. In and out. Look at me. See me. You're safe."

She gave a deep, shuddering breath as the tightness eased and the air flowed smoothly once more. She gazed helplessly up at him, hating her weakness but knowing she wasn't strong enough to overcome it. Was she?

She'd overheard Doc Summerston tell Greer and Taggert that she'd given up. Funny, she'd never really thought of it in terms like that. Dying didn't mean giving up, did it? No one ever bothered to tell her she was alive until Doc issued a sharp reprimand that she was killing herself.

Sean hadn't given up, and he was dead.

But you're alive. The tiny voice whispered in the back of her mind.

Oh God. Did she want to live?

"Come here," Taggert whispered as he gathered her into his arms.

The blanket slipped to her waist as she leaned toward him. He simply plucked her from the couch and sat down with her on his lap. Greer sat beside them and propped her legs over his lap.

"Bad dream?" Greer asked softly.

"Blood," she blurted. She shuddered violently. "It was everywhere." She raised her hands to stare at them and then rubbed them frantically over her pants legs. "It was all over my hands. I couldn't get it off."

Taggert pressed his lips to her hair and rubbed his hand down the length of her arm. "It's okay, Emmy. It was just a dream. You're safe."

"Make it go away," she whispered.

He squeezed her tight, and she snuggled further into his embrace. It was ironic that for so long she would have given anything to be here in Taggert's arms, close to Greer. All that was missing was Sean.

She stiffened and bowed her head, shrinking from his embrace.

"Don't," Taggert said huskily. "I know you hurt. But don't push me away. Not like I..."

...pushed you away.

The words hung between them in the thick silence that ensued. She didn't want to go there. Not now. She simply couldn't have this conversation. It was much easier to pretend that day never happened, that she'd never bared her soul and that Taggert and Greer hadn't rejected her.

Slowly she laid her head back on his broad chest and stared mutely at Greer. His hand ran over her leg, pausing occasionally to offer a light squeeze.

What had changed? They confused her, and she was too exhausted to figure them out.

"Emmy," Greer began, his voice hesitant, "sweet pea, you've got to start living again."

She flinched and looked away, but Greer reached forward, cupped her chin and forced her gaze back to him.

"We miss him too."

She went very still in Taggert's arms. No one had said Sean's name since her arrival. No one had mentioned him even indirectly.

"I'd like to go to bed," she croaked.

Greer's lips firmed, and he looked like he'd argue. He pulled away from her and ran a frustrated hand through his hair.

"All right, Emmy. But tomorrow things are going to change."

She heard the warning in his statement, but that was tomorrow, and it was all she could do to deal with today. Tomorrow...that was a long time away, and she'd take it one day at a time.

Chapter Five

The gentle strains of a guitar woke Emily from her sleep. She blinked fuzzily, wondering if it was just part of a dream. It was still dark outside, but a quick glance at the clock told her dawn wasn't far off.

A haunting melody, so simple and beautiful, floated over her ears. Her chin trembled. It was the first song she'd recorded—a song she'd written long ago when she and the Donovan brothers had spent a spring afternoon in the rain. *Mountain Rain.*

She closed her eyes and let the chords take her back to the nights spent round a campfire, Sean playing the guitar while she sang. Taggert and Greer sat by the fire, their long legs stretched out, their brims pulled low over their foreheads and their worn boots reflecting the flicker of the flames.

Drawn to the music, she eased out of bed and walked into the hallway to stand at the top of the stairs. Clad in only her flannel PJs, she followed the sound of the guitar down to the living room and realized it was coming from the front porch.

Her legs shook, and she had to steady herself by reaching down to grasp the arm of the couch. Who was playing? And moreover, her song?

The words to the song floated through her mind, and she was reminded of earlier, happier days. Carefree.

She opened the front door and stepped into the chilly morning air. The music stopped, and she found herself staring at Taggert, his hand frozen over the strings as he stared back at her.

"I didn't mean to wake you," Taggert said.

"I didn't know you played."

He glanced down at the guitar, and it was then she realized it was Sean's.

"I don't play well. Been fiddling with it for the last year."

"It sounded beautiful," she said in a low voice.

He looked back up at her, his gaze roving over her face until she could feel it caressing her cheek.

"Will you sing if I play?"

Her hand flew to her throat and she shook her head forcefully. "No. I c-can't."

"Why can't you?" he persisted. "Emmy, it's been a year. Yours is the most beautiful voice I've ever heard in my life. You have a talent that astounds me, and you're wasting it."

She shook her head again, unable to voice her terror, to admit her guilt, that it was because of the voice he loved so much that Sean was dead. She hated it. She couldn't even think about singing without her throat closing in on her.

She sank down onto one of the rockers. "Play for me," she begged.

His fingers stuttered over the strings for a moment, clumsy at first, and then he strummed the first chords of *Montana Memories*, a song she'd written specifically for the Donovan brothers. Did he know? Had he guessed?

She wrapped herself in the beauty of the music, allowing it to give her comfort when nothing else had. When the last note died and the skies began to lighten in preparation for sunrise, she sought his gaze and asked the question burning a hole in her mind.

"Why?"

His brow furrowed. "Why what?"

"Why did you come after me? Why did you bring me back here? Why...do you and Greer act as though I mean something to you...more than being your brother's widow?"

He sucked in his breath and carefully laid the guitar aside. His hands wiped along the tops of his legs and then gripped the area just above his knees. He looked...nervous. That puzzled her. Taggert was brash, temperamental, outspoken, opinionated, but she'd never seen him nervous.

"We made a mistake," he said in a raw voice. "One that's cost us a lot. One we'll regret making the rest of our lives."

"We?"

"Greer and I, but he's not here, so I can only speak for me. *I* made a mistake, Emmy. I pushed you away. I was surprised, even a little appalled that you claimed to love all of us, that you wanted to be with us. I was angry—jealous—and so I sent you away."

She stared at him in shock. Had he changed his mind? *Now?* After four years?

"Don't you see, Emmy? If I hadn't sent you away, you could have been with us. You would have never turned to Sean the way you did and the two of you wouldn't have left here. You would have been happy and wouldn't have spent so much time avoiding us. You and Sean would have stayed here and not in a hotel in town, and you damn sure wouldn't have been walking back to the hotel from the café the night Sean was killed."

Oh God, it hurt. She couldn't breathe. She wanted to deny that he was at fault, but she couldn't find the words. Her mind screamed *no, no, no* in a never ending litany, but instead of saying it, she got up and walked back into the house, leaving Taggert calling after her.

She walked past the living room, through the kitchen to the back door with no destination in mind. She let herself out, shivering when her bare feet made contact with the cold ground.

She went in the opposite direction of the stables, through the gate and down the worn pathway to the pond. The water looked dark and forbidding in the faint light, and she hurried on until she topped the slight rise beyond.

She came to a stumbling halt by the large oak tree that sheltered the headstones beneath. Some of them old, dating back a hundred years, and one much newer.

It wasn't necessary for the sun to shed its light over the engraving. She knew it by heart. *Sean Donovan, beloved brother and husband.*

163

Pain. Unrelenting pain. A tiny crack formed in the thick ice protecting her. Spreading rapidly, splintering in all directions. Unstoppable.

Panic swelled in her chest. A garbled noise caught in her throat. She couldn't breathe and oh God, it *hurt*. She needed help. She was going to explode. Something was terribly wrong. She was losing control and felt her insides straining against unbearable pressure.

She tried to take a breath and then another. Her eyes flooded with tears and sobs piled up deep inside her chest. The agony was unbearable. She was going to break. Maybe she was having a heart attack. How could it hurt so much?

A horrible noise echoed across the hillside, startling her, and then shockingly, she realized the sound came from *her*, from the very bowels of hell.

Another followed, and she fell to her knees as finally, she shattered.

Her arms clutched her belly as the sobs came tearing out of her soul. Her hands moved to her throat in an effort to stem the horrible tide of grief.

When she felt wetness, she pulled her fingers away in bewilderment to see her tears shining on her palms.

She leaned forward to touch Sean's name, to trace the etching on the marble headstone, made blurry by the tears running in streams down her cheeks.

"I'm sorry," she whispered hoarsely. "God, I'm so sorry. I loved you so much. You were everything to me."

Her head fell forward as the horrible, wracking sobs spilled from her lips. The sound was so harsh, so ugly that she covered her ears, but still, the noise permeated every pore.

She sank lower until she curled in a ball on the ground next to Sean's grave, her entire body heaving with the force of her cries.

Before she hadn't felt enough, and now she felt too much. It overwhelmed her, and she couldn't survive this. Sean was gone. He wasn't coming back. She'd killed him.

"Emmy, ahh sweetheart."

Firm hands glided over her body, moving her, repositioning her, and then she was lifted into the air. She turned into Taggert's chest, clamping her lips tight to stop the sounds of raw agony tearing their way out.

She grabbed at him, seeking his strength, knowing she could no longer do this alone.

"It wasn't you," she rasped out between sobs, the words barely recognizable. "Wasn't your fault. Mine."

"Shhh, you're talking crazy," he said as he gripped her tighter.

Her body swayed and bounced as he began the walk back to the house. To her immense relief, the awful noise stopped, but the tears tracked endlessly down her face, wetting his shirt.

Taggert halted suddenly, and Emily heard Greer demand what the hell was wrong.

She couldn't find the strength to look at Greer. Her strength was gone. She'd thought herself weak before, but now she realized the fortitude it had taken not to break before now, to face each day, even as numb as she'd been, and survive.

The next thing she knew, her clothing was being removed, and she couldn't even summon a protest. Her vision was blurred by the torrent of tears. She couldn't stop them. Now that they'd finally come, she had no idea how to turn them off.

Her hands fluttered helplessly to cover herself, but neither Taggert nor Greer was concerned with her nudity. She was thrust into a hot shower, and she reached for the walls to brace herself when she realized that Taggert had come in with her, still fully clothed.

They stood there under the hot spray until some of the bone-numbing cold began to wear off. Her shivering gradually lessened, and some of the heat seeped into her skin.

She bowed her head, letting the water run over her hair and down her body. Taggert simply held her, his hands firm around her shoulders, lending support she badly needed.

And then Greer reached in for her, pulling her away from Taggert and out into the cold again. Greer wrapped a towel around her, rubbing briskly, and then he stilled for a moment and gently touched the end of the towel to her cheeks, wiping away the tears.

Silently, more fell, and she wondered how many more she could possibly shed. Would it ever end? But the ache hadn't diminished. She opened her mouth to speak and realized why the horrible noise had stopped. Her voice was gone. Nothing more than a raspy exhalation sounded. Had she broken that too?

"Shhh, don't try to force it," Greer said.

He leaned forward, wrapping his arms around her, and pressed his lips to her forehead.

"This was a long time coming, Emmy. It's only going to get worse before you get better."

He pulled away and looked down at her pale, gaunt face, watching helplessly as the tears fell faster than he could wipe them away.

He'd never felt so damn useless in his life.

Yes, he'd wanted Emily to break. Finally. She was operating on autopilot, scraping by while her reserves were fast depleted. She couldn't go on like she had forever. But the alternative was seeing his beautiful Emmy completely and utterly shattered.

He wrapped the towel around her once more, tucking the ends at her small breasts. Taggert was drying off behind them, and Greer didn't spare him a glance as he herded Emily out of the bathroom toward the bedroom.

He rummaged in her still-unpacked bag, cursing when he saw that she barely had any clothing and her one pair of pajamas was dirty and wet.

Easing her to a sitting position on the bed, he tilted her chin upward. "Wait right here, sweet pea. I'll be back."

He strode into his bedroom and snagged one of his flannel shirts then returned to Emily's room where she sat on the bed, her eyes vacant and tearful. One hand was massaging her throat absently, and a grimace worked at her mouth.

She'd hurt herself. He'd never forget the sounds she made. He'd heard her all the way from the house, and the raw edge of grief mixed with her cries had sent a chill down his spine.

"Here, put this on," he urged. "I'll have Buck make you some soup. It'll feel good on your throat."

She reacted listlessly, as if it took all her strength to shrug out of the towel. He helped her into the shirt and quickly buttoned it up.

Taggert walked in and Greer looked up to see distress in his older brother's eyes. Tagg wanted to say something. Greer could see it. He was battling with himself, not knowing whether it was the time.

Greer shook his head, hoping Taggert got the message. Whatever it was could wait. Emily was at her end. There was no way she could process anything Tagg had to say anyway.

Greer tucked Emily into bed, pulling the covers up so she would be warm. She was still crying, her shoulders shaking, but no sound escaped from her lips. He leaned down to kiss her and whispered a silent prayer that she would make it out of this.

When he stood, Taggert was still standing by the door, his hand rubbing a stressed path through his hair. Greer motioned him out of the bedroom, and the two met in the hall.

"She's blaming herself," Taggert said. "Goddamn it, Greer. She lost it when I told her that if I'd never sent her away Sean would still be alive. I did this to her. She went to pieces at his grave, and she *apologized* to me. Said it was her fault, not mine."

Greer blew out a long breath. "It had to happen, Tagg. Whatever the reason for it, she couldn't keep on in denial, just existing day to day like some damn ghost. We'll figure out why she blames herself later. Right now I'm just glad she's finally letting herself cry."

"Why is it that I'm always the one to hurt her?"

The self-condemnation in Taggert's voice was strong, and as much as he didn't like the idea of his brother in pain, Greer's focus was Emily.

He put a hand on Taggert's shoulder. "Put it away, man. You're not doing yourself or her any good. She needs us both right now. I'm going to go down and get her some soup. She's cried herself hoarse."

"I'll stay with her until you get back," Taggert said as he turned back to Emily's door.

Chapter Six

Crying females had always made Taggert uncomfortable, but this wasn't a woman pouting or crying because she hadn't gotten her way. It wasn't an effort at manipulation or an upset that she'd get over in a few minutes.

He was completely and utterly baffled as to how to help her. Should he hold her? Touch her? Not touch her?

Did he tell her he loved her—had always loved her—or would that just pile more on her when she couldn't stand up under what she already bore?

He stood by her bed, running his hand through his hair for the tenth time. Christ, but there weren't rule books for these situations. What if he did or said the wrong thing?

In the end, the decision was made for him.

Emily turned her face and stared up at him, the silent trails down her cheeks ripping his heart right out of his chest.

She tried to talk, but it came out in a hoarse cough. Instead she held up her hand.

He grasped her trembling fingers and pressed a kiss to her knuckles as he slid onto the bed beside her.

With a muted, strangled sob, she turned into him, clutching him as if he were her lifeline. And maybe in a way he was.

"It's going to be all right, Emmy," he whispered against her hair. "I swear it."

She shook and fluttered against him like a wounded butterfly. He eased one arm underneath her then pulled her closer to his body as he leaned back against the pillows.

Her mouth worked against his chest, and he knew she was trying to talk again. After the horrible screams that had assaulted his ears, he couldn't imagine she had anything left.

"Shhh," he said as he rocked her back and forth. He rubbed his hand up and down her back, making little circles at her shoulder blades then pressing firmly against her spine. "Don't talk. Give your voice a rest, Songbird."

She shuddered against him and turned her wet cheek into his throat as if seeking more of him, his warmth and strength. It was all he had to offer her right now, and he couldn't deny her anything.

His mouth found her temple and he nuzzled her hair back before kissing her soft, pale skin.

"I just want you to listen to me, Emmy. I love you. I let you go once. I'm not letting you go again."

She went very still against him and slowly raised her head, her luminous blue eyes wide as she stared back at him.

"I'm not saying I have everything figured out. I think we have a lot of hard work ahead of us. But I need you to know that I'm not walking away this time."

A sound at the door turned Taggert sharply away. Guilt crept over his shoulders, and he angrily shook it off. Greer was standing there, his expression indecipherable as he held a tray with a bowl of soup and a glass of tea.

Nothing Taggert had said would surprise Greer, but Taggert still felt like he was sneaking one over. And that pissed him off.

Greer carried the tray to the bed, and Taggert touched Emily's cheek, returning her gaze to him.

"Sit up for us and eat some soup. You don't have to take it all, but it'll make your throat feel better."

She pushed against him and struggled upward. He helped her until she was sitting up in bed, then he plumped the pillows behind her back to give her support.

Greer slid onto the bed on her other side and settled the tray over her lap.

"Eat up," he said gently.

He glanced briefly over at Taggert, but Taggert didn't see any judgment or condemnation in his brother's eyes. Just concern for Emmy.

Greer reached out and caught a tendril of her hair that fell forward as she bent to blow on a spoonful of soup. He tucked it behind her ear and trailed a fingertip over her cheekbone.

She raised her head slowly to stare at him, and Taggert sucked in his breath at the multitude of emotions expressed in her gaze.

She was searching for answers that Greer hadn't supplied so far. There was fear and uncertainty cast deep in the shadows of her eyes.

Greer sighed. "Not now, Emmy. Not here. Neither one of us is up for what I have to say."

Her gaze skirted sideways to Taggert. His first instinct was to rush in, talk for Greer, state his case since he knew damn well what his brother wanted, what he felt for Emily. Anything to make her smile again or at least erase some of the pain from her eyes.

But he kept silent because he knew this was huge. This wasn't just about him and Emily. It was about him, Emily *and* Greer.

Greer just better hurry the fuck up.

The two brothers sat in silence while Emily ate her soup. When she was finished, she leaned back against the pillows with a weary sigh. The tears that had stopped briefly while she ate slipped like silver strands over the hollows of her cheeks.

The discomfort in Taggert's chest grew until it was a physical ache. He looked to Greer for help, but his brother just quietly collected the tray and headed for the door.

Anger tightened Taggert's features, and he battled the urge to go after Greer and ask him what the hell his problem was. But he didn't want to leave Emily. Or was that what Greer was trying to tell him? That they should leave Emily alone?

Jesus Christ, now he was looking to his younger brother for guidance?

He felt a million years old. Too old for Emily, too old to feel so helpless.

Fatigue whispered through his veins, mixing with sorrow. He loved Emily, had missed her, but he missed Sean too. Somehow, he'd imagined that one day Emily and Sean would come back home even though he'd resigned himself to never having Emily as anything more than a sister-in-law. As much as he wanted Emily, he'd trade a future with her to have his brother back, because then Emily would smile again.

He glanced down at Emily to see her eyelashes flutter and finally come to rest on the dark smudges beneath her eyes. She looked beautiful and delicate, so very fragile that he was afraid to touch her for fear she'd shatter.

Carefully shifting his weight so as not to disturb her, he moved further down the bed and put his arm over her waist. She responded to his touch by snuggling into him, her cheek nuzzling his chest. Her head bumped his chin as she sought to get closer, and finally she tucked herself into the curve of his body like a cat seeking warmth.

He held her like that for the longest time, listening to the soft sounds of her distress even as she slept. He caressed and held her, offering her comfort the only way he knew how. By being here.

When finally she quieted, he melted into the bed in exhaustion. He hadn't realized how tense he'd been through the entire ordeal or how tightly he was wound.

Her even breathing whispered across his chest, and he touched her cheek to find that while it was still damp, there were no new tears. Maybe she'd finally cried herself out.

He rested there for a while, enjoying the feel of her in his arms. Oh, he'd held her plenty of times over the years, but never this way. He'd never wanted her to guess the extent of his feelings, and then when she'd married Sean, he'd stopped touching her at all beyond a casual kiss on the cheek the few times they'd seen each other.

Where was Greer? It wasn't like him to bolt. He was the levelheaded one in the Donovan family. Taggert and Sean were the two short fuses, quick to blow and quick to get over it. Greer...he liked to brood. Which was probably what he was doing now.

Taggert sighed and eased away from Emily. She didn't even flinch when he got up. He tiptoed across the floor and let himself out of her bedroom to go in search of Greer.

*
**

Greer shoved his hands in his pockets and stared at his brother's grave. He hadn't been out to visit in a while. Maybe he'd been as much in denial as Emily had. Seeing her shattered and scattered to the wind brought back the grief he'd tried to bury. Now it felt like a festering wound about to open.

It had always been the four of them. Looking back, he couldn't even see when it had started to unravel. He hadn't opened his eyes to the possibility of Emily marrying, wanting a family. A career. Somehow he'd just taken for granted that she'd always be here, a part of his life, not changing.

He shook his head at his stupidity. If only he could have that day back again. If he'd only had some warning, some idea of what Emily was thinking—feeling.

After he and Taggert had sent her away... He flinched and tightened his lips in a line. *Sent away* implied some calm, civilized action. They'd rejected her, and she'd fled in tears. The next thing he knew, Sean and Emily had eloped and she'd signed a recording contract that would take her away from Montana—and him and Taggert.

Where had it all gone so terribly wrong?

"You don't come out here often."

Greer turned to see his brother standing a few feet away, his gaze resting on Sean's grave.

"How would you know?"

"Because I do come out here," Taggert said. "Usually once a day."

"This is such a mess. I don't know how to fix it. I don't know how to get beyond my own anger and grief to help Emily with hers."

"I miss him. I miss them both," Taggert said as he moved closer to Greer.

"They should have been able to feel like they could come home. We took that away from them. I thought by ignoring the issue, it would go away."

Taggert remained silent, his lips pinched.

"The four of us were family," Greer said painfully. "Sean accepted... He accepted what you and I didn't. That Emily loved us. We failed her, and now to find out she blames herself for Sean's death. It's more than I can stand, Tagg. I've got to find out why, even if it makes her face everything that hurts her the most. She can't go on like this, carrying so much guilt that she buckles under the weight. None of us can. We've got to face this...what's between us and what was. Nothing can ever be right again until Sean is laid to rest."

"I know," Taggert said quietly. He turned to look at Greer and then back again at the grave. "What do we do?"

Greer blew out his breath and tugged one of his hands free of his pocket. "I know you think I'm a cold son of a bitch."

Taggert made a sound of surprise.

"I mean with Emily. I let you comfort her. I made her some soup then split."

Taggert raised an eyebrow in acknowledgement but didn't say anything as he stared back at his brother.

"You know what I regret?" Greer looked down at one scuffed boot for a moment before he refocused on the hillside, looking beyond the neat graves to the mountains in the distance. "That day that Emily came to see us. I could tell she was upset about something. But all I wanted to do was take her in my arms, haul her up to my bedroom and make love to her. I felt like a first-class jerk. She was young. I'd sworn to never act on my feelings beyond friendship. I had this idea that I was being noble and self-sacrificing." He snorted. "What a crock of bullshit. I gave her that pompous speech about how she was mistaking friendship for something else and then I proceeded to really patronize her by saying I'd always love her but she was too mixed-up about her feelings to possibly know her mind."

He shook his head bitterly.

"Even now, all I can think of is taking her to bed and showing her just how much I love her. She's hurt, she's grieving, and I can't get close to her without wanting to make love to her. How big of a bastard does that make me?"

"Christ, if you're asking my blessing," Taggert said in disgust.

Greer clenched his fingers into fists and turned on Taggert. "Fuck you. I'm not asking you for any goddamn favors."

"Look, I'm sorry," Taggert said wearily. "This is one big goddamn mess. I don't have the answers. I never did or we wouldn't be standing here over Sean's grave arguing and feeling like the two biggest dumbasses this side of the Mississippi."

"Agreed," Greer clipped out. "Fuck me but I don't know what to do."

Taggert toed a line in the soil with the tip of his boot then kicked up a clump of the grass. "Seems to me like you ought to at least talk to Emily. Let her know your feelings and all that bullshit. Jesus, this is a hell of a conversation to be having with my younger brother. You know what I mean, though. Talk to her, for fuck's sake. We've got a second chance here. Let's not blow it."

"She loved Sean," Greer said quietly. He turned to stare at Taggert, needing his confidence. "What if what she felt for us was girlish infatuation, what we feared she felt at the time? Or what if her love died when we pushed her away? She and Sean were happy. I don't believe for a minute he was some substitute for what she couldn't have."

"She loved...loves us all," Taggert said. "It seems simple enough now, though back then it sounded so farfetched."

"Or maybe we just want to believe it now."

"Look, believe what you want to believe," Taggert said impatiently. "I'm not going to try and convince you. I get that you're worried. I get that you're having second thoughts now that she's here and we're not talking about abstracts and possibilities. But if you love her—if you want her—how the fuck can you stand by and do nothing?"

"You make it sound so simple."

"It is simple. Pull your head out of your ass, for God's sake."

Greer chuckled, suddenly feeling a little lighter. "You do have a way with words, Tagg."

"Well Christ, you're getting positively moody on me."

"Okay, okay, I get it. I'm a dumbass."

For a moment, his gaze flickered back to Sean's grave, and a spasm of pain squeezed his heart.

"I miss him, man," he said softly.

Taggert followed his gaze to the headstone, his expression sad. "I miss him too. He was too young to die."

Chapter Seven

Emily woke in darkness, her senses more alert than they'd been in a long time. For a moment she just lay there, staring up at the ceiling, tears crowding her eyes. How easily they came now when before they'd been locked behind an impenetrable barrier.

Strangely, she didn't hurt quite as much as she had. In some ways she supposed it had been, like cutting a festering sore to allow the infection to drain away. Poison. It had built in her system until she'd been staggered by her grief and pain.

She turned her head, seeking confirmation of the time, and gasped when she saw a dark outline by the window. He turned when he heard her, and it was then she saw it was Greer, pale moonlight spilling over his solemn features.

"I'm sorry I scared you," he said quietly.

She couldn't very well say he hadn't since her heart still pounded like a jackhammer.

"What are you doing here?"

She rubbed her throat when the words came out in a barely audible croak. She'd really done a number on her voice. Frank would have had a heart attack if he could hear her.

Her hand froze as she thought about Frank—and the fact she hadn't talked to him in nearly a year. She'd been too busy running.

Greer flipped the lamp on, illuminating the bed in its soft glow. He sat on the edge and turned, sliding one knee onto the mattress as he stared down at her.

She swallowed nervously and wrung her fingers until they were numb. He looked so serious. So grave. This was the first time she'd really faced him since that day four years ago when she'd blurted out her feelings. No wonder he and Taggert had reacted the way they did. It hadn't been well done of her at all. Nearly hysterical after the confrontation with her father, she'd felt as though her options had run out.

How many times had she wished she could have that day back?

Greer picked up her ravaged fingers and brought them to his lips. He kissed each one, his eyes glowing vibrantly in the light.

She watched in fascination at the tenderness he displayed, at the regard that went beyond simple affection for a girl he once knew. For a sister-in-law.

She couldn't wrap her brain around it. First Taggert with his declaration of love—had she imagined it? Was she finally losing what was left of her mind?

Why now?

The same question echoed over and over. What had changed?

"Do you want me to stay with you, Emmy?"

His warm, husky voice vibrated over her skin, leaving her awash in want. Need. So much need.

"Because if I stay, I'm going to make love to you."

She swallowed and then her lips parted in surprise. Torment blazed in his eyes. Guilt. Why guilt? Did he feel like he was betraying Sean? Should *she* feel like it was betrayal?

Closing her eyes against the sudden rush of tears, she bit her bottom lip to stem the tide of emotion that bubbled in her throat. She had no business making promises with her body that her shattered mind couldn't keep.

But oh how she longed to say yes. To give in to the craving for his touch.

"I suppose you think it makes me a bastard that you're here crying—grieving—over Sean and all I can think of is making love to you," he said harshly.

She hung her head but shook it slowly. Gathering her courage—courage she hadn't possessed since the day she'd left her father's rage to confess her feelings to the Donovan brothers—she looked back up, trying to infuse strength into her spine.

"We need to talk," she said softly. "About a lot of things. Taggert needs to be here."

"Okay," he agreed.

Was it relief she saw in his eyes? She supposed she sounded positively sane compared to the way she'd functioned for so long. She'd surprised even herself with her calm and firmness.

She glanced at the clock and saw that it was three in the morning. Had Greer been standing there at the window all night? He looked tired, but more than that, he looked older than she remembered. The kind of old you got by experience, not by true age. He looked as weary as she felt.

"I'm hungry," she announced.

He cocked one eyebrow in surprise.

She offered a tremulous smile. It was true, much to her shock. In fact, she was starving.

"Buck'll be pissed that we invaded his kitchen," he said with a grin.

"I want some peanut butter toast," she said wistfully. "And a tall glass of cold milk."

"Come on." He stood and held a hand down to her.

She let him pull her up and then noticed she was wearing just his shirt. With Buck due in the kitchen in an hour, not to mention the ranch hands that would be in for breakfast and to collect their sack lunches, she could hardly run around like this.

She extricated her fingers from Greer's hand and dug into her bag for a pair of sweatpants. As she pulled them on, Greer watched her, frowning.

"We need to take you into town so you can buy some clothes and other stuff you need."

She shrugged and nodded. Everything she had was still in the apartment. Taggert and Greer had said they'd take care of having her stuff stored, and to be honest, she had no emotional connection to it. She'd moved there with the basics, only what she could carry herself, and the rest she'd had delivered to the apartment. It could all rot for all she cared.

"We'll go after breakfast."

Again she nodded and then followed him out of the bedroom. Her step was lighter, and for once she didn't feel overwhelming fatigue at the idea of facing the day.

Greer turned on the light in the kitchen, and she went to the pantry to dig out the huge bulk-sized can of peanut butter. Snagging a loaf of bread, she retreated and set the items on the counter while she fished in the drawer for a knife and a spoon.

Greer set the sugar bowl in front of her, and she grinned her thanks.

"Want some?" she asked.

He gave her a horrified look. "I'll just eat plain butter toast."

"You don't know what you're missing."

She slathered a generous amount of peanut butter on both pieces of bread and then sprinkled several spoonfuls of sugar over the surface. Behind her, Greer turned the oven on broil, and when she was done, he opened it for her to slide the toast onto the rack.

While she watched her toast, he popped his bread into the toaster then leaned against the counter watching her.

When the peanut butter began to bubble and the sugar caramelized just slightly, she reached in with her fork and pulled the toast to the edge of the rack before sliding it onto a waiting plate.

Greer got a glass down, handed it to her and took her plate to set it down on the bar. After pouring milk, she slid onto a barstool across from where Greer stood buttering his toast.

"I never could understand how anyone could eat that," he said as he eyed her concoction.

She took a careful bite so as not to burn her lips and sighed in contentment.

"It was always Sean and mom's favorite."

She swallowed and nodded, willing the food not to get stuck in her throat.

"He made it for me," she said softly.

Greer turned his attention back to his toast and then tossed the knife into the sink.

Uncomfortable silence stretched between them. Emily ate mechanically, trying to savor the comfortable taste, but the more she chewed, the more difficulty she had forcing the gooey peanut butter down.

She chased the first piece down with half a glass of milk and shoved the saucer away, giving up on finishing. Whatever spark that had ignited her hunger was doused by the memory of Sean standing in the kitchen licking peanut butter off the knife as he made her toast.

"What are you two doing up?" Taggert asked as he ambled into the kitchen.

Her gaze tracked down his torso at the faded T-shirt and well-worn jeans that clung to his body, outlining his lean hardness. If she remembered right, he was still wearing what he had on the night before, which meant he hadn't been to bed.

A glance at his tired eyes confirmed her suspicions. He and Greer both looked tired. And worried.

"Emily was hungry," Greer said. "We came down before Buck took over and barred everyone from the premises."

Taggert grunted and took a seat next to Emily. He glanced sideways at her saucer. "You gonna eat that?"

She smiled faintly and slid the plate along with her half-full glass of milk at him. She stole a look at Greer as Taggert wolfed down the toast. There was an impatient set to his stance as if he was being held up and didn't like it.

Before, in the bedroom, when she'd looked into his eyes, she'd found the courage to speak up, to state the need for them to talk, and she'd had every intention of asking the questions that burned in her mind. But now, faced with both of them, her courage waned.

Another peek at Greer told her that he was as ill at ease as she was. The least she could do was meet this head-on and quit hiding. She'd done enough of that in the last year.

She cleared her throat, swallowing some of the soreness away, and then she massaged it with her hand, more in a gesture of nervousness than an attempt at comfort.

"We need to talk."

She glanced sideways at Taggert as she spoke so he'd know she was including him.

He set the now-empty glass down in front of him and turned those dark eyes on her. There was cautious reserve set deep in the brown pools. Almost like he was building himself up for what was coming.

Now that she had their attention she had no idea what to say. She licked her lips and opened her mouth, but nothing came out.

"I—"

The back door slammed, and she jerked around in her seat to see Buck standing there, his eyebrows up as he looked at her and then the others.

"What in Sam Hill are y'all doing up at this hour? Breakfast won't be on the table for another hour."

Taggert looked guiltily down at the empty saucer in front of him then hastily shoved it toward Greer. Emily's shoulders shook. Taggert looked like an errant child caught with his hand in the cookie jar.

"I can still eat," Taggert said.

Buck snorted. "Of course you can. You've still got one hollow leg to fill. It's a wonder your parents didn't go bankrupt trying to feed you boys."

Emily stole another peek at Greer, who looked even more annoyed. His gaze told her that the interruption was not welcome, that he was seething with impatience, that he was tired of waiting.

Buck's appearance was a welcome reprieve to her.

"You going to eat?" Buck asked her as he dug into the cabinets for the pans he needed.

She started to shake her head but stopped when she met three disapproving stares. "Uh, okay," she agreed. More wouldn't kill her, and who knew, maybe it would go down better than the toast.

Buck puttered around the kitchen, efficiently preparing a breakfast large enough to serve the half dozen hands that lived on the ranch. Emily avoided the gazes of Greer and Taggert. She needed all the courage she could muster, and she wasn't going to waste it on a few stolen glances.

The hands filed inside just as the first rays of light filtered through the kitchen window. The foreman Rand stopped at Emily's stool and smiled at her.

"It's good to see you again, Miss Emily. It's been a long time."

She smiled. Rand had always been polite, extremely courteous and shy around her.

"Hello, Rand."

"Will you be visiting long?"

She stilled, unsure of how to answer his question. Of course he'd assume she was visiting. The ranch had never actually been her home even if she'd spent most of her time here when she was younger.

"She's not leaving," Taggert said in his don't-argue-with-me voice.

It certainly seemed as if he were sending her a message rather than answering Rand's innocent question.

Rand smiled and nodded. "Welcome home, then."

"Thank you."

The hands called out their greetings, some of them echoing Rand's welcome home. There weren't any new faces. The most recent hire had been years ago when Emily was still a permanent fixture at the ranch.

Taggert and Greer were good men to work for. Their hands' longevity was a testament to that.

Taggert's words lingered in her mind. He didn't want her to go. Greer didn't want her to go. But did she have a future here? And in what capacity did they want her to stay? Greer had been blunt. He wanted her. What did she want? What did she need?

God, but she missed Sean's smile. His understanding. The way he made love to her. The way he made her feel. She tried so hard not to feel guilty. He wouldn't want her to. He'd be the last person to want her to languish over his memory. Unfortunately, knowing it and practicing it were not the same. Not when every waking moment reminded her that if she'd made different decisions so many lives wouldn't have changed.

Lost in thought, she ate quietly, not really listening to the conversation around her. One by one, the hands got up, collected their sack lunches and disappeared out the back door to go to work.

"Make me a list, Buck, and we'll pick up what you need while we're in town," Taggert said as he leaned back in his seat.

She blinked when Greer turned toward her.

"Go get dressed, Emmy," he said. "You can ride in with us and do your shopping."

Chapter Eight

When Greer had first suggested replacing her wardrobe, she hadn't considered that it would mean going into Creed's Pass. She hadn't set foot in the town since she'd fled after Sean's death.

Now she stood in front of the small all-purpose mercantile, her fists clenched at her sides as she glanced furtively down the main stretch of town.

Her gaze alighted on Tilly's motel, and she flinched, closing her eyes in pain as that night came back. Her and Sean laughing. Walking along hand in hand from the corner café after dinner, returning to their room.

They hadn't stayed at the ranch. They never did. Not since they'd married and the visits back had been so awkward. That was her fault. It was she who couldn't bear to face Taggert and Greer and pretend that nothing had ever happened.

The man had come out of nowhere, the knife glinting in the light from the streetlamps. Sean stepped in front of her to fend off the attack and took the blade to his chest.

The attacker's hand wrapped around her throat, squeezing as she screamed until he silenced her.

Alerted by her screams, several nearby people rushed into the street. Her attacker had dropped her but not the knife, and then he'd run. Never to be found. Was he still out there?

She'd dropped to Sean's inert figure, her hands pressing against the terrible wound in his chest. Blood, so much of it, spilled onto the street.

He'd known. God, he'd known. He looked up at her with such love in his eyes. Then he'd told her he loved her before taking his last breath.

Her breath released in a silent stutter, and she squeezed her eyes shut, determined not to lose her composure.

"Emmy?"

Taggert's concerned voice reached past the oppressive weight of her grief. She turned to see him standing there, his dark eyes filled with so much understanding it was nearly her undoing.

"I should have thought," he said. "We've been back into town so many times that I forgot this is your first time back."

She shook her head as if somehow she could deny the agony that stabbed as sharp and as deep as the knife that had ended Sean's life.

"I'm okay," she managed to get out. "Let's go in."

He touched her arm reassuringly, and Greer opened the door so they could walk in.

She couldn't muster much enthusiasm for clothes shopping. She chose a few pairs of jeans and simple T-shirts and browsed the two racks of dressier clothing, which were nothing more than nicer western shirts and a few denim skirts.

Wanting to be done with it, she piled the clothing over her arm and headed for the cashier. She stopped short when she saw her father standing at the register paying for his purchases.

His gaze swept over her. There was a brief flicker of recognition, but he turned away as if she were nothing more than a stranger. No acknowledgement, no greeting.

A knot formed in her throat. It shouldn't hurt. It shouldn't bother her one iota that the unfeeling bastard had snubbed her. He'd made his feelings plain a long time ago. She was dead to him. She just hadn't expected him to act as if she were nothing at all.

Why should it be easy for him? Why should he get away with acting like an ass? She'd done nothing to deserve his scorn, and she was tired of feeling guilt for perceived wrongs. There were plenty of real ones without adding the imaginary kind.

"Dad," she said evenly.

He froze, and for a moment, she thought he'd look at her again. His shoulders stiff, he collected his sack from the counter and turned away to walk toward the door.

"Nice to see you too," she called.

He didn't miss a step.

"Emmy, don't," Greer said, his voice hard. "Don't put yourself through that. He's an unforgiving bastard, and he's not worth your breath."

Her gaze followed her father until he disappeared from view. It shouldn't hurt. No. But it did. Her own family didn't accept her. Didn't want her.

Taggert stepped in front of her, blocking her view of her father's departure. He touched her cheek with gentle fingers, his eyes soft as he looked down at her.

"Don't torture yourself, sweet pea."

She nodded her agreement and turned to toss her clothing onto the counter.

"Glad you're back home, Emily," Will Ludlow said with a smile as he rang up the items.

"Thank you, Will."

At least the townspeople didn't seem to blame her for bringing violence into their small, tight-knit community. In her more paranoid musings, she'd wondered if they'd welcome her back or want her to stay away. Nothing ever happened in Creed's Pass. Until the day a crazy fan took his obsession too far.

Greer collected her bags for her, and the three of them walked outside.

"I need to drop our grocery order off and then we'll have some time to kill before it's ready. Want to go eat at the café?" Taggert asked.

Emily froze. Her fingers were icicles against her arms, and she gripped tight, trying to infuse them with warmth.

She shook her head. No, she didn't want to go back there. It was the last place she and Sean had been together.

"Can we just go?" she whispered.

"I can send one of the hands back for the supplies," Greer murmured.

Taggert put an arm around Emily's shoulders and directed her toward the truck.

She sat staring out the window on the drive home. The scenery passed in a blur, not really registering in her consciousness.

"Why does he hate me so much? He's *always* hated me."

"Forget him," Taggert growled.

She shivered as she remembered the sting of her father's belt. Never would she forget the helpless rage he invoked in her. She hated that trapped-animal feeling. He'd treated her no better than an animal to be kicked when its master was displeased.

"What are you thinking about, Emmy?" Greer asked softly from the backseat.

"His belt," she said honestly before she could think better of it.

"His *what?*" Taggert demanded.

She shook her head and turned away to look out the window once more.

Greer scooted forward, draping his arms across the backs of the two front seats. "Talk to me, Emily. What the hell did you mean?"

She closed her eyes and curled her fingers into tight fists. Maybe it was time they knew the truth. Maybe then they wouldn't think she'd recklessly run off with Sean because she was in a pique over their rejection.

"The day I came over..." She swallowed. She hadn't realized how painful it would be to revisit this part of her past. "My father had beaten me because Sean took me to talent night over at the honkeytonk. It was the night I met Frank."

"He *beat* you?" Greer asked in a horrified voice.

"What are we talking about here, Emily?" Taggert demanded.

"Please, just let me finish," she begged.

They fell silent but their faces were masks of anger, their lips drawn into tight lines.

"I just wanted to get away so I worked up the courage to tell you how I felt. I was young and stupid. I didn't really think through it all. And then when you sent me away I went home to another beating. This time he didn't just use a belt."

"Son of a bitch!" Greer spit out.

"Sean came over to see me. I didn't want him to know, but my father had gone into town and Sean came in anyway. He was so angry. I've never seen him so angry. He told me he'd never let me stay another night in that house. He wanted to take me back to the ranch so I told him what happened and that I couldn't go back there."

She closed her eyes, tears slipping silently down her cheeks as she remembered the events of that night.

"He packed me a bag and then told me he loved me, that he'd always love me and take care of me and that we were going to Vegas to get married and that I was going to call Frank and tell him I wanted to talk about my career."

She turned in her seat so she could see both Taggert and Greer and they could see her. "I didn't marry Sean to get back at you. I didn't do it to punish you, and I didn't do it in some fit of childish temper. I loved him just like I loved you. I'd always loved him. I couldn't stay there with my father anymore, and when you told me we couldn't be together there was no reason for me to stay in Creed's Pass any longer."

"Goddamn it!" Taggert exploded, his hands pounding the steering wheel. He braked hard and pulled the truck to the side of the road, and then he sat there, hands locked on the column, his jaw clenching and unclenching spasmodically.

To her shock, when he finally turned to her, tears burned bright in his eyes.

"Why didn't you tell us, Emmy? Why would you keep something like that from us? *Why?*"

"I didn't want anyone to know," she said painfully. "I didn't want *Sean* to know."

"We could have helped you. We would have taken you out of there," Greer rasped. "We would have never let you stay there if we'd known. Yes, he's an uptight asshole. Everyone knows that. We knew he made your life hell with his narrow-minded bullshit, but goddamn it, Emily, we would have never let you stay there if we knew his abuse was physical."

"He was my legal guardian," she said in a shaky voice. "What could you have done? He was my father."

"Bullshit," Taggert swore. "I would have killed the bastard for ever touching you."

"How many times?" Greer gritted out.

She didn't pretend to misunderstand the question. "Whenever I displeased him," she said dully.

Taggert turned away, his face ravaged by grief. "I'm going to kill him. So help me, I'm going to hunt him down and kill him."

Emily put her hand on his arm. "No, please, Taggert. He can't hurt me anymore. Just leave it be. I wouldn't have told you at all, but I wanted you to understand why I married Sean. I wasn't trying to punish you and Greer. I loved Sean with all my heart, and I'll never be able to forgive myself for all the sacrifices he made. I was the reason he died, Tagg. Not you."

The interior of the truck closed in on her. Hot and suffocating. She needed air. She needed to breathe. She needed to get away from the horror etched into Greer's and Taggert's faces.

Fumbling with the door, she yanked the handle and nearly fell out in her haste to get away. Ignoring Greer's shout, she stumbled into the ditch, crossed it and leaned on an old wooden post that was barely holding up the barbed wire fence.

She bent over as her stomach rolled and clenched violently. She gagged once and went to her knees, breathing heavily through her nose to control the overwhelming nausea.

Enough. It was enough. She was so tired of pain. Tired of never feeling like she was going to live again. Happiness seemed like a once-upon-a-time story that never made it to the end.

"Emmy, Emmy, please baby, don't cry."

Greer wrapped his arms around her as he knelt beside her on the hard ground.

"I just want it all to go away," she said. "I can't do this anymore, Greer. I can't."

Taggert dropped down on her other side, his hand tangling in her hair as he pulled her head to his shoulder.

"Come home with us, Emily. It'll be okay, I swear it. We'll get through this. Together. We're never leaving you."

She raised her head to look at him at the same time he lowered his lips. They met in a heated rush, and she tasted tears—his or hers?

His hands moved clumsily over her cheeks until he cupped her face. He deepened the kiss, his tongue sliding like warm velvet over hers.

It was urgent, it was calm. It was anguished and loving. Salt lingered on their lips, and she knew it was a mixture of both their tears.

"I love you," Taggert whispered in an aching voice. "I love you so damn much, Emily. I need you. Please let us take you home."

Greer's hands ran over her shoulders, and he squeezed reassuringly. Then his mouth caressed the curve of her neck as his fingers slid the strands of her hair out of his way.

She dared not breathe. She didn't dare hope. So much had been taken from her she refused to believe that what she wanted most was within her grasp. And then she remembered the price she'd had to pay to have it.

"Don't think, Emmy. Don't analyze. Let us take you home. We need to talk," Greer said quietly against her ear. He kissed her hair and stood, urging her to her feet.

Taggert rose and reached for her hand. For a moment he stood rubbing his thumb in a pattern over her knuckles. The slight calluses on his fingers rasped over her skin, and she trembled in his hold.

Her mouth quivered, and she resisted the urge to rub her hand across her swollen lips. She could still feel his mouth on hers. Tender. So much intensity just waiting to burst free.

Did she have the courage to face them again? Trust them with her heart? As she stared into Taggert's eyes, she was filled with so many conflicting emotions. Fear. Joy. Sadness. Hope. Love... So much love. It hurt every bit as much as her grief. She wanted to be able to express her love, but she was terrified, and it felt like a betrayal of Sean.

Taggert lowered his head again and touched his lips to hers in a simple, heartfelt gesture she felt to her core.

"Come home, Emmy. That's the first step."

Chapter Nine

Emily got out of the truck and hurried toward the house. Her instinct was to hide, just as she'd been hiding for the last year. The back door swung shut behind her, the sound cracking through the silent house. She hesitated for a moment, not knowing where to go, and then she headed up the stairs to her room.

She was inside, her door safely closed. She let out a long breath, one she'd held because it hurt to breathe. And then the door swung open behind her.

She whirled around to see Greer and Taggert standing there, determination and fire in their eyes.

"No more running, Emmy," Taggert said.

He crossed the distance between them, grasped her shoulders in his big hands and crushed his mouth to hers. Even as his lips devoured hers, his hands dug underneath her shirt, pulling, his movements jerky and desperate.

His palms covered her breasts, and she went still against him. The sweetest of pleasures surged through her veins. His touch. How she'd longed for his touch. It was everything comforting and beautiful. Strong. Masculine.

She leaned into him, wanting him closer, seeking his warmth. Cold. She'd been cold for so long, and now it was like walking into the sun after a long winter without any heat.

Her shirt came off and then Greer's lips pressed gently against her shoulder. She flinched in shock and turned, seeking confirmation that he was there too. She glanced between the brothers, unbelieving of their acceptance. There was no anger, no disgust.

Heat and arousal made their eyes glow. There was an almost drugged, drowsy satisfaction in their depths as if they'd waited as long as she had for the simple pleasure of their touch.

Her lips parted, and she swallowed rapidly. Then she tried again.

"Please," she whispered. "Don't do this if you'll hate me afterwards."

"Ahh Emmy," Greer said, his voice breaking. He turned her to face him, his fingers caressing the line of her jaw. "I'll never hate you."

He lowered his head and brushed his lips across hers. Just one simple gesture. Then he returned, kissing her lightly again as if judging her reaction.

When she teetered toward him, he slid his hand around her neck, cupped her nape and pulled her to him.

He kissed her like a man starving. He wasn't gentle, and yet he was. She couldn't explain it if she wanted. There was such an urgency. He devoured her lips, but there was such love and caring that tears burned her eyelids.

His tongue delved deep, licking gently over hers then going deeper, wrapping around hers, exploring every part of her mouth. She sucked air wildly through her nostrils because he stole every puff that she tried to drag past their lips.

When he finally tore himself away, he was breathing just as harshly as she was. His gaze fell to her breasts, and then she was pulled backwards into Taggert's embrace. Her back met his chest and his heat scorched her skin. His arms wrapped around her waist, and his palms skimmed up her belly to her cup her small breasts in his hands.

She swallowed nervously and chanced another look at Greer. What she saw incited a flutter deep in her belly.

He reached out and put his fingertips under her chin.

"Sweet Emmy," he murmured. "I think you know what's about to happen."

Her pulse ramped up, and she could actually feel the blood pounding at her temples and at her neck. Her breaths came out all jittery now, and she felt curiously lightheaded.

"Are you afraid?" Greer asked gently.

Taggert's fingers brushed over her nipples, coaxing them into painfully hard points. It was hard to focus when her entire world was blurred.

"No," she said hoarsely. "I'm not afraid. Never of you and Tagg."

Taggert kissed the curve of her neck as his hands covered her breasts, gently squeezing.

"Do you want us, Emmy?" Taggert whispered close to her ear. "If this isn't what you want, if you aren't ready, then tell us now. We'll back off even though it's the last thing we want."

Were they going to take her together? She'd entertained some vivid fantasies involving the Donovan brothers in the past, but she'd never been sure of them. In her dreams all three had loved her, kissed her, made sweet love to her, separately, at the same time. Now that it was a startling reality, she was a little bewildered by how fast and *normal* it all seemed.

Then she saw the same uncertainty in their eyes. The slight awkwardness. Hesitation. But so determined. Her heart softened and the ache grew stronger. This was as new to them as it was to her, but they were determined to show her their love.

She curled one arm up and over her head to wrap around Taggert's neck. Then she simply extended her other arm to Greer. He moved closer, and she pulled him to her, raising her lips to meet his again.

He kissed her back as his fingers fumbled with her pants. For several long seconds the only sounds that could be heard was the rasp of jeans, rapid breathing and the rustle of clothing.

Seeing the two of them naked was a shock. Her gaze wandered appreciatively over hard, muscled bodies. Taggert was whipcord lean with narrow hips and broad shoulders. His chest was smooth with a faint line of hair that ran down his midsection and circled his navel.

She blushed, unable to control the heat that washed up her neck when her gaze lowered to the juncture of his legs. His cock jutted upward from a dark nest of hair. Long and thick, the head stretched tight.

Greer was the shorter of the two, thicker and built stockier, if you could call his muscular build stocky. A light smattering of hair covered his chest, lending the dips and lines a more rugged appearance.

He stood, legs apart, his erection heavy and distended. He watched her as she watched him, his gaze intense.

She wanted to touch them both. She wanted to melt into their arms, feel their heat against her skin. She wanted them to never let her go again.

"Emmy."

She turned her head at Taggert's softly spoken request.

"Come here," he said as he extended his hand.

She went willingly, curling her fingers trustingly into his. As he pulled her to him, she skimmed her palm over his taut belly and up the hard wall of his chest. The roll of his muscles told her he wasn't unaffected. He trembled against her and sucked in his breath.

"Do you have any idea how long I've waited for you?" Taggert whispered as he ducked again to take her mouth.

There was more urgency this time, as if he no longer had the patience for gentle wooing. He feasted on her. There was no other word for it.

Unable to resist the temptation, she lowered her hand, reaching down to cup him intimately. He flinched and let out a moan when her fingers curled around his rigid length.

She stroked carefully, enjoying the different textures, the roughness and the softness, the plump vein on the underside and then the supple roll of his sac as she massaged.

He thrust against her hand, his body pressing against hers. And then Greer's palm stroked lazily over her behind, his finger teasing her cleft and the sensitive region just below the small of her back.

She turned, her other hand going out to cup him just as intimately as she held Taggert. It was a shock, the sensation of steel in both her hands. So much power, and yet they were as vulnerable to her as she was to them.

Each caress brought her pleasure but gave them more. She explored their lengths, marveling at their differences and similarities. She would take both of them into her body. She'd have it no other way, for they both occupied her heart, her soul. Now she needed a physical bond.

"Love me," she begged.

With a groan, Greer pulled her to face him. His hand stuttered clumsily over her face, but she didn't care. His movements were jerky, but he was so tender, so cognizant of just how big a turning point this was.

He lowered his mouth, taking her lips in the softest of kisses.

Behind her, Taggert framed her shoulders then trailed his lips up the curve of her neck, nibbling a path to her ear.

It was as if a drug invaded her blood. The dual sensations of hungry mouths feasting on her skin sent her pulse soaring. Lightheaded. She was perilously close to falling. Her legs went weak then buckled.

Two pairs of hands caught her, held her, even as Taggert's and Greer's lips never left her body. She sighed, little breathy sounds of contentment she hadn't uttered in so long.

She'd missed this. Having such an erotic connection with a man. It had been so long since desire had warmed her veins, simmered in her depths just waiting to be called to the surface.

Lonely. She'd spent the last year being so lonely she ached. It still hurt to think of all the nights she'd spent in numb silence, her only memories of Sean and his love.

Hot tears sloshed over the rims of her eyes and spilled down her cheeks. It wasn't even sadness that prompted her emotional outburst. She was quite simply overwhelmed.

"Don't cry, sweet pea."

Greer cupped her face and kissed away the damp trails. Then his mouth fused hungrily to hers again. He pressed forward and Taggert pulled her back. They bumped into the bed and went down in a tangle of arms and legs.

She came to rest on her side, Taggert melded to her back, his palm sliding sensuously over her hip, her waist and up to cup her breast. Greer leaned up on his elbow in front of her, and he stroked his hand through her hair, pulling each strand and letting it dangle from his fingers.

He lowered his hand to her belly, and she trembled as he traveled lower to the juncture of her legs. He trailed a fingertip through the short curls and hovered tantalizingly over the hood of her femininity.

Then he pressed. Just a gentle push and slid past her folds. His fingertip fluttered over her clit. Once, twice.

A low moan escaped her and she arched her pelvis forward, seeking more of his touch.

Taggert simply held her, his hands coaxing over her skin like a balm. Safe. Comforting.

She existed in a sensual haze, their heat wrapping around her like the strongest of bonds.

Taggert slid one hand over her behind and then between her legs. He lifted, inserting his knee between her thighs, opening her wider to Greer's advances.

Greer's fingers sank lower, gliding through her wetness until he circled her opening, tracing the sensitive mouth, teasing.

Taggert petted her, caressing a line from the small of her back over the plump flesh of her behind and then lower until his fingers were mere centimeters away from where Greer's delved into her wetness.

They took turns, Greer's long finger easing inward then retreating. He spread her fluids over her flesh until her clit slid easily under his touch. Then Taggert eased a finger inside, teasing and touching the walls of her pussy.

One inside, stroking, the other stroking her clit. A long burned-out fire came to life, catching the wind and spreading wildly through her veins.

Greer leaned down and tugged a nipple into his mouth, sucking gently in rhythm with his fingers. Her hair slid over her back as she arched, offering herself more fully to him.

Her dreams, her most secret fantasies had nothing on the reality of having these two men make love to her.

The rush of her impending orgasm left her breathless, that long, sharp build-up, the strain and tension and the delectable wait for the inevitable explosion. Too long her desires had lain dormant, but now they roared to life, her body awakened. Fierce need assailed her, pulling and stretching her until she cried out for mercy.

But she wanted none, and they knew it.

Her breath tore from her lips. She panted and arched her body, twisting and writhing. Taggert added another finger, plunging them into her tight passage. Greer pressed against her clit and rotated, finding just the right amount of pressure. His teeth grazed her nipple and she flew.

Her scream rippled through the room, primal and hoarse. Greer's mouth crashed down over hers, swallowing her cry of pleasure, and he continued to ravage her, taking as much as she would give.

She clung desperately to him, clutching his shoulders as she raised her mouth to meet his. Taggert's teeth sank into her shoulder, and she let out a gasp. He sucked hard, and she knew she'd have a mark. His mark.

Greer's fingers left her quivering clit, and he eased his hand over her belly, leaving a faint trail of her moisture. He cradled one breast, plumping it in his palm as his thumb brushed over the sensitive nub.

She closed her eyes and sank back against Taggert. His arms came around her, holding her steady as she sagged. Then he simply rolled her over, taking her from Greer.

Impatiently he pushed at her legs, hoisting them up, bending them at the knees then nudging higher still until she was completely open and vulnerable to him.

He rose over her, positioned himself at her opening and in one push, thrust himself to the hilt.

Her eyes flew open, her body arched and spasmed. She struggled wildly as she tried to process the overriding sensations bombarding her from every quarter. God, he was big. Thick and heavy. She was tight around him. So tight she didn't know how he'd manage to move. But move he did.

He planted a hand on either side of her head, his eyes locked with hers. Fire and determination lit their depths. Love. Passion. He had the most beautiful eyes.

Slowly he dragged himself out, until only the blunt head of his cock rested just inside her entrance.

"Please," she whispered. "Take me, Taggert. Love me. Make me yours. I've always been yours."

His jaw tightened, and he closed his eyes as if fighting for control. But she didn't want his movements to be measured. She wanted him raw and passionate. She wanted him as crazy as she was.

She reached down to touch him. Slid her finger up his length then back to where they were joined. If possible he grew even harder.

"Emmy, stop," he rasped. "God, what you do to me."

She smiled up at him. "Take me, Tagg. Don't hold back. You won't hurt me."

She accentuated her words by trailing her hand back up to cup his sac. Squeezing gently, she rolled the heavy weights in her palm.

With a tortured groan, he surged forward, ripping himself from her grasp. She pulled her hand away and reached for his arm, his shoulder, anything to steady herself with.

His sac rubbed erotically against her behind as he strained to get deeper within her. Her legs doubled back, trapped between their bodies, kept her wide open to whatever he wanted to do.

A shift on the bed had her turning her head. Greer. She'd nearly forgotten about him, but he lay there next to her, his gaze locked on her. Their eyes met and he caressed her cheek, brushing back her hair as Taggert withdrew and stroked forward again.

There was an unspoken promise in his eyes. He would have her next.

She shuddered and twisted, restless as pleasure rose again from deep inside. No longer locked behind a wall of grief and pain, she soared. She'd forgotten what it felt like to feel the wind in her face.

She reached for Greer's hand, and she gripped the back of Taggert's neck with her other hand. She rose to meet each thrust, gasping as he grasped her buttocks, lifting so he could achieve greater depth.

He was hard where she was soft, and they blended seamlessly together. Back and forth, he plunged, his body cupped protectively over hers.

"Don't stop," she urged. "Please don't stop."

"I won't baby. I won't."

Taggert leaned down, letting her legs fall to the sides. His chest lowered until her breasts were flattened against it. His tongue tangled wildly with hers.

His hips rose and fell, and she strained upward, reaching, wanting release again. It was different this time, not as lazy as before. It was sharper, faster, more impatient, and before she could open her mouth to beg—for what she wasn't even sure—the room blurred and she fell long and hard.

Taggert emitted a hoarse shout and then an agonized groan. He tightened over her, and he thrust frantically until finally he went still, his cock still wedged deep inside her.

His hips twitched spasmodically, and he collapsed onto her, his forehead resting against hers. After a long moment, his harsh breathing slowed and he gently kissed each eyelid.

"I love you," he murmured.

Her heart clenched, and she closed her eyes, absorbing the moment. His love. The sated, sluggish feeling that crawled through her veins.

She felt Greer's fingers trail over her arm in a lazy, reassuring manner, and her senses reeled at the idea that he was there, waiting.

Taggert kissed her again and then carefully rolled away. He rose from the bed and went to the bathroom, returning a moment later with a towel cupped over his groin. He carefully wiped and then gently cleaned the sticky semen from the insides of her thighs.

When he was done, he tossed the towel away and lay on her other side. She was flat on her back, her gaze too unfocused to do more than trace random patterns on the ceiling.

Greer's hand rested on her belly, rubbed gentle circles before moving to palm first one breast and then the other. Instead of rising as she expected, he simply reached for her, pulling her up and over him until she blanketed his body.

She loved the feel of him underneath her. Hard, big, so strong. His hands stroked her body until she swore she purred like a sated cat. She arched into his caresses then dropped her head to kiss him.

"So sweet," he murmured. "You taste just like I dreamed you'd taste."

She smiled and nipped at his bottom lip, sucking it between her teeth. Then she all but crawled up his body so she could position her breasts at his mouth. She wanted his lips around her nipples, wanted to feel the erotic pull of his mouth.

"Can you take me?" he asked hoarsely. "I don't want to hurt you, Emmy. If you're tired or sore I'll wait."

Ignoring his question, she shimmied back down his body until his cock nudged impatiently between her legs.

"The question is, can you take me?"

His eyes gleamed and sparked as he stared up at her. "Do you worst, love."

With a smile, she reached down and tucked his cock to her opening, rising up as she did. He was as big and hard as Taggert, but God he looked longer. She glanced nervously at him then back again.

His hand rested on her waist but he waited, not pushing.

"I won't hurt you, Emmy," he said softly. "Take as much of me or as little of me as you want. It's all up to you."

She eased down, feeling him stretch her as she lowered herself onto him. He reached to hold her, to offer support and she grasped his arms for leverage.

Her knees dug into his sides, and she closed her eyes before rising to give her better position to take all of him. The sensation of him filling her was delicious. So hard, big and thick.

Already she panted, her body coiling into a tight ball of intense sexual heat. She came down forcefully, gasping as she stretched more when he pushed deeper.

"Take it easy, baby," Greer chided as he lifted her hips to ease the burn.

"No," she whimpered. She wanted it all. All of him. All he had to give.

She released his arms and placed her palms flat on his chest, rose over him and slammed down, taking him into her body in one heated rush.

His fingers curled into her hips at the same time a breathless curse slipped past his lips.

"Ride me, Emmy. Make me yours."

Her fingers curled into the hair on his chest. She rose and fell, gripping him with her knees. She rotated, bucked and took him hard.

Her hair slid forward, a curtain over her shoulders. The strands tickled Greer's skin, and he wrapped his hands in them, gathering until his fists rested on her shoulders. Then he extricated his fingers and let them slide down her body until he cupped her breasts, rolling the sensitive peaks between his thumb and forefinger.

Her pussy fluttered and convulsed wetly around him, and unbelievably her orgasm rose when just moments before she'd been limp and sated.

"Come with me," she whispered. "When I do."

"Always. Always with you."

She closed her eyes as he raised a hand to her cheek. She nuzzled into his palm, enjoying the simple pleasure of his touch.

Fluidly she arched over him, undulating, finding a smooth rhythm that had them both straining. Their harsh breaths filled the air, and when she opened her eyes, her unfocused gaze found Taggert, still lying on the bed, his eyes glowing with lust. And love. For her. All for her.

She reached for his hand even as she gripped Greer with her other. She stared at them both with all her love for them to see. The words stuck in her throat. She was too gripped by emotion to force them past stiff lips. But she could show them.

She guided Greer's hand down to where they were joined, and he slipped a finger through her folds until he found her swollen little nub. His fingers spread the hood, baring her clit to his touch. He stroked, just light little touches but it was enough to send her right over the edge.

She jerked, gripping Taggert's fingers until they were bloodless. A low cry of desperation burst from her chest. It *hurt*. God, the tension was so great she was going to shatter.

Up and down, she slammed against his body, driving him deeper, harder.

"Emmy!" Greer cried.

His finger pressed hard against her clit, and she shattered. He arched convulsively into her, and she was too tired, too devastated to continue the ride. So he held her hips and did the work as his release flooded into her.

Long after she'd slumped forward, his hips rose, his thrusts easing in and out of her. And then he wrapped his arms around her, holding her so close she could feel the frantic beat of his heart.

He kissed her hair and then her temple. He raised his hands to pull the heavy curtain away from her face, and she lay limply over him, absorbing his strength.

"Ours now," he murmured. "Ours, Emmy."

She smiled and glanced lazily up at Taggert who lay there still watching. She raised her hand and he laced their fingers together before letting them fall to the bed beside him.

"Yours," she said simply.

Chapter Ten

Emily lay between Greer and Taggert, one arm and leg thrown over Taggert and her head resting on his shoulder. Spooned behind her, Greer rested his hand possessively on her hip and he kissed her bare shoulder.

Peace. For the first time in a year peace filled her. Sweet. Unending. So exquisite she wanted the moment to last forever.

With a wistful sigh she snuggled a little deeper into the crook of Taggert's arm.

Some of the constant ache she'd lived with ever since Sean's death dissipated as she felt the steady reassurance of Taggert's heartbeat and Greer's warm lips brushed across her skin.

And then, because she couldn't stand another moment without saying it, she whispered, "I love you."

They both went still beside her, their bodies tense. Not even the sounds of their breathing could be heard. The silence hurt her ears. It was harsh. A white void that filled her with insecurity all over again. It was too easy to go back to that awful day when her world had irrevocably been turned upside down.

"Do you mean that, Emmy?" Greer asked as he stroked the curve of her behind.

Taggert raised his head to stare into her eyes. There was such hope reflected in his gaze. And fear. She found herself staring at the same insecurity that rocketed through her chest.

"I've always loved you. That's never changed. It didn't change when I married Sean. I loved him. I loved you. I'll always love all of you."

Greer put his lips to her shoulder again and left them there. She felt the slight tremble as if he were trying valiantly to come up with just the right words.

Taggert shifted and came up on one elbow. He touched her cheek, his finger tracing the line of her jaw and then lightly feathering across her lips.

"I love you too, Songbird. I think I've always loved you."

Her heart swelled, and she swallowed to alleviate the discomfort. An ache bloomed but a different kind of ache. Not the sharp, incessant pain of grief and longing. This was overwhelming. Hope budding and unfurling like a flower seeking the sun.

"I love you," Greer whispered against her skin. "I'm so sorry I hurt you."

She closed her eyes against the sting of tears. It wasn't fair. How could she hope to have it all when she didn't have Sean?

"Emmy, look at me."

Taggert's command, tender and coaxing, penetrated the fog swirling in her mind. She forced her gaze to his, her lips trembling even as he continued to stroke his thumb over her mouth.

"Tell me why you blame yourself for what happened."

Her pulse jumped and stuttered. She tried to shrink away, but she was caught between the two men. There was nowhere to run.

"Sean gave up so much for me. For my dream. He loved me. Protected me. He died protecting me."

Greer kissed her nape, and his fingers curled over her shoulder in a gesture of comfort.

"He grabbed my throat—the attacker—he was so angry. He kept saying I'd ruined everything. He was..." She could feel his hand tightening around her neck. Feel the pressure as he squeezed. Remember the absolute knowledge that she was going to die. "He had to be some obsessed fan or someone like my father who felt my career was an abomination," she finished in a barely audible voice. "My singing, my *gift*, killed Sean. I should have been happy to have just been with him and away from my father. We could have had a wonderful life, but I was so determined to prove my father wrong. My anger and my resentment killed the man I loved more than anything."

Taggert sucked in a stuttering breath. His hand fell away from her face for a moment, and she refused to look up at him. She didn't want to see judgment in his eyes.

"Is that why you won't sing?" Greer asked.

Her hand flew to her neck. Her pulse jumped crazily against her fingertips.

"I can't," she said honestly.

"You will, Songbird," Taggert said. "Right now you're afraid, but when you feel safe again, you'll sing."

She shook her head, but he leaned down and kissed her, refuting her denial.

"It's not your fault," Greer said as Taggert pulled away. "You can't second-guess your entire life. Sean was proud of you. He loved you. He wouldn't have had it any other way. You know that, Emmy. If you look past your hurt and grief, you'd admit to yourself that he'd have no regrets."

"No, he wouldn't," she said quietly. "But I do."

"So do I," Taggert said. "But I can't torture myself forever over them. All I can do is try to make things right. With you. I want the chance, Emmy."

She lay back, staring at the ceiling as she listened to Taggert's and Greer's rough breathing beside her.

"Are you sure?" she asked even as her chest swelled with hope. "Is this something you both want or is this a sympathy move for your dead brother's wife?"

"That's a shitty thing to say," Greer said in a low voice.

She pushed herself up, crawled to the end of the bed and turned so she could see them both.

"I'm not trying to be shitty. I have a right to ask these questions. Have you and Taggert even considered what kind of life we'll have? God knows I didn't give it any thought before I came barging in here four years ago throwing my feelings around."

She hated the hint of vulnerability that shadowed her voice. Hated even more that her hands shook.

Greer elbowed up and shifted his body so he was closer. The muscles in his shoulders rippled as he reached for her. She put her hands out to ward him off, but he caught her fingers and threaded them through his.

"What we've considered is that we'll have a life with you. That's all we care about. Will it be easy? Hell, I don't know. I've never even tried to wrap my brain around a situation like this. Did I accept it overnight? No. I wish I had. Then maybe you and Sean would be here. It took me a long damn time, but I know what I want, Emmy. I want you."

"Oh Greer," she whispered. "Don't blame yourself. What I wanted—what I suggested was so out of bounds. You can't blame yourself for thinking I was crazy."

"I'll make you a deal." Taggert's eyes glittered with grim determination. "You don't blame yourself and we won't blame ourselves."

"The point is, we can play the blame game for eternity," Greer said. "But it won't change a damn thing. Sean's gone. We can't bring him back no matter how much we want to."

Pain slashed through her chest, and tears clouded her vision. He didn't say it to be hurtful, but the resignation in his voice got to her in a way nothing else had. Sean was gone. He wasn't coming back. Ever.

She rolled away, unable to face either of them. She clutched her arms and bowed her head, willing herself not to break again. There was nothing left. She didn't have the strength for another emotional outburst.

Strong arms surrounded her, holding her, offering her love and support.

"Emmy."

Said so tenderly her heart clenched, her name slid over her ears and straight into her soul. She turned her face up to see Greer looking at her with the pain of so many memories burning in his eyes.

"We loved him too. We miss him. But he's not coming back. You're alive. You have to live. You can't go on like you have. Taggert and I love you. We want you to stay with us. We know it won't be easy. We don't even know what to expect. It's new to us and we'll have to work at it. Together. Give us the chance we didn't give you four years ago. Let us love you."

She raised haunted eyes and looked straight through Greer's soul. He felt her pain. It was a tangible, terrible thing. Her grief spilled over into the room. Her guilt. If only he could take it away. He couldn't. But he could love her. He could cherish her. Offer her all the things he should have given her four years ago.

He glanced over at Taggert and saw the same grim resolve reflected on his face. Emily was theirs. They might not have always acknowledged it, but it didn't change the utter truth. She belonged to them. She'd always belonged to them.

She sagged against Taggert in a gesture of surrender. Fatigue hollowed her eyes. Making love to her when she was so fragile had probably been a bastard thing to do but he—they— had been unable to resist any longer. They'd waited a damn long time. They weren't waiting anymore.

Taggert pressed a tender kiss to the top of her head and snagged his fingers in her long hair.

"Lie back down, Emmy. Rest. I'll be here. Sleep and we'll face tomorrow together."

She closed her eyes and then allowed Taggert to ease her down on the mattress. She crawled onto the pillows and curled into a tight ball. She fell asleep before either man could recline beside her. Instead they sat toward the end of the bed watching the soft rise and fall of her chest.

Greer drew in a deep breath and avoided Taggert's thoughtful stare. Hell, he was sitting on a bed in his underwear with his brother after they'd made love to the same woman. It didn't get any weirder than that.

He slid off the bed and stood abruptly, his back to both Taggert and Emily.

"She's right you know," Taggert said in a low voice. "Have we really considered the life we'll have? We've talked some but mainly we've avoided the issue, believing it'll all work out. But will it?"

Greer cursed under his breath. He didn't appreciate Tagg's cold logic. Not now. He didn't want reality. Didn't want to face any harsh truths. What he wanted was to keep Emily safe from the world. From her bastard father and the prying eyes of others. But that wasn't possible. They lived on a ranch where a number of other hands lived as well. How would they look at Emily knowing he and Taggert both shared her bed and her love? Would they think she was some easy lay, there for any man's taking? He'd kill any son of a bitch who ever acted on that impulse.

"We can only control the way we deal with things. We can't make others accept it. We can't keep them from speculating. Any life we have with Emily will be open to the public if she goes back to singing, and if I have my way, she will sing again. She stands to lose more and be hurt more by her relationship with us. If she can deal with it, then I sure as hell can take whatever heat we get."

Taggert nodded, some of the tension easing from his brow. "You're right. If Emily is willing to put so much on the line to be with us, then I can man up and do the same. I just don't like the idea of her being hurt. She's been hurt enough."

"Her father could be a problem."

Hatred for Cecil Patterson left an acid taste in Greer's mouth. The idea that he'd beaten Emily filled him with such rage that it was all he could do not to go give the old man a taste of his own medicine.

"He won't say anything," Taggert said. "He'll pretend Emily doesn't exist, but he won't shoot off his mouth because it will hurt his standing in the community, or so he thinks."

"The people of Creed's Pass have been good to Emily. They've always been proud of her fame. I'd like to think they won't turn their backs on her because of us."

Taggert's expression turned thoughtful. "No reason to flaunt our relationship in front of them. Word will get round quick enough, but that doesn't mean we need to give them any more to gossip about."

"I agree. I wouldn't be comfortable making a spectacle of our relationship anyway."

Emily stirred and turned over, curling once again into a small ball. Taggert smiled, a soft gesture that told Greer how much his older brother felt for her. Taggert reclined on the bed and pulled her against him. Greer suddenly felt like a voyeur, an intruder in something intimate.

He turned toward the door. He needed a cigarette in the worst way. "Think I'll head down. I won't be able to go to sleep anyway. See you at breakfast."

Chapter Eleven

Arousal stirred deep within her and fluttered outward in exquisite waves. Emily opened her eyes just as Taggert moved over her, parted her thighs and settled his heavy erection at her entrance.

He lowered his head and captured her lips in a more demanding, less gentle measure than before. She responded eagerly to his possession. This is what she waited for. For him to take her. She wouldn't break no matter how delicate she may appear. She needed this more than she needed her next breath.

"We didn't use protection, Emmy," he murmured over her lips. "Neither of us did. I don't have it now. I need to know how you feel about that. About having our babies. We should have asked, should have protected you better. You're fragile right now. I need to know if it's too soon. You could be pregnant already."

She smiled up at him and wrapped her arms around her neck to pull his mouth down to hers again.

"I want a normal life," she admitted. "I want all the things I wanted with Sean. I want a family. Children. I want you and Greer and this ranch. I don't ever want to leave. Make love to me, Tagg. Give me your child."

He groaned low in his throat, a tortured sound that told her of his fight to maintain control.

"I love you," she whispered. "Love me too."

"Aww Emmy, I love you more than anything."

He reached down and gently touched her clitoris. He traced the line of the hood that protected the sensitive bundle of nerves, and then he reached lower, testing her readiness with one fingertip.

With a sigh of pleasure, she arched into him, bumping into the head of his cock. He stiffened and then thrust forward, easing into her wetness.

Inch by inch he sank deeper until his body met hers. She cradled him, holding him as tightly as he held her. There was such a sense of rightness, of homecoming. It was impossible for her to tell him just how much she'd missed him, how she'd dreamed of a moment just like this. But she could show him. She could love him back with every part of her self.

She kissed his jaw and then his neck. She tasted him, running her tongue from the curve of his shoulder up to the spot right behind his ear. He shuddered against her and moaned, but he moved closer, seeking more of her mouth.

The muscles in his back rippled and bulged under her fingers, and she lovingly traced the lines, enjoying his strength. Hers. He was hers in a way she'd never dreamed of him being.

Back and forth, his body rose and fell, and she held him to her by wrapping her legs around his hips. In this moment there was no pain, no sorrow. She was free from the relentless ache of the past year.

Hope. She had a future. Here in Taggert's arms. He and Greer would protect her and love her. She'd give them her love, children. They'd be a family just as she'd always wanted.

Oh Sean.

Sweet, sweet Emmy.

She could hear his voice as if he whispered directly in her ear. She could see him smiling tenderly down at her.

Be happy, my love. Be happy.

Tears leaked from her eyes, and she buried her face in Taggert's neck even as she shook with the sweetest of orgasms. It was mind-blowing, an explosion to rival a volcano. It was heartrendingly beautiful. It was what she needed.

They love you too. Just as I do.

"I know," she whispered.

"What do you know?" Taggert asked as he kissed away the tears.

"That you love me."

"Do you really?"

She smiled and reached up to stroke his face. "Yeah. I do."

He kissed her fingers and rubbed his face back into her palm.

"This time it's forever, Songbird. We won't let you go again."

She swallowed and sucked in a deep breath. It was hard to breathe when her chest was about to cave in.

"No, you won't let me go," she said with conviction.

She could see the resolve in his eyes, and in this moment she believed with all her heart that he meant every word of his declaration.

In the early hours of the morning, Emily stepped out the back door and wrapped the light shawl around her shoulders. She'd left Taggert sleeping, and she hadn't seen Greer on her way down. Buck was due in the kitchen any moment, and she didn't want to get stuck for breakfast.

There was something she needed to do.

With every step closer she got to the small graveyard, her heart grew a little heavier. The eastern sky had lightened just enough that pale lavender coated the headstones and outlined the large oak tree. The branches hovered protectively over generations past and those whose present had ended all too soon.

She stared at Sean's grave and then slowly knelt on the cold ground in front of the granite stone that marked his birth and death.

With trembling fingers she traced his name.

"I'm home, you know," she said conversationally.

It sounded quite absurd, but it felt good to talk to Sean again, and she knew he could hear her. Knew he was with her. She could feel the warmth of his arms around her.

"Taggert and Greer came for me, but then you probably knew they'd eventually drag me back to the MPR. You'd approve, no doubt. They share your stubbornness, or maybe you share theirs."

She stared at the stone and paused, content to listen to the early morning sounds of the world around her awakening. She could almost hear the gentle strains of his guitar as the strings came alive at his fingertips.

"They say they love me," she said softly. "Only you'd know how much that means to me and how it scares me to death. You know how much I love them. Like I loved you. I always hated you knowing it because I felt like it wasn't fair. But you always understood. God, I loved you for that. Never with anyone else was I able to completely be myself. You loved and accepted me. Every part, good and bad. I'll never have another friend or lover like you, Sean. I hope you know that. I'll never forget you, and I'll never stop loving you. But I want you to know that I'm going to start living again. I want the babies that you and I planned. I want a family and I want to be home again. I'm just so sorry I kept you from your home and family for so long."

She leaned forward and kissed the cool marble and closed her eyes. It all felt so final, and she knew for the first time, she was letting go. Acknowledging that Sean was gone. It hurt. God, it hurt. He was gone and she'd never see him again. How was she ever supposed to get over that kind of pain?

Again she felt his gentle warmth surround her. Love, so much love, and she smiled through her tears.

"Still kicking my ass, huh."

Sing for me, Emmy. One more time. Just for me.

She felt the whisper in her mind, and for the first time didn't feel the paralyzing fear that accompanied the thought of singing.

The lyrics to *Montana Memories* danced on her tongue, and her throat quivered in anticipation.

And then she opened her mouth and the melody spilled out into the early morning air. Pure and beautiful. Haunting. It carried on the breeze and straight to heaven.

For you, Sean.

She closed her eyes and sang from the depths of her heart. She poured every ounce of her love into the words. She remembered the first time she'd ever met the Donovan brothers. All the times Sean had picked her up when she fell, tended her scrapes, rebraided her hair so her father wouldn't scold her. The times he took her swimming. The night he came for her and took her away from her father. The night they got married, just two scared kids determined to forge their own path in life.

She felt a warm touch on her cheek, but when she opened her eyes, all she could see were the sun's rays as they shone through the branches of the oak tree.

And then a great weight lifted. She felt freer than she'd felt in so long. The sun's rays warmed her but hope burned hotter. Sean would always be a part of her life. A treasured memory. She'd love him always. But now she had something else to live for. Herself. Taggert and Greer. Her future.

It was always there, Emmy. You just had to reach out and take it.

Sean's chiding voice made her smile. Oh yes, it was just like him to scold her.

She ran down the hill toward the ranch, her hair flying in the breeze. She laughed and God, it felt so good to be happy again.

Greer met her at the back gate, a scowl on his face as he waited.

"Where the hell have you been, Emmy? No one saw you leave. You could say something, damn it."

She launched herself at him, laughing like an idiot. He was forced to catch her, and she wrapped herself around him, peppering his face with kisses.

He staggered back under the impact, but caught himself and stood steady.

"What the hell's got into you?"

She grinned and kissed him again. "Take me to bed. I'll show you precisely what's got into me."

His grip tightened on her ass, and she felt the current race through his body.

"Hell, Emmy, sun's up. Work to be done. Buck has breakfast on the table."

"You could play hooky," she said innocently. "I'd make it worth your while. Or you could just take me behind the barn. Or better yet *in* the barn. I always wanted to make out in the hayloft."

"The hell I will," he muttered.

He swung around, arms tight around her and strode back toward the house. The hands hadn't made their appearance yet, and he simply strode past Taggert, bypassed the kitchen and headed up the stairs.

She almost giggled but thought better of goading him.

He shoved his bedroom door open, walked forward and dumped her on the bed then returned to kick the door shut. He took his hat off, then reached for the buttons on his shirt. She watched in fascination as he methodically removed every stitch of his clothing.

When he was naked, he advanced on the bed, his cock jutting upward, stiff and painfully erect. She licked her lips, and he stopped with an inarticulate groan.

"Goddamn, Emmy," he muttered. "You're killing me, you know that?"

She gave him an innocent look and then crawled forward to meet him as he got to the edge. She cupped his balls, fondling and rolling the supple flesh in her palm. Then she guided him to her mouth, sucking him inward.

His hands tangled in her hair, and his breath escaped in a hiss.

"Jesus that feels good."

She smiled and took him deeper, enjoying his taste and the sensation of so much hardness on her tongue. Steel encased in softness. The contrast fascinated her.

She grasped the base of his penis and rolled the foreskin up and down in unison with the movements of her mouth. His fingers dug into her scalp and then gentled, and he stroked through her hair, murmuring his love and approval as she coaxed him close to release.

One drop slipped onto her tongue, and she increased her pace, but he cupped her chin and eased away. She looked up to see the strain on his face. He was so close. Why had he pulled away?

"Strip," he gritted out.

Her eyes widened at the guttural command but she hastily complied, pulling at her clothes and shimmying out of her pants. In seconds she was naked.

He grasped her shoulders and fell forward, pushing her to the bed as his weight pressed down on her.

"You make me crazy," he rasped. "Do you have any idea how much I want you? How long I've wanted you? I can't go slow, Emmy. Tell me you want me too. I can't hold back."

She opened herself to him, wrapping her legs around him.

"I want you, Greer. Please, make love to me. I love you."

"You have no idea what a miracle you are to me," he said as he positioned himself. "I don't deserve a second chance, but God, I want one. I need one."

She touched his lips, pressed one finger over them to silence him. Then she lifted her hips, taking him inside her. He lowered one hand to cup her buttocks and held her in place as he thrust.

It wasn't smooth or even practiced, and that was what she loved most about his lovemaking. There was an urgency to his actions that made him almost clumsy. His hands shook on her skin, and his thrusts alternated between smooth and slow and quick and rough.

Their mouths met, tongues tangled, hot, breathless. His lips left hers and traced a frantic line over her jaw and down her neck.

"My Emmy," he breathed just as his teeth sank into the curve of her shoulder. "Say it again. Tell me you love me."

She smiled. "I love you, Greer. Always."

"Never leave again."

She stroked his back and closed her eyes as her orgasm built. "No. Never."

He lowered himself, covering her body with his. Only his hips moved as he arched over her, rising and falling as he dove deeper into her body.

The friction was nearly unbearable. Hot. Electric. Wave upon wave of pleasure flowed through her body, fanning out in a hundred different directions.

Sweet, like a song, hovering and balancing with just enough volume and then rising.

"Greer!"

Her cry was ripped from her lips, and she clutched at his shoulders, her fingers digging into his skin.

"My love," he murmured.

She tensed, her muscles squeezing, her groin clenched, and she tightened around him like a vise. He thrust hard and fast, his hips slapping against hers.

She couldn't stand it. Not anymore. With a harsh cry, she wrapped herself so tightly around him that she couldn't breathe, and then she flew.

Greer's breath blew warm over her ear, the sound ragged. His cry mingled with hers as they fell over together.

Floating. Spiraling gently downward. She was surrounded by warmth and softness.

He pulsed deep within her and he remained still, keeping them locked together.

Home. Such a beautiful word. One that brought such comfort. She was finally home. With those who loved her.

Chapter Twelve

"Emmy, honey, can you come downstairs?" Greer asked outside her door.

Emily put her brush down, tucked her hair behind her ear and stepped out of the bathroom to see Greer standing there with his hands tucked into his pockets.

He looked uneasy, almost nervous, and that worried her.

"Greer?"

He relaxed and reached to take her hand. "Nothing to worry about. Promise. There's someone here to see you."

She cocked her head to the side, apprehension tracing a chilly path up her spine.

"Who?"

He grimaced and then said, "Frank."

Her eyes widened, and she took a step back.

Greer stepped forward again and tentatively put his hand on her shoulder.

"Are you angry?"

She shook her head but wasn't sure whether she was or wasn't. No, she wasn't angry. She was afraid, and *that* made her angry.

"No. I'd like to see him," she murmured. "I should have stayed in contact with him."

Greer's expression softened. "He's been worried about you, sweet pea. He just wants to make sure you're okay. Talk to you. There's no pressure, I promise."

He extended his hand, and she took a deep breath before sliding her palm over his. He squeezed reassuringly and tugged her toward the door.

Taggert was in the living room with Frank when she and Greer entered. Taggert immediately rose, his gaze searching her features for—what, fear? Worry? She was such a coward. But with his and Greer's strength and support, she could face anything.

"Emily, my dear," Frank said as he walked to where she stood trembling beside Greer.

He waited a moment as if to gauge her reaction, and then he enfolded her into his embrace.

"You've had me worried sick," he said gruffly.

She sighed, rested her head on his shoulder a moment and then pulled away.

"I know. I'm sorry, Frank. I should have called. I just couldn't... I just couldn't deal."

"And now?" He peered at her over his glasses, his stare probing. "How are you now?"

"Better," she said quietly.

He smiled. "That's great. You and I have a lot to talk about, Emily Donovan."

"Frank," Taggert growled. "You promised."

Frank raised an eyebrow as he turned in Taggert's direction. "I promised I wouldn't badger her. I just want to talk. No harm in that."

"I won't sing," she said flatly. "I haven't sung in a year. I'm not sure I could even if I wanted to."

The memory of the haunting melody she'd sung from her heart at Sean's grave shifted painfully through her. That was private. For Sean. She wouldn't do it in public again.

Frank's expression softened. "Come out on the porch and talk to me, Emily? I can't stay long. My return flight is in a few hours. I have to be back in Nashville."

She nodded reluctantly. She owed him this much. It was too bad he'd come all this way for nothing, but it finally solved the issue of her facing him again. Better to have it over with so she could dispense with the demise of her career.

***

Taggert stepped onto the porch as Emily stood watching Frank tear down the long dirt driveway toward the main gate.

"Everything okay?" he asked.

She turned, and he could see the haunted grief in her eyes again. Eyes that for the space of one night had been clear and beautiful. He sighed. He and Greer had a long road to travel with Emily.

Her long blond hair lifted in the back, carried on the light breeze blowing over the porch. It was like liquid sunshine. He'd always loved her hair. In the past it had always been indicative of her carefree personality. When she smiled, she glowed, the silvery strands adding to her warmth. It served as a reminder of all he and Greer wanted to get back. But could they ever truly go back?

"Yes," she said simply. "He won't return."

Taggert held out his arms, and she went willingly, burying her face against his chest.

"I don't mind if you never want to sing to crowds again. Or go into the recording studio. But baby, you love to sing. It's part of who you are."

She stiffened and curled her fists, gathering his shirt tight in her grip.

"It's part of who I *was*," she said dully.

He brushed a kiss across the top of her head, wishing he knew what to say, what he could do to make it all better. It wasn't that he had to hear her sing again, though he wanted it more than anything. Singing was just Emily. It had always been Emily. There was never a time she wasn't humming a tune, plucking her old guitar or scribbling lyrics down on every scrap of paper she could find.

It hurt her not to sing. He knew it as much as he knew anything else. She'd never fully heal until she could put what happened to Sean behind her and embrace her gift again. Even if it was just for her and she never made a public appearance again.

His fist curled in frustration. He wanted nothing more than to make the bastard who'd done this to his family pay. Bleed. The irony was that he was out there. Free. While Taggert's family suffered.

"Come inside. It's time to eat, and you know Buck gets cranky when we keep him waiting."

She glanced up, her lips twisting into a rueful smile. "Not going to lecture me on getting on with my life and not letting that bastard win?"

"Is that what Frank told you?"

"Yeah." She sighed. "He's right. I know he's right, but it doesn't change anything, Tagg. Do you understand that?"

The pleading in her voice tore at his heart.

He tugged her into his arms and rested his chin on top of her head. For a long moment he just stood there, staring out over his land. His and Greer's land. Sean's land.

"I understand, Emmy, I do," he finally said. "I know this can't be rushed. It's hard for me. I'm a guy. Guys want to fix things. I can't fix this, and it's killing me."

He felt her smile against his chest.

"Don't give up on me?"

He pulled away and nudged her chin up with his knuckle. "Never, baby. Do you get that? Greer and I aren't going anywhere, and neither are you."

Her eyes were wide and luminous, shining with a silken veil of tears. But her smile lit up his entire heart.

"I love you, Tagg. Do you have any idea how good it feels to be able to tell you that and for you to accept it?"

His throat swelled, threatening to shut down his ability to speak. He wasn't sure what the hell he'd say to that anyway.

He kissed her instead. Clumsy. Desperate. Needy. He was all those things when it came to her. How was he ever supposed to pull it together when she shattered him with a simple word?

He held her close so that their breaths stuttered erratically over each other's lips. His fingers trembled as he stroked her cheek, the tips tangling with the single strand of hair that refused to stay behind her ear.

"Let's go eat," he said, his voice cracking.

She smiled, kissed him again as if she knew just how hard it was for him to process the barrage of emotions, and then she pulled away, taking his hand as they entered the house.

"Everything all right?" Greer asked when they walked into the kitchen.

Taggert eyed his brother and gave him a short nod.

"What did Frank have to say?"

Emily shrugged. "You know what he wanted."

"Did he come out and ask you to come back?"

Greer's voice was mild, but Taggert detected a hint of...what, insecurity? Worry? He cocked an eyebrow in his brother's direction, but Greer ignored him as he continued to stare intently at Emily.

Emily's shoulders sagged. "No, but he didn't have to. I knew what he wanted. He lectured me about hiding away from my destiny and then he pulled out the Sean card."

Taggert tuned in. "Sean card? What the hell is that?"

"Yeah, the Sean-wouldn't-want-you-to-live-this-way speech."

"He's right about that," Greer said quietly. "The question is how long are you going to ignore what's so clear to the rest of us?"

She shook her head and threw a bewildered look at Taggert as if expecting help from his quarter. Hell, Greer was dead-on, but she'd already been hit over the head during Frank's visit. There was no reason to rehash it all.

"What do you want from me?" she asked helplessly.

Greer crossed the room, cupped her cheek and stared down at her with a fierceness that even had Taggert taking a mental step back.

"I want you to live, Emmy. I want you to be with me. Sean is gone. Do you understand that? He's not coming back, and he'd be the last person to want you to keep grieving for him."

Emily flinched as though Greer had struck her. Raw pain and rage flared in her eyes, and she wrenched away from his grasp.

"I get it, Greer. Believe me I do. I was there remember? I watched him die. I had his blood all over me. I'm not likely to forget that he's gone. I don't ever need you to remind me of that."

She was furious. Her entire body trembled. Her hands shook, and she curled her fingers, raising her fists in what looked like a fighting stance.

And then just as quickly she folded inward. Her face crumpled and her knees buckled. She slid bonelessly to the floor, her sobs searing over Taggert's shocked senses.

Taggert dropped to his knees beside her, but Greer was already there, folding his arms around her huddled body.

"Shhh, sweet pea. It's okay. It's going to be okay. I swear."

Emily raised her tear-streaked face to stare up at Greer. "I know he's gone, Greer. I sang for him today. Only for him, though. I didn't know it would feel so good."

Taggert closed his eyes and cursed the timing of Frank's visit. Maybe she'd come around on her own, but she was raw and hurting, and then Frank had arrived determined to make her *see the light.*

Greer rocked her in his arms, holding her tight as he moved back and forth. "He loved your singing, Emmy. He was so proud of you. You were the reason he learned to play the guitar. It was his way of sharing your gift with you. Don't take that away from him. Don't take it away from us."

"It killed him," she whispered.

"No, baby. No."

No longer able to keep silent or remain back, Taggert pressed forward, putting his hand on her shoulder. Her eyes, deeply wounded, sought him out, looking, asking.

"Emmy, you can't think that. Your attacker was a sick bastard. Do you understand that? It wasn't you. It was him."

She looked away, and Taggert blew out his breath in frustration. Then she looked back, a pleading expression in her beautiful eyes.

"I know that. I do, Tagg. But every time I close my eyes I see him, I hear his voice, and I know that if I'd never sung Sean would still be alive, and that's hard for me to come to terms with even if it's stupid, and I know it's not logical but guilt isn't logical. God I wish it was. I wish I could just turn it off. I felt

Sean today. I felt him, and I knew he wanted me to sing, and so I did. I even thought I could go on, but then Frank came, and all I could feel was that panic inside and the knowledge that I couldn't take a chance on losing one of you just because I want something so inconsequential as to sing again. Isn't that insane?"

The speech came out all run together and ended in a laugh that verged on hysteria.

"Emmy. Songbird. Our Songbird."

The words spilled past stiff lips and cracked with emotion. Taggert swallowed and stroked her hair, hoping he could come up with the right thing to say.

"It doesn't have to be now. It doesn't have to be tomorrow. But one day, baby. One day you'll feel safe. You'll sing. And we'll be here to help you fly."

Chapter Thirteen

Supper was quiet, and Emily could feel the stares of Greer and Taggert. A heavy sigh escaped her before she could call it back.

She'd honestly thought she was through with the emotional breakdowns. Her visit to Sean's grave had been freeing. And then Frank's visit had brought old fears back.

"Emmy, what are you thinking?"

She glanced up to see Taggert studying her intently.

"I'm okay. Promise. I'm sorry for freaking out on you. Again. It seems it's all I can do lately."

"Cut yourself some slack," Greer said in a gruff voice. "You've been through a lot."

She pushed her food around the plate, grateful that Taggert had dismissed Buck and the hands to eat in the bunkhouse. The last thing she felt like doing was pretending her world wasn't crumbling around her.

Be a little more dramatic, why don't you?

She made a sound of disgust.

"My world is not ending," she muttered.

Taggert's lip lifted in a half smile. "I should hope not. Greer and I aren't that bad."

She laughed, relief soaring through her chest. It was so easy to love him. The idea that she could finally be open with that love floored her.

Slowly she lowered her fork, her pulse speeding up as the two brothers watched her.

"Take me upstairs," she said huskily. "Please. I need you. Love me."

Taggert picked up her hand and brought it to his lips. "I do love you."

Greer shoved his plate aside and rose abruptly. When he reached for her, his hands shook. She took his hand and brought it to her mouth just as Taggert had done to her.

The work-roughened fingers brushed across her skin, and she closed her eyes, imagining them on her body, caressing her, touching her intimately.

"Take us upstairs, Emmy. Show us what you need."

Need? She needed them. Their love. She needed them to hold her and stand between her and the nightmares.

Taking both their hands, she twined her fingers with theirs and tugged them toward the stairs.

She was nervous. Her food churned in her stomach. Maybe she'd never really quite get over the idea that Taggert and Greer were here with her. Loving her.

They followed her into the bedroom, and they stood waiting as she slowly turned around to face them. Her heart fluttered wildly, and she swallowed as she curled and uncurled her fingers at her sides. Then she squared her shoulders and took that step.

In her wildest fantasies, she'd done this a million times, but the reality threatened to steal her breath away. Her hands shook and her fingers were clumsy as she worked at the buttons on Greer's shirt. She worked down, her gaze never leaving his face, watching as his eyes flared and simmered like coals.

When she reached his belt, she left the shirt and yanked at the buckle. In a few seconds she had his fly open and she pulled impatiently at his shirt until it was free of his jeans.

Drawn to the bare expanse of skin, she placed her palms on his tight belly and let them glide upward to his chest and then to his shoulders. Inhaling, she pressed her lips to the hollow of his chest, closing her eyes as his scent filled her.

He didn't touch her or make the effort to undress her as she did him. He seemed content to let her lead and for him to follow. Part of her wanted to tear off his and Taggert's clothing and indulge in hot, passionate lovemaking, ending it almost before it began. She was eager to feel their hands and mouths on her body. But the other part of her wanted to savor the sweet, slow symphony, to indulge in hours and hours of exploring their bodies while they pleasured her.

She wanted it hard and fast. She wanted it hot and edgy. She wanted it long and slow. Sensual and loving. Her mind blazed with the possibilities.

"Do you want help, Emmy?"

Greer's huskily voiced question brushed over her ears and elicited a trail of goose bumps down her back. She'd been standing here, her mouth against his skin, unmoving while she imagined the many ways she wanted to be made love to. Her lips curved into a rueful smile, and she shook her head. She wasn't a complete coward.

Stepping away, she slid her hand down his belly, into the springy hair at his groin until her fingers circled his length. He flinched and rocked back on his heels when she went lower to cup his balls.

"Take your pants off," she murmured, suddenly eager to see him.

His thumbs hitched into the waistband of his jeans, and he yanked. The denim gathered around his feet, leaving him deliciously exposed. Not waiting for her dictate, he shrugged out of his shirt, allowing it to fall behind him.

Her gaze was riveted to his lean hips and to the dark hair at his groin. His erection jutted outward, an invitation. She dropped to her knees and reached to circle him with both hands.

She stroked. Up and down, enjoying the way he came to life in her palms. He grew harder, pulsing over her fingers. Her tongue darted out. A taste. She wanted to taste him, to bring him the ultimate pleasure.

She circled the head, teasing, with light little licks, keeping him from the depths of her mouth. When he tensed and let out a groan, she smiled, confident in her ability to drive him wild.

"Stop teasing me, damn it," he rasped. "Suck me, Emmy. Swallow me whole. Do something, but stop tormenting me."

In response she took him deep. His fingers tangled roughly in her hair and he thrust forward, wanting deeper.

His taste danced on her tongue and his scent filled her nostrils. He was in her, on her, living inside her heart and soul. They were both frantic, and she didn't know who was doing the most work. Her fingers dug into his hips as she pulled him closer. His hands twisted in her hair, holding her as he bucked against her.

And suddenly he left her. She rocked back, her hand going to the floor for balance. His harsh breathing filled her ears as he gasped for breath.

"Not yet. I don't want it to end yet."

She understood, and she gifted him with a wavering smile. He'd been close. She turned, wanting to find Taggert. She wanted to undress him too and run her hands and mouth over his hard body.

He was already naked, standing a few feet away, his hand coaxing his cock to full erection. She watched in fascination as he rolled the foreskin up and down and how thick and long he looked when he pulled it all the way back.

Before she realized what she was doing, she licked her lips, and Taggert let out a harsh expletive.

"You're killing me, Emmy. I want your mouth, baby."

"Then come and take it," she challenged.

He was there before she could blink. He put one hand on the top of her head to hold her in place while he positioned his cock at her lips with his other hand.

"Open for me."

Dutifully she complied, and he slid inside as soon as she parted her lips. He wasn't as content as Greer to let her dictate the pace. He thrust hard and deep, and his fingers curled tighter into her hair. He released his grip on his cock and gently touched her face, his fingers feathering over her jaw and then to her neck as he fucked her mouth.

"If you only knew how many times I've seen you just like this in my fantasies."

Greer's voice startled her and her gaze shot sideways to see him standing there watching, his hand pumping his cock as he watched her suck Taggert.

"On your knees. Only it's my cock in your mouth. Your hair streams down your back like moonlight, and you're looking up at me with the world in your eyes. If you only knew, Emmy."

She glanced up at Taggert to see the agreement in his expression. He thrust back and forth, his jaw clenched tight, but his gaze never left her. There was lust, but there was so much more reflected there for her to see. Love. And hope.

He rose up on tiptoe, his face creased in agony. And then, like Greer, he pulled away, leaving her gasping for breath, her body trembling with awakened passion.

Greer grasped her shoulders and lifted her to her feet. His lips came down on hers even as he walked her backward toward the bed. He pushed. She fell. He came down over her, his body covering her like a sheet of fire.

His knee wedged between her legs, pushing them apart. She couldn't think, couldn't breathe. All she knew was his mouth ravaging hers, tasting her, drinking from her. He settled between her thighs, his cock nudging impatiently at her opening.

"Take me," he whispered into her mouth.

She wrapped her legs around his waist and arched into him. He thrust hard, and the first shock of his entry nearly shattered her. He was in her so deep, so full, that it stole her breath. She raced to catch up, to process the bombardment of sensations battering her from every angle. But he didn't wait. He rode her, driving her into the mattress, taking everything she offered until her sob of pleasure filled the room.

She was on the brink, ready to dive over. Her vision blurred, and she dug her fingers into his shoulders, ready to take the leap.

He slowed, and she whimpered her protest. Then he stopped, his cock lodged as deep in her as he could go.

"Do you trust us, Emmy?" he whispered.

Her gaze flew to his. She was shocked he'd even ask. But there was something in his eyes. Something edgy and dark that excited her. It was then she knew what he was really asking.

"You know I do. Always. With my life. With my heart. Everything."

He closed his eyes and rested his forehead against hers. Then he withdrew and backed away, leaving her sprawled on the bed, her entire body quivering on the verge of release.

And then Taggert was there, kissing her sweetly. He picked her up, holding her to him as he continued the long, hot sweeps of his mouth over hers.

"I'm going to put you back down. I want you on your knees. We're going to ease into this, baby. And if you want us to stop at any time, say so."

She swallowed, not in fear but in anticipation. Bubbles rose from her stomach and into her throat, dancing their way onto her tongue. She shivered as his dark eyes bore into her.

Carefully he put her back down on the bed, and as he'd directed, she turned and got to her hands and knees. The mattress dipped as Greer got on the other side of her. He reached up to push her hair away from her face and let his thumb linger close to her mouth, almost as if he were imagining what it felt like to have her mouth around his cock again.

She closed her eyes, losing sight of Greer when Taggert pressed his lips to the small of her back. He worked down, pressing tiny kisses over the seam of her behind. Then he gently parted the globes, exposing the tiny entrance. Shockingly, his tongue probed delicately at the opening. She gasped, and heat flooded her face until she thought she might burst into flames.

"Taggert!"

He chuckled softly and continued to tongue the sensitive ring until she shook uncontrollably. When he pulled away, she almost protested, but she was too mortified. She was unbelievably turned on, and if he so much as touched her clit, she would orgasm on the spot.

Warm gel smoothed over the same area he'd just spent so much time licking. He smeared it generously around the opening and then tucked a finger inside. The shock sent her forward, and Greer caught her before she fell. Her eyes widened, and her mouth opened but no words came out.

Taggert took his time. He rubbed, touched, petted and smoothed the lubricant until she was a mindless, boneless puppet. Never once was he too forceful or did he go too fast. It was enough to make her crazy.

She burned. Her mind filled with edgy forbidden images. Taggert deep in her ass while Greer fucked her mouth. Oh God. Taggert in her ass while Greer fucked her pussy. She shuddered and locked her arms so she wouldn't collapse. She'd imagined it so many times. Them taking her at the same time. But she'd never thought it would happen.

"Taggert," she pleaded.

"Shhh, Emmy. You're not ready yet. I'd never do anything to hurt you or frighten you. We'll take it slow. I want it to be good for you."

"Just do it!" she wailed.

Greer laughed softly. "Always so impatient, Emmy."

Taggert's fingers stroked silkily in and out of the tight ring of her anus. She wiggled and then she rocked back to take him deeper, but he only withdrew and then issued a light slap to her ass with his other hand.

"Taggert, please!"

Again he leaned down and kissed the small of her back before finally easing his fingers away. His palms glided over her hips and then one hand left her. Her breath caught in her throat as she felt the first brush of his penis.

"Listen to me, baby. I'm going to take this really slow. When I push in, I want you to push out. Don't fight it. Relax and let me in."

She bit her lip and nodded, not trusting herself to speak.

He pressed forward. Her eyes closed and her head fell back as the pressure increased. It began to burn, a delicious stretching sensation that sent shockwaves through her pussy. Her nipples hardened painfully.

"Push against me, Emmy," Taggert said hoarsely.

She bore down, and he pushed. Suddenly he was inside and she cried out.

Taggert swore. "Did I hurt you? Do you want me to pull out?"

"No! God, no. Just give me a minute," she gasped.

It was too much. She sucked in mouthfuls of air and tried to steady the pounding of her heart. Her fingers dug into the covers and gripped until her knuckles turned white. He was there, inside her. He felt huge, and she was half afraid he'd move, and then she was afraid he *wouldn't* move.

Taggert kissed her shoulder. "It's okay, Emmy. I won't move. Not until you tell me to. Just tell me what you need, baby. We've got all the time in the world."

She stayed there, her knees dug into the mattress, her hands locked around the sheets. She sucked air into her nose and let it out in long exhales. When the burning subsided, another ache took over. A low throbbing that set her insides on fire.

Restlessly, she pushed back. Taggert caught her hips and held her still. They both moaned and she wiggled impatiently.

"Move," she whispered. "Now, Taggert. Please, I need it."

Slowly he pulled back. The relief was overwhelming. God, it felt so good. He paused, caressing the curves of her hips. Then gently he pushed forward again.

"Holy hell," she breathed.

Greer cupped her cheek and turned her face so she could see him. "He's going to do this for a while, sweet pea. Nice and easy. Until you get used to it. We don't want to hurt you. All we want is to give you more pleasure than you've ever known."

Her lips trembled. Taggert slid in and out with more ease now. Her body opened to take him, and she found herself pushing back to meet his thrusts. She was on edge. Fiercely so. She was riding a razor's edge of pleasure, so sharp. She needed more. Needed something she wasn't sure of.

"Touch me," she said. She needed him to touch her so she could come.

"No, baby," Taggert denied. "Not yet. If you come now, this won't feel good to you anymore."

Greer moved in closer, tucking a finger under her chin to direct her gaze upward. "We're going to take you at the same time, Emmy. Do you want that? Do you think you can handle it?"

Oh God.

"In a minute Taggert's going to pull out and you're going to climb on top of me. I'm going to slide into your pussy and when you're ready, when you think you can take us both, Taggert's going to be inside you too."

"You're okay with that?" she whispered.

He smiled crookedly. "It's pretty damn cool in a porny sort of way. One of those things I always wanted to try but never thought I'd get the chance."

She smiled back and shook her head. And then Taggert pulled out, the shock of his withdrawal ricocheting up her spine. She felt empty, and her nerve endings were going off like firecrackers.

"Come here, sweet pea."

Her eyes widened when she saw Greer recline, his erection jutting upward toward his navel.

As well as she was able when her entire body shook uncontrollably, she crawled to his outstretched arms and allowed him to position her over his body.

"You take me," he said. "Take me inside you."

She circled his rigid cock in her hand, marveling at the size and thickness. Shifting her position so she was over him, she tucked the head to her softness and carefully eased down, her eyes widening as she took him inch by delicious inch.

He watched, his eyes glittering dangerously. He looked like a predator waiting to strike. And then he was inside her. Wholly, deeply inside her.

"Ride me, Emmy. Take your time and get used to having me there. Tagg and I will never do anything to hurt you, I swear. This is all for you. Always."

"I love you," she whispered, overcome at the tenderness in his voice.

He held his hands up and she laced her fingers with his, holding on as she undulated her body, taking him on a slow, decadent ride. Pleasure rose and surrounded her. Such a sweet song.

She leaned forward, guiding his hands to her breasts, wanting to feel his fingers toying with her nipples. He needed no urging. He palmed the globes and brushed the puckered peaks with his thumbs, teasing her repeatedly.

The bed dipped, and Taggert's hands glided sensuously over her back and down to her ass. Her breath caught and stuttered clumsily from her lips. Greer continued to toy with her breasts, playing with the nipples, drawing them into stiff points.

"Nice and easy, Emmy," Taggert soothed. "This is for you. Tell me if anything hurts or scares you."

Her gaze connected with Greer's. She saw the love in his eyes. The solemn promise. No, they'd never hurt her. Never again. She hoped they both knew how much she trusted them to keep that promise.

Taggert spread her, soothing more of the lubricant over her burning flesh. She moaned in anticipation. She'd wanted this for so long. Had fantasized about it. Had experienced it in her sweetest dreams.

He positioned himself at her anus. Greer stilled his thrusts. Then tenderly, Taggert pushed forward, opening her slowly and carefully around his cock. Her eyes flew open. Her hands fell to Greer's shoulders, and she held on for dear life as Taggert pushed harder.

It was more difficult than before with Greer lodged inside her pussy. There wasn't room for Taggert and yet he pressed relentlessly until her body surrendered and opened for him. And still it was so tight, so agonizingly tight.

Her breaths came in shallow, rapid spurts. Her eyes glazed over, the room blurring around her.

"Just a little more, baby and I'm there. You'll have us both."

She barely registered Taggert's husky words. She was falling too far, too fast.

"Lean forward," Greer whispered. "Lean into me."

She did, allowing him to catch her, to hold her. The position gave Taggert a better angle, and he thrust hard, seating himself the rest of the way in.

"She's not going to last," Greer warned.

"Then let's go now," Taggert rasped out.

They began to thrust. Taggert did most of the work, his movements working her up and down Greer's cock. Greer arched his hips while Taggert held her in place.

No, she wasn't going to last. She was gone the moment Taggert had entered her. Pleasure, sharp and hazy, surrounded her. It was like being drunk or high. She couldn't think. Couldn't speak. All she could do was feel. And feel she did.

She went a little crazy in their arms. She twisted and writhed, and through it all they held her. They whispered their love. Kissed her and caressed her as they pounded into her, branding her body with theirs. They possessed her. They showed her all too well who she belonged to and that they belonged to her now.

Higher and higher she soared, and now she knew what they'd meant when they'd told her she'd fly again. In their arms she'd always have the freedom to fly. Here, she was safe. No one could touch her. The nightmares fell away, ripped from her memory and replaced by their absolute love.

"Love you, love you, love you," she said brokenly. It was all she could say, all she could think.

"Ahh Emmy, I love you too," Greer said gently as he gathered her close in his arms, his body trembling with the aftershocks of his release.

Behind her, Taggert finally went still. He leaned into her for the longest moment before brushing a kiss across her shoulder. Then he withdrew and stepped away.

Greer rolled with her in his arms until she lay beside him. He was still buried inside her and he made no move to separate himself from her.

"Are you all right?"

She nuzzled his chest with her lips and snuggled deeper into his embrace. "I couldn't be more all right."

"Come take a shower with me, Emmy," Taggert said from the side of the bed. "As soon as we're cleaned up, I'll take you back to bed, and you can sleep to your heart's content."

"Mmm."

Greer chuckled and carefully slid out of her body, ignoring her murmured protest. He patted her affectionately on the rear and then rolled away.

"Go take your shower, sweet pea. But hurry. You wore me out, and I sleep better with you in my arms."

Chapter Fourteen

The murmur of voices woke Emily from the most wonderful dream. Before she opened her eyes, she was content to exist in that plane between sleep and awake, enjoying for once images devoid of blood, pain and death.

When she finally pulled herself away from the veil of sleep, she saw that the sun was already peeking through the curtains and Taggert and Greer were hurriedly dressing a few feet from the bed.

She yawned indelicately and propped herself up on her elbow to stare at the two men who held her heart in their firm grasp.

"I don't suppose you're coming back to bed."

Taggert turned, tucking his shirt into his jeans. An expression of regret crossed his face, and he walked over to where she lay.

"Sorry, baby. We've got a fence down and a few cows have already gotten out. We're heading out with some of the hands to do repairs."

She yawned again, and he touched her cheek with his fingertips.

"You go on back to sleep. I'll make sure Buck leaves you something to eat on the stove."

With a nod, she snuggled back into the covers, keeping her eyes open only long enough to watch them go.

Heavy pressure on her back jerked her from sleep. She lifted her head up, and she tried to turn, but a hand slammed her face back into her pillow.

Her cry was muffled, and then a heavy body lay over her, pushing her further into the mattress.

"Not a word. You make a sound and I'll slit your throat."

Shock made mush of her brain. She knew that voice. Who was it? *Think, Emily, think, for God's sake.* She could barely breathe. She struggled wildly, but he yanked her arms behind her and quickly tied her hands together.

Fingers snaked into her hair, balled into a fist and jerked her upward. The flat of his other palm slapped across her mouth, stifling the scream she tried to launch. It was then she saw him from the corner of her eye. *Rand.* Oh my God.

Her eyes went wide, and he yanked her against him as he dragged her from the room. When she kicked at his legs, silver flashed in his hand, and the sharp blade of a hunting knife pressed to her neck.

"You'll die right here, right now," he hissed. "Stop fighting me."

"Why?" she croaked out when his hand relaxed against her mouth.

He tightened his grip once again, ignored her question and hurtled down the stairs, her flopping like a rag doll the entire way down.

"Rand, stop, please," she gasped when he shoved her out the front door.

"Shut up! Just shut up."

He pushed her toward his work truck, opened the door and threw her across the seat. Her back landed against the passenger door. He climbed in next to her and flashed the knife once again.

"Why are you doing this? Are you *insane*?"

She was too stunned to do more than stare at him. Then she realized the stupidity of her inaction and fumbled clumsily for the door handle with her bound hands.

There was supposed to be evil in his eyes, wasn't there? Something to tell her he was some desperate wackjob. But all she could see was ruthless determination.

He gunned the engine just as she managed to crack the door. He reached over and grabbed her around the neck even as he wrestled with the steering wheel.

"Shut it!" he shouted. "Shut it, or I swear to God I'll make you suffer. You won't escape, Emily. Not this time."

He swerved wildly on his way up the long drive and the door slammed, knocking her forward on the seat. He anchored her against him. When she turned, trying to bite him, he doubled his fist and punched her in the jaw.

She went sprawling. Her head cracked against the dash and her behind slid off the seat, wedging her between the glove compartment and the passenger seat.

"That's a good place for you," he grunted.

She lay there, helpless, her hands tied behind her, stuck on the floorboard.

"Why?" she rasped out. "What the hell are you doing, Rand? Taggert and Greer will kill you for this. You have to know that."

He ignored her, staring out the windshield with that same grim...determination. What was he so determined about? This was all some joke. A really twisted, sick, dumb-as-shit joke, but a joke nonetheless.

Rand was quiet, respectful, and he'd always had a smile for her. What the living hell had gotten up his ass?

She cleared her throat and tried a different tactic. "Rand, what's going on?" She purposely softened her voice and tried to make herself sound...accommodating. God, she was actually trying to sweet-talk this bastard. "Why are you so angry with me?"

Could she sound any more pathetic? She was so through being pitiful. Enough was enough, damn it!

"Just shut the hell up so I can drive. I have to get away before they come back. They'll fix that fence soon enough."

He was almost talking to himself, not even acknowledging her awkward-as-hell position on the floorboard.

"Did you sabotage the fence?"

He shrugged. "Seemed the easiest way to get them out of your bed and out of the house."

Her cheeks went warm, and rage shot through her veins.

Then he turned to stare at her. "Yeah, I know all about you, whore. You couldn't leave well enough alone. You already destroyed Sean. You should have stayed away from Taggert and Greer."

"Dear God, is that what this is all about? You disapprove of my relationship with Greer and Taggert so you're taking me away?"

She could hardly control the incredulity in her voice. He was off his goddamn rocker.

"Rand, stop the truck. Let me out. Now."

He slammed on his brakes, and for a moment she thought he was actually going to listen to her.

Then he turned, his eyes sparking with fury.

"You don't get it, do you? You don't get to make demands. You twist a man's balls, have them dangling from your fingertips. It should have been you who died. Not Sean. I won't make another mistake."

Nausea rose in her throat. Tears of anger swam in her eyes. No way. He couldn't mean what she thought he did. She tried to open her mouth but all that came out was an inarticulate sound of rage.

She licked her lips, frustrated that she couldn't get her tongue to work.

"Nothing to say?" he mocked. "You didn't have much to say that night either. You deserve to die if for no other reason than for causing Sean's death."

She closed her eyes. None of this made sense. Rand had worked for the Donovans forever. Since he was a young man out of high school. What could possibly have made him hate this way?

The truck rattled to a stop. Rand got out and walked around to open her door. Without any care, he yanked her from her awkward perch, and she stumbled, trying to get her feet under her. Her hands were completely numb from the tight bonds around her wrists.

Where on God's green earth were they? They'd gone the opposite way of town. There were no houses, no buildings, nothing but rock formations jutting from the earth and the base of a large hill that sloped sharply upward, a precursor to the mountains in the distance.

Rand shoved her forward and she went down to her knees, the rocks digging into her shins.

He hauled her upright and all but dragged her beyond the maze of rocks and boulders. A cave. He was taking her into a freaking cave.

A low moan escaped her. She hated the dark. She never slept in the dark. Not since Sean died.

"Please," she whispered. "Not in here. I'll die in here."

"That's the idea."

Her mouth fell open, and he shoved her through the tight opening into the yawning mouth of darkness. This time when she stumbled, he let her fall. He knelt beside her and coiled rope around her ankles.

Panic hit her hard. He really meant to leave her here. Where Taggert and Greer would never find her.

"Why did you do it?" she rushed out. "Why Sean? I thought you liked him. He was always so nice to you. He gave you a home and a job."

Rand's fingers tightened around her ankles, and she could positively feel the rage billowing off him.

"It was supposed to be you," he seethed. "Not Sean. Never Sean. But he stepped in front of you, took the knife."

Cold settled over her like a suffocating blizzard.

"But why?" she croaked.

"You pulled them apart. You took Sean from the ranch. You turned brother against brother. The Donovans are good people, and you destroyed their family. I heard you that day when you pranced into the house talking about loving them all, wanting to be with them all. Couldn't blame them for being appalled and sending you away. It's what they should have done. What kind of a woman proposes something like that?"

"Someone who loves them," she said faintly, too shocked, too numb to filter his explanation. Sean had died because of her. She'd always known it, just hadn't realized how much she'd been the cause of his death. It hadn't been random at all.

Oh God.

"Love," he said scornfully. "What does a whore know about love? You tempted them with your body. You took Sean away. But that wasn't enough. You had to come back, luring them with that pitiful smile. I won't let them be dragged down by you again. They deserve better than that."

"They love me," she said in a steady voice. "You'll hurt them if you kill me."

There was a pause, almost as if he considered that. Then he laughed harshly. "They'll forget you. You aren't the keeping kind. You were good for a lay, I guess."

His words shouldn't hurt. He was a maniac. Taggert and Greer did love her. They did. But would they find her in time? Would they ever find her?

"I'll just tell them you left," he said matter-of-factly. "Shouldn't come as a surprise. You left before. Women change their minds all the time. Can't be trusted."

"What the hell is your problem?" she snarled. "Did your mommy abuse you? Not hug you enough? Did your girlfriend dump you? Leave you for another man?"

He drew back, almost as if shocked by her outburst. Then he slapped her hard across the mouth.

"Your father was right to beat you. Your kind needs discipline. You need correcting. The Donovans will be better off without you."

He shoved a rag into her mouth and then put masking tape over her lips. As he stood, he kicked her once in the side.

"If Sean hadn't died for you, I'd make your death quick, but you deserve to suffer. You deserve to lie here thinking about all the lives you've destroyed."

With that he turned and stalked out of the cave, leaving her lying in the dark.

Chapter Fifteen

It was late when Greer drove through the back gate. He stopped to wait for Taggert to shut it and get back in the truck. A few seconds later, they pulled up to the house and got out, dusting themselves off as they headed to the back door.

As they mounted the steps, Rand opened the door and glanced uneasily at them. The hairs on Greer's neck prickled and he stared sharply back at his foreman.

"Something wrong, Rand?"

Rand's cheeks flushed a dull red. Man had always been quiet and almost painfully shy. But he was a good, hard worker and he'd never given them any reason to complain. They could definitely use more like him.

"It's Miss Emily." He stepped back to allow him and Taggert inside.

"What about her?" Taggert demanded.

Rand looked as though he'd rather eat dirt than have to say what was on his mind.

"Well, uh, she left."

Greer reared back. "What?"

Rand was openly nervous now. He was sweating bullets, and he twisted his hands together.

"She went down to Sean's grave. She does that a lot. When she came back, she went upstairs then came down with her bag. Asked me to take her to town. I didn't want to," he added in a rush. "But when I suggested she wait for you to get back, she said she'd walk if she had to. I didn't think you and Taggert would want her going alone so I drove her."

Greer's hands were shaking. He couldn't even get his thoughts together. Gone? What the hell?

"Did I screw up?" Rand asked as he rubbed his palms on his jeans.

"No, Rand, you did right," Taggert said in a tight voice. "But we need more information. Anything she said. Don't leave a word out. We need to know where you took her."

Greer dragged a hand through his hair and leaned back against the wall. "Why did she leave?"

Rand colored again and shoved his hands into his pockets. "She didn't say. I mean she didn't talk to me. She was upset. I could tell she'd been crying. Maybe the visit to Sean's grave put her over the edge? I took her to the motel. She wouldn't listen to reason. I tried all the way into town, but she wouldn't even look at me."

Taggert let out a curse that made Rand flinch. Then he turned to Greer. "Let's go." At the door he glanced back at Rand. "How long ago did you take her into town?"

Rand shrugged. "Couple of hours."

"And you only just now saw fit to tell us?" Greer asked incredulously.

"I didn't want to disturb the work on the fence. Already lost enough cattle."

Trust Rand to be focused on work. Of course he wouldn't understand the seriousness of Emily taking off in a fragile emotional state.

Greer followed Taggert to the truck and the two tore down the drive. Taggert's hands gripped the wheel, and his face was locked in stone.

As they neared town, Taggert finally turned to Greer. "What the fuck, Greer? When we left this morning, Emmy was fine. She seemed happy. What could possibly have happened? She's visited Sean's grave several times since she's been back but she's never taken off on us."

"I don't know," Greer said in frustration. "Let's hope she's at the motel."

*
**

An hour later, a cold sweat gripped Taggert's entire body. Panic hovered, and it took everything he had not to give in to it. No one had seen Emily. Or Rand, for that matter. But if Rand had dropped her at the motel on the edge of town, he wouldn't have gained a lot of notice. And if Emmy didn't want attention drawn to herself, all she had to do was go the opposite way. But how?

He met Greer back at the truck, helpless rage snaking through his veins.

"What the hell do we do? No one's seen her. She's not in Creed's Pass."

Greer's face hardened, but Taggert could see the worry in his eyes.

"Maybe she got a ride into Hodges. Hell, Tagg, I don't know. I don't understand any of this. It's late and I don't know what we should do. One of us should go back to the ranch in case she comes back. We don't know if she planned to leave permanently or if she just got upset."

"Buck and Rand can wait up," Taggert said. "You and I can keep looking for her. They'll call if she shows up at the ranch."

"Tell them to sit on her if she shows," Greer said in a low growl.

"Let's go find our girl," Taggert said.

Chapter Sixteen

Dawn had long since come, bringing with it the grim realization that Emily was gone. Not just gone but vanished. For hours, Taggert and Greer had searched every conceivable location. They'd questioned motel owners, cab drivers, they'd gone to the airport and every spot in between. She simply wasn't anywhere they looked.

They both needed sleep, but they also knew that with each passing minute, Emily was further away. Hell, she could be across the entire country by now.

"Maybe the best thing to do is go home and wait," Taggert muttered. He was dead on his feet after a long day repairing a fence line and then all night spent searching for Emily.

Greer didn't look any better. He wore a haunted look that Taggert hadn't seen since the night they'd been called with the news of Sean's death.

Greer raised a hand then let it fall to his side, his shoulders sagging.

"She left us."

Taggert flinched at the betrayal in Greer's voice. It was a feeling he'd tried damn hard not to experience himself, but how could he not? One minute Emily was pledging her love, her commitment to them, the next she had hotfooted it to parts unknown. The big question was why?

"It doesn't make sense," Taggert said wearily.

He climbed into the truck and turned home. They were several hours from the ranch. It would be afternoon before they got there. He was hungry, he needed a shower and he needed sleep. Mostly he needed Emily. In his arms. Back home where she belonged.

"Nothing makes any goddamn sense," Greer muttered as he slouched in the seat.

The two didn't talk on the drive home. They didn't even look at each other. They stared out the window at the passing scenery, and Taggert focused relentlessly on the road.

Why had she left?

The question haunted Taggert. He couldn't have been that wrong about Emmy. Not their Emmy.

By the time he pulled up to the house, dusk had bathed the world in shadows and pale shades of lavender. Without a word, they got out and trudged inside where they were met by Buck and Rand.

"No luck finding the girl?" Buck asked.

Greer shook his head and continued on past the two men.

"Get some rest. Both of you. We'll look again in the morning. I'll sit by the phone. If she calls, I'll wake you up," Buck said.

Taggert raised his hand in acknowledgement and went up the stairs to his bedroom. His bed was still unmade, the covers twisted and shoved to the side. The fitted sheet had popped off and was dragged halfway across the bed. What the hell?

Had Emily woken up in the midst of a nightmare? Had she been driven from bed by past demons, visited Sean's grave and taken off on impulse?

He stood by the bed, staring down at where he and Greer had made love to her just two nights ago. Where was she now?

Not bothering to undress, he fell over the bed, eyes closing as soon as his head hit the pillow. He could smell her. He inhaled deeply and curled his fingers into the sheets.

A few hours was all he needed. Then he'd find Emmy. He had to.

Taggert woke with a start, unsure of what had disturbed him. Christ, it was light again already. How long had he slept? He rolled, wincing at the soreness in his muscles.

A beam of reflected sunlight flashed across his window, and he frowned. The sound of a vehicle reached his ears.

His pulse picked up a notch and he hurried to the window, lifting the slats of the blinds with one finger. His frown deepened when he saw Rand's truck driving slowly down the driveway.

An uneasy feeling slithered through his veins. Why did it bother him?

Rand was the last to see Emily. Rand was the one who had taken her from the ranch. Into town. Where no one had seen her. Where the hell was he going right now? Could be nothing. But his gut was screaming.

Responding to his gut, he raced down the stairs, not bothering to get Greer. He didn't have time if he wasn't going to lose Rand.

He bounded off the front steps and threw himself into the truck, his fingers fumbling with the ignition before he ever got the door closed.

He peeled out of the yard and hit the dirt drive with a cloud of dust billowing behind him. He forced himself to slow. Last thing he wanted was to get too close to Rand and spook him. And if Rand was doing a legitimate errand, he'd apologize later for the ugly suspicions that had suddenly taken root.

Everything about Rand's earlier demeanor took on new light. When he'd faced them with the news that Emily had left. Maybe he hadn't been reluctant and worried about their reaction to her being gone. Maybe he was nervous because he was the cause of Emily's disappearance.

Nausea rose in his throat, and he forced himself not to succumb to the dark thoughts tormenting him.

He caught sight of Rand up ahead and immediately slowed to allow Rand to take the corner. When he rounded the curve, he saw Rand pull out on the main road and head away from town.

"Bastard," Taggert whispered.

If Rand was responsible for any harm or fright to Emily, Taggert would kill him.

He kept good distance between them though it made him frantic to think of Rand getting to Emily so far ahead of him, but he couldn't let Rand know he was on to him.

And what if he's doing something perfectly innocent?

Then Taggert would be wrong, and hopefully Emily was safe wherever she was, but he wasn't taking any chances.

For half an hour he followed Rand until he saw him turn off the road. Taggert immediately slowed and waited. What the hell was Rand doing out here? It was the middle of nowhere. Only rocks, hills and...caves.

Oh shit. No. No, no, no.

Taggert hit the gas and careened up the road to the spot where Rand had pulled off. He bumped over the rough terrain, his head hitting the ceiling. His hands slipped off the wheel but he grabbed on again and raced over the barely discernible trail.

When he caught sight of Rand's truck he no longer worried about discovery. He roared up and slammed on the brakes beside the other vehicle.

Goddamn it, Rand was already gone from sight. No matter, he'd been up here plenty of times as a boy. There was only one real possibility as far as a cave. Or at least it was the only one he knew about, and he prayed Rand didn't know of any others.

He hurried around rocks, up the hill to where the boulders became larger and hid the entrance to the small cave. It couldn't really be called a cave. It was more of an enclosure. An area dug out of the side of the hill with no path further into the earth.

As he neared the carved out entrance between two rock outcroppings, he slowed, listening for Rand, for Emily, for any hint of activity.

Carefully he edged closer, his hand sliding along the rough surface. Still, he didn't hear anything. With a decisive lunge, he burst into the opening, prepared to fight Rand. But he didn't see the man anywhere.

It was dark, but not so dark he couldn't see the figure lying on the ground. Still. So very still. Emily.

Forgetting Rand, forgetting everything but the agony burning through his mind like a blowtorch, he dropped to his knees beside her.

"Emily. Emily!"

He started to tear at the ropes tying her hands, then stopped and pressed his fingers into the side of her neck. Then she moved. A slight turn, but he felt it and relief crashed through him like a tidal wave.

"Emmy, oh my God, my sweet Emmy."

His voice was nearly destroyed. *He* was nearly destroyed. In the dim light, he barely made out the tape covering her mouth. With trembling fingers he pulled at it, wincing when it didn't come immediately free.

With a murmured apology, he yanked, pulling it away in one clean motion. She immediately shoved the rag out with her tongue and coughed hoarsely.

"Taggert."

It barely came out in a whisper, but he'd never heard a sweeter sound.

"Shhh, baby. Let me untie you so I can get you the hell out of here."

"I didn't think you'd find me."

She sounded weak and tearful, and her fear tore at him, ripping what little control he had away from him.

He went nuts trying to get her hands and feet free, and as soon as he succeeded, he yanked her into his arms, rocking her back and forth as he absorbed the feel of her heartbeat.

"Rand is here. He's close. I need to get you out of here, baby."

She shuddered and went still against him.

"He's crazy, Taggert. Not clinically crazy. The bastard knew exactly what he was doing. He killed Sean."

She grabbed hold of his shirt with both fists, and her entire body trembled with rage.

Taggert's brain exploded with the impact of her statement.

"What?"

"Later," she said hoarsely. "Please. Let's just go. He's so determined to save you from me. There's no telling what he'll do if he finds you here."

Taggert couldn't even wrap his brain around all she was saying, but one thing registered. The need to protect her. To get her home.

He hastily got up and pulled her to a standing position beside him. She stumbled and let out a cry of pain.

"My feet," she gasped. "Hurts!"

Taggert swore. He couldn't afford to tie up his hands by carrying her out. Not when Rand could show up at any time.

"Hold on to me," he said gently. "You'll get the feeling back as soon as the blood starts circulating good again. Just hold on to me and we'll take it nice and slow to the truck."

She clutched at his arm, and he started forward, careful not to rush too much, but damn it, they needed to move.

She hobbled along, making little breathy sounds of pain that seared his soul. But she didn't stop, and she didn't complain.

Her hand went up to cover her eyes as soon as they stepped into the sunshine. She turned away, and he could see how pale she was and the deep shadows under her eyes. God. She'd been here for almost two days. Two fucking days while he and Greer had been chasing all over the damn state. He was going to kill Rand with his bare hands.

He killed Sean.

Emily's words sawed like a dagger. Was it possible?

"I knew you couldn't stay away."

Rand stepped from behind a rock. His eyes were wild, his clothes dirty and rumpled. And he held a gun pointed directly at Emily. "I saw you following me. Why couldn't you just leave her alone?"

Taggert shoved Emily behind him. She nearly went down, but he held tight to her arm.

"What the fuck is this?" Taggert asked furiously. "You lied to us, you son of a bitch. You kept her in a goddamn cave for two days. You *know* she hates the dark. Why?"

His fingers flexed and curled. He'd never wanted to hurt another human being as bad as he wanted to tear Rand apart right now.

Rand eyed him warily but he kept the gun trained in his direction.

Emily closed her eyes and shifted her feet back and forth as she stood behind Taggert. Anything to try and regain sensation. She was useless in her current state.

"She should have never come back," Rand bit out.

"You don't get to decide that," Taggert roared. "Did you kill my brother, Rand? Is Emily right? Did you kill Sean?"

Emily gripped Taggert's arm tighter and tried to see around him, but he pushed her back again.

"It was supposed to be her," Rand said in a bleak voice. "It was never supposed to be Sean. He stepped in front of her. It was too late for me to stop. I hated her for making me do that. Sean didn't deserve to die. I wanted to save him from her."

Every muscle in Taggert's body stiffened. He bristled with rage. So much fury. She felt it like an inferno.

"Save him? Save us? Where do you get off interfering in our lives? Who gave you the right? You goddamn bastard, you killed my brother!"

"It wasn't what I wanted. I never wanted to hurt him. Or you and Greer. But now you give me no choice. If you'd just stayed at the ranch, I would have disposed of Emily, and you could have gone on with your lives. It's unnatural what you and Greer are doing with her."

She heard the click of the safety, and she felt Taggert's swift intake of breath.

No.

Not again. Never again.

It was supposed to be her last time. She wouldn't allow another man she loved to die because of her.

"Forgive me, Taggert," Rand whispered.

She pushed at Taggert and caught sight of Rand raising the pistol. God, he was really going to do it. He was going to shoot Taggert down in broad daylight.

Rand's hand trembled, but his gaze never wavered. She saw his finger tighten on the trigger.

"No!"

She hooked her foot between Taggert's legs and shoved with all her might. He stumbled away, and she turned to face Rand, placing herself between him and Taggert.

"Emmy, no!" Taggert cried.

Anger flared in Rand's eyes, and then he simply pulled the trigger.

Pain exploded over Emily. She went flying backwards, her body hitting the ground with enough force to jar her teeth loose. She lay gasping for air but couldn't draw any into her lungs.

Taggert's roar echoed in her ears. Dimly she heard Rand cry out. Then she heard another shot. She couldn't move. Couldn't make her arms or legs obey her commands.

Pain. So much pain.

The metallic taste of blood seeped into her mouth. Where had it come from?

She coughed and felt the warm liquid slosh over her tongue. She spit, revolted by the taste and the sensation of it filling her mouth.

"Emmy! Emmy, oh God, baby."

She blinked as a shadow fell over her body. Taggert. She tried to say his name, but like her arms and legs, her tongue just wouldn't cooperate. Was she dying?

"No. No, baby you aren't dying," Taggert said fiercely.

Evidently her tongue worked after all.

"Rand," she managed to get out between coughs.

"He can't hurt you anymore. Oh Jesus, Emmy."

His hands fluttered over her body, and she could see the panic in his eyes. It was bad. But then she knew that.

She smiled, ignoring the blood seeping from her mouth.

"So glad you came," she whispered. "Love you."

"Emmy, listen to me. I've got to pick you up. It's going to hurt like hell, but I've got to get you to the hospital."

She nodded, his face blurring above her.

"You stay with me, okay? Swear to me you'll stay with me."

"Swear," she slurred.

Why couldn't she breathe? She sucked in huge mouthfuls of air, but she could only manage the smallest bit into her lungs. And it hurt. God, it hurt so much. She didn't want to breathe, but she panicked when she held her breath for too long.

Taggert slid his arms underneath her, murmuring apologies and prayers the entire time. His words faded in and out, or maybe it was her fading. How could she tell?

She was lifted into the air, and agony seared through her body like a bolt of lightning. She gasped then choked as blood filled her mouth. She gagged and coughed and that sent another surge of pain through her chest so fierce that her eyes rolled back into her head.

The next thing she knew she was lying on the seat of Taggert's truck, and Taggert was shouting at her to stay with him.

Blackness crowded her vision, closing in on her like night. She struggled to stay awake, to stay with Taggert as he demanded over and over. It hurt too much, though. It was easier to slide toward the dark.

"Tagg..."

"Yes, baby, I'm here. I'm here, Emmy. Don't leave me. Don't leave me, honey."

"L-love you. So...so much. Always...have. Tell Greer. Love...him...too."

She was sliding. Endlessly. No handholds. No way to hang on.

Chapter Seventeen

When Emily opened her eyes, she knew something wasn't right. It was too quiet, too peaceful, and there was no pain. She wasn't even lying down, but then after glancing down, she wasn't exactly standing either.

For the love of God—literally—don't let this be one of those out of body experiences people talked about when they died.

A chuckle had her whipping around, well, as much as one could when she had no sense of physical being.

Sean. Standing there with a big ole smile on his face, worn jeans—his favorite pair—boots and a threadbare T-shirt. Looking just as gorgeous and as full of life as he'd ever looked.

"You're not dead, Emmy," he said.

"Sean," she whispered. Tears filled her eyes. Her nose stung, and her throat ached.

"Hey, love," he said in a husky voice. "Still causing trouble, I see."

She smiled through her tears and then threw herself into his arms.

Oh it was the best feeling in the world. It wasn't a dream. She could feel his arms around her when she thought never to feel them again. He even smelled just like he always did.

She pulled away and looked up into his eyes. "Kiss me."

His mouth lowered to hers. This was a gift like none she'd ever expected to receive. How many times had she begged God for just one more time in Sean's arms? One more chance to tell him how much she loved him and how much she missed him.

"I love you," she whispered into his mouth.

He gripped her shoulders, his thumbs rubbing a pattern over her skin. "I love you, Emmy. I've always loved you. Now we need to have a talk."

She groaned. "Don't spoil things. I don't want to talk. I just want to be with you."

His eyes were so serious. He cupped her cheek and held her face between his hands.

"Taggert and Greer need you, Emmy."

She shook her head, only focused on the miracle of seeing—of talking—to Sean again. How could she even think of leaving him?

"I had three wonderful years with you, Songbird. Three years I'll cherish for eternity. I don't regret anything. You weren't to blame for my death."

She looked away, tears slipping down her cheeks.

"Emmy, look at me."

She raised her gaze again, overwhelmed at the love and understanding she found in his eyes.

"You weren't to blame. If I had it to do all over again, I wouldn't change a thing. It was my time. It's *not* your time."

"I don't want you to go."

"I'll always be with you. Wherever you are, I'll be."

She rested her head on his chest, savoring the connection to him that time and his death hadn't erased.

"I love you."

His hands slid over her back and into her hair. "I love you too. Always. Taggert and Greer love you. They always have even if they wouldn't admit it. They need you, Emmy. They can't lose us both."

He tilted her head back up so she looked at him again.

"I'll never leave you. Do you know that? I'm always here."

Tears slipped rapidly down her cheeks as she stared wordlessly up at him.

"I don't want to say goodbye," she choked out.

He smiled. "Then don't. Say you love me and then go back. I'll be waiting for you. When it's your time, I'll be there."

"Oh Sean. I do love you so much."

She threw her arms around him and held on desperately. This time...this time she knew she wouldn't see him again until it was her time.

"I know, Songbird. I know. I never doubted for a moment that you loved me. Now go. Taggert and Greer are worried. They're scared of losing you, and you've been a very difficult patient."

He smiled a little as he said it and stroked her cheek with one finger.

"Do one more thing for me."

"Anything."

"Sing."

She swallowed then nodded. Sean leaned down and kissed her tenderly on the lips. She closed her eyes and basked in his love. When she opened them, he was gone.

Chapter Eighteen

They wouldn't leave her alone, and it was seriously pissing her off. She'd been poked and prodded in places that didn't bear mentioning. Awareness was slow to come and with it the realization that Sean was no longer holding her, kissing her.

She retreated from that reality and let herself be surrounded by the beckoning fade.

"Goddamn it, Emily, don't you dare leave me. You fight, damn it. Don't you fucking give up."

Greer. What was he doing here? And why was he so angry with her? It wasn't like she shot herself.

They need you, Emmy.

Sean's gentle reminder echoed softly in her fragmented mind.

She sighed, or at least she thought she did.

"Emily, I swear to God, I'm going to kick your ass."

She smiled. She couldn't help it. So like Greer to threaten to kick her ass if she died on him. Where was Taggert? Wasn't like him to miss out on a chance to snarl and bellow.

"Emily, please. Fight, baby. Don't leave us."

Ah there he was. He sounded… She flinched away from the grief she heard in his voice. He thought he'd already lost her. Just like he'd lost Sean.

You were right, Sean. I can't leave them. I'm so sorry.

Don't be sorry, love. I'll wait for you. Go now. They're worried.

Sean's warmth and strength surrounded her, urging her, pushing her back to the voices calling for her.

I love you. I'll miss you.

She felt his smile all the way to her toes.

I love you too, Songbird.

A gasp of pain escaped as suddenly she was brutally thrust out of the shadows. Noise surrounded her. Beeping, loud voices, the sound of wrappers tearing, hurried footsteps. And pain. God, the pain.

"We're here, Emmy. You stay with us," Greer said.

Not going anywhere.

She tried to stay aware, but the pain was horrific. She felt a gentle hand on her cheek. Taggert. Comforted by the knowledge he was there and she wasn't alone, she surrendered to the heavy drag of oblivion.

Quiet surrounded her. She was dimly aware of pain, but it seemed muffled and a little fuzzy. It was a welcome change from the way she'd been thrust so rudely into chaos before.

Her eyelids weighed about two tons, and by sheer force of will she managed to pry them open. Thankfully the room was mostly dark with the only light showing from the hallway. The entire front of her room had windows looking out to the nurses station, and she could see medical personnel bustling back and forth between the station and the other rooms. She must be in ICU. Things must have been bad.

Slowly she registered her surroundings. Greer sat next to the bed, his head back, eyes closed. On her other side, Taggert sat bent forward in his chair, his head between his hands. He was completely still, and she wasn't sure if he was also sleeping or just at his wit's end.

Guilt hit her hard. While she'd been begging Sean to let her stay, Taggert and Greer had been fighting for her life. Sean was right. She couldn't give up. They needed her, and she needed them.

For once the idea that Sean was no longer here didn't fill her with relentless grief. She felt him as surely as if he were standing at her bedside. He'd made her a promise, and she knew he'd never go back on his word. He'd be there when it was her time. Until then she had a lifetime to look forward to with Taggert and Greer.

She opened her mouth to call out to Taggert and frowned when absolutely nothing came out. Her throat hurt. Probably had a damn tube shoved down it. She licked her lips and tried again.

"Taggert."

It came out in barely a whisper, but Taggert's head immediately popped up. So much relief washed over his face. He leaned forward, his hands reaching for her and then he seemed to think better of touching her. He looked down and then back at her almost as if he didn't have the first clue what to do.

She smiled and moaned when that simple action sent pain rocketing through her body.

That woke Greer up. He jolted forward, his feet hitting the floor with a thump.

"Emmy," he breathed.

Taggert scooted his chair to the edge of her bed. He tentatively touched her arm, and her gaze fell down her body, her eyes widening at the bulky bandages decorating her chest.

"Hi," she croaked out.

Taggert smiled, and then his face completely crumbled. Tears shimmered in his dark eyes, and he picked up her hand, pressing it to his cheek.

"Thank God," he choked out. "You had us so worried."

"We should call the nurse. They've been waiting for you to wake up," Greer said.

"No, not yet. Please. Just let me lie here for a minute while you two talk to me."

Greer took her other hand and rubbed his thumb over her palm.

"How long have I been here?" she asked.

Taggert grimaced. "Four days. You were taken here after surgery. I was beginning to think you planned to sleep for the rest of the year."

The memory of that gun staring her in the face made her flinch. "Rand?"

Greer's face blackened. "Dead."

"Oh."

She attempted to turn more so she could see Taggert better but quickly abandoned that idea. Hurt too damn much to move.

"He didn't shoot you?"

"No, baby. You took the bullet meant for me," he said fiercely. "I shot him. He can't hurt you anymore."

"Pity," she murmured. "Would be nice to see him go to prison for a long time."

Greer muttered a few choice words under his breath.

"Better this way. He's out of our lives and it'll save the taxpayers the expense of a trial," Taggert said with a scowl.

She smiled. "I knew you'd say something like that."

"I'm so pissed at you," Greer growled.

She raised one eyebrow. "I know. You sounded mad when you were shouting at me not to die. I didn't shoot myself, you know."

Taggert actually smiled.

Greer wasn't smiling, though. "You ever pull a stunt like that again and I swear I'll tan your ass."

"Trust me. Getting shot again isn't high on my list of priorities."

Taggert sobered and gripped her hand a little tighter.

"I couldn't let him take someone else I loved from me," she said softly. "Now will one of you tell me how bad it is? I don't remember much."

Both men scowled.

"You almost died. You *did* die," Greer said bleakly "He shot you in the chest. You lost an enormous amount of blood and the bullet nicked your lung. Damn lucky it missed your heart."

"I take it I'm out of the woods now?"

"No," Taggert clipped out. "There's still risk of infection, pneumonia and a whole host of other complications. You're going to be here a good while, and even when you get to go home, it's going to be a long recovery."

She sighed. "Guess you two will have to hover, huh."

"Damn straight," Greer said.

She squeezed both their hands with as much strength as she possessed, which wasn't much. "I'm not going anywhere. Promise. I have it on good authority it's not my time."

"That's good since we don't have any intention of letting you go," Taggert said gruffly.

"Think you can put up with me for the next fifty years or so?"

"Fifty years is only the beginning, Emmy." Greer leaned over and brushed his lips over her forehead. "It's only the beginning."

Taggert touched the inside of her wrist then lifted her hand to kiss each fingertip. "I'm kind of liking the sound of forever."

Lightness bubbled even amidst the pain raging through her body. For the first time in a year, her future looked bright and free of the shadows that had haunted her soul.

Her smiled came easier this time and was missing the agony caused by her wounds. She glanced between the two men and saw some of their worry ease.

"I can deal with forever."

Greer took her lips in a gentle kiss. "We're going to hold you to that."

Epilogue

The delighted squeal of four-year-old Macy, as she bolted from the back porch, put matching smiles on her fathers' faces. Taggert swung her high into the air before settling her atop his shoulders. Her chubby little hands smacked against his cheeks as she held on for dear life.

"Hey, short stuff. Your mama still writing?"

"Uh huh. She's talking to herself again."

Taggert looked at the swing on the porch to see Emily hunched over her guitar, pencil between her teeth and a notepad on her lap. It was a pretty funny sight given the advanced stage of her pregnancy and the fact that her lap wasn't near what it used to be.

He swung Macy down then tossed her into the air to Greer who caught her as she screeched in approval.

"Do it again! Do it again!"

Greer tucked her under one arm and mounted the steps to the porch. Emily looked up and let the pencil fall from her mouth.

"You're back!"

The welcome in her eyes never failed to turn Taggert's heart over in a series of somersaults.

"You must be deep in your writing if you couldn't hear Macy's squeals. I'm pretty sure they heard her in Canada," Taggert said.

She smiled at the wiggling bundle in Greer's grasp. "I'm trying to get this song finished today. Words are coming faster than I can get them down."

Taggert sat on the swing next to Emily and brushed a kiss across her temple. Then he let his hand slide over the swollen mound of her belly. The baby rolled, causing a ripple in her dress.

"How is the little one today?"

She smiled and her entire face lit up as she covered his hand with her own. "He's good. He's been up all afternoon. I'm hoping that means he's getting his days and nights back in order."

"God, me too," Greer muttered. "Would be nice to sleep at night."

Emily leveled a stare at Greer. "I'm the one he keeps up at night, thank you very much."

Taggert chuckled. "And you, in turn, keep us up, thank you very much."

She scrunched up her nose. "Sorry. It's hell being eight months pregnant. I figure if I must suffer then so should you."

Greer sat in one of the rockers and plopped Macy into his lap. "You hear that, short stuff? Your mama has a mean streak in her."

"Daddy mean, Mama nice."

Both Greer and Taggert jerked their heads up in surprise at that announcement. Emily had the grace to flush. Then she laughed and made a shushing sound at Macy.

"You, my dear, have a big mouth."

"Ah so Mama has been spreading propaganda," Greer said with a grin.

"It's never too early to teach them the way of things," Emily said primly.

Taggert chuckled and pulled Emily into his side. She let the guitar slide forward and propped the end against her leg. A breeze elicited a shiver from her, and she snuggled a little closer.

He sighed, and it was the sound of a deeply contented man. Life was good. He wasn't the sort to get all maudlin, but even he had to stop every once in a while and marvel at the gifts he'd been given.

The rapid bump bump against his side had him looking down.

"Active little rascal isn't he?"

Macy slid from Greer's lap and crawled onto Taggert's.

"His name is Sean," she pronounced.

Emily, Taggert and Greer all shared a bittersweet smile. There had never been any doubt that their son would have Sean's name. Emily had shared the experience she'd had when she'd hovered between life and death in the hospital as she'd lain recovering from the extensive wounds.

Greer and Taggert both cherished the unselfish gift their brother had given them, and they were eternally grateful to Sean for loving Emily when she'd so needed support.

"Yes, munchkin, his name is Sean," Emily said as she reached to pull her daughter onto her lap. "Put your hand here and say hello to your brother."

Instead of putting her hand on Emily's belly, Macy leaned down and smacked her lips noisily against the mound. Emily's delighted laughter rang out through the air.

Taggert was enchanted, and Greer was no less so. Yes, life was good. Emily had embraced her singing career though she didn't keep the hectic tour schedule she had before. There was no longer a reason to stay away from the place she called home.

Much of her time was spent songwriting. She recorded most, but other artists also picked up her titles. In her most recent venture, she'd released an album of lullabies, all of which she'd written when she was pregnant with Macy.

Taggert's favorite times, however, weren't of hearing her songs on the radio, though his pride knew no bounds over her success. No, the times he cherished the most were when she took her guitar and sang for her family.

Their songbird had traveled a long, winding road home, but she was here and that was all that mattered.

About the Author

To learn more about Maya, please visit www.mayabanks.com. Send an email to Maya at maya@mayabanks.com or join her Yahoo! group to join in the fun with other readers as well as Maya: http://groups.yahoo.com/group/writeminded_readers.

Their final mission will be to win her love.

Amber Eyes
© *2009 Maya Banks*

A beautiful, vulnerable woman appears at the high country cabin where Hunter and Jericho live between assignments. They are captivated by their stunning, reticent visitor and vow to protect her—and uncover what she's hiding. Neither is prepared for the unbelievable. Their beautiful innocent is a cougar shifter who's spent a lifetime alone.

In the shelter of their love, Kaya blooms, finally willing to trust—and embrace her humanity again. Then Hunter and Jericho are called away on a mission that goes terribly wrong. Now, pregnant, and alone once more, she must find her way in a world she doesn't belong to—and hope that the two men she loves will find their way home.

Warning: This title contains explicit sex, adult language, sweet lovin', multiple partners and ménage a trois.

Available now in ebook from Samhain Publishing.

It was supposed to be an easy mission. But nobody told her that.

Into the Lair
© *2008 Maya Banks*
Falcon Mercenary Group Book 2

Ian and Braden Thomas return to the U.S. to extract Katie Buchanan, the sister of the teammate who betrayed them. She could very well be the key to taking down the man responsible for turning Ian and Braden into unstable cat shifters. Unfortunately, they're not the only ones after Katie.

Katie has no intention of going quietly or of offering her trust on a silver platter. She's got troubles of her own that don't include two pain-in-the-ass men who claim her dead brother sent them. She's too busy trying to stay one step ahead of Ricardo de la Cruz, the brother of a man she killed.

As the bodies pile up, Ian and Braden are only sure of one thing: Katie makes them crazy. Something about her calls to their inner predator. They both want her, but she's made a practice of making bad decisions and trusting the wrong men. And by the time she realizes that she can trust these two warriors, it might just be too late.

Warning: Blood, gray matter, guts and gore. Ass kicking, potty mouths, acerbic wit. More mean people, mean people dying, mean people getting what they deserve. Sex...explicit sex, rough sex, ménage a trois, voyeurism, light bondage. Oh, and avalanches.

Available now in ebook and print from Samhain Publishing.

GREAT
CHEAP
FUN

Discover eBooks!

THE FASTEST WAY TO GET THE HOTTEST NAMES

Get your favorite authors on your favorite reader, long before they're out in print! Ebooks from Samhain go wherever you go, and work with whatever you carry—Palm, PDF, Mobi, and more.

Samhain
Publishing ltd

Breinigsville, PA USA
05 April 2010
235553BV00001B/2/P